THE EYES OF
A STRANGER

THE EYES OF A STRANGER

JACKIE HYMAN

ST. MARTIN'S PRESS

NEW YORK

THE EYES OF A STRANGER Copyright © 1987 by Jackie Hyman. All rights reserved. Printed in the United States of America. No part of this book may be used or reproduced in any manner whatsoever without written permission except in the case of brief quotations embodied in critical articles or reviews. For information, address St. Martin's Press, 175 Fifth Avenue, New York, N.Y. 10010.

Library of Congress Cataloging-in-Publication Data

Hyman, Jackie, 1949–
    The eyes of a stranger.

    I. Title.
PS3558.Y467E94   1987   813'.54   87-26599
ISBN 0-312-01017-6

First Edition

10 9 8 7 6 5 4 3 2 1

For Sylvia and Arthur

MONDAY

1

He drove by the elementary school about noon, knowing he wouldn't be noticed in the slow-moving traffic of Citrus Avenue.

In front of the school, a line of wiggling young bodies clattered toward the playground behind their teacher. A little girl with fuzzy gold hair turned and saw him and for one moment their eyes met, and then another little girl grabbed her hand and the contact broke.

The car drifted past. He could make almost no noise at all when he wanted to. He passed the library and pulled up alongside the high school, halting in the shade of a pepper tree.

They were sitting on the grass beneath a palm tree about a hundred feet away, eating lunch out of white paper bags from the McDonald's across the street. The two boys had their backs to him, but between their heads he could see her, framed, as in a movie.

Today the shoulder-length blonde hair was pulled back with two clips, or maybe they were combs, and spilled down over the shoulders of the delicate white blouse. Her mouth glistened from whatever she was drinking out of that paper cup, not bothering with a straw.

One of the boys shifted, leaving a clear view of her breasts

3

pressing outward through the thin blouse. You'd think they'd leave a permanent mark.

She wore a gold chain around her slim neck.

"Mary, Mary, quite contrary, how does your garden grow?" His mother laughed tipsily, her hand stroking lightly down his pajamas as he lay in bed. "Cockles and mussels, alive, alive, oh." Louder laughter, ringing against the scarred walls. He shifted pleasurably against her hand and she drew it away, slapping it with stinging suddenness against his cheek. "Bad boy!" The pain brought tears to his eyes.

Today was going to be perfect. It had to be today. The need ached and swelled in him. His palms grew moist on the steering wheel. He could already see the puzzled look in her eyes, the way she would half-smile as if trying to figure out the joke. He could already feel the pulse of her throat.

Slowly he took his foot off the brake and idled forward until he reached the entrance to the high school parking lot.

2

"**H**ave you noticed recently that your shoes don't match?" Barry Wheatley tried to keep a straight face as he waited for Diane's reaction.

"The mates hurt my feet," she said calmly. Her right shoe was black with an open toe and the left one was gray with a black stripe, but the heels looked as if they were almost the same height, and they were probably both real leather—Diane liked quality, when she could afford it. "I won't go out of the building this way; trust me. And don't change the subject."

She was standing in the doorway of his office, the newsroom clickety-clacking behind her. Something in the way she braced herself, blocking the door as if ready to fight for what she believed in, made him want to give her anything she asked. A damn fool, that was what he was.

"Maybe you ought to investigate the shoe industry," Barry said. "That's more along the lines of a consumer reporter, don't you think?"

Diane shook her head impatiently, silver earrings glinting at the movement. She had exquisite earlobes. Barry could almost feel the velvet of them. But he knew that if he tried, she'd leap away like a startled fawn.

"Close the door," he said.

5

Diane glanced at her watch. "I'm going to be late picking up Lara at the high school."

"You want an audience? Guy wouldn't like you moving in on his territory."

She glanced over her shoulder. Nguyen "Guy" Chang, the *Daily Record*'s police reporter, was sitting a dozen feet away staring fixedly at his computer screen. Not writing anything. Probably listening. Chang made everything that went on in Citrus Beach his business, especially everything that went on in the managing editor's office.

Diane closed the door and sat down on top of the late edition of the Citrus Beach *Daily Record*, which occupied the chair closest to her. Through the glass front of the office, Chang could still see them, but at least he couldn't hear them. "Just because I want to investigate a phony psychic doesn't mean I'm gunning for a news job."

"Aren't you?" Barry thought about lighting a cigarette. He thought about losing the twenty-five dollars he'd dropped into the office pot two weeks ago. He thought about not smoking for the remaining two weeks and decided he'd give it a try.

"Barry, I got a complaint about this psychic, and I think it's justified. Have you ever listened to his radio show on Wednesday nights? The man's a con artist." When she was excited about something, Diane's hands started to wave like a conductor's.

"Who was the complaint from?"

"She wouldn't give me her name—she said she was embarrassed. She 'donated' a hundred dollars to find her daughter and he said the girl had run away to Los Angeles. Big help."

Barry shrugged. "Anybody who believes in a guy called Eduardo Ranier deserves what she gets. Diane, your job is to write a consumer column about incredible shrinking sweaters and people who sell solar-powered toothbrushes door-to-door. Fake psychics are out of your territory."

"I want to do it." Her mouth tightened. "You know how I

6

feel about people like that, people who take advantage of worried parents . . ." There was a slight tremor to her voice.

He was going to fold; how could he help it? He knew, even if only at second hand, the memories that lay behind that tremor. "Well, the column comes first. Go after the man in your spare time, if you insist." She gave him a smile, but her eyes stayed sad. "Speaking of which, what are you doing for lunch tomorrow?"

"Buying a new pair of shoes." She stood up, pausing with her hand on the doorknob. "Look, Barry, after Saturday . . ."

"I'm not going to make a pass in Sammy's."

She considered. "That was the only silk blouse I had where all the buttons matched."

"I'll look in my carpet again, I promise," he said. "Don't tell me. I know. They're real mother-of-pearl."

She sighed. "All right. One-thirty at Sammy's."

As she opened the door, the noises filtered back—the click of terminal keys, the endless ringing of phones—and Barry picked up a thick whiff of smoke, which filled the newsroom despite the handful of smoke-eater ashtrays he'd scattered around. Breathing it was almost as good as smoking his own cigarette.

The general effect in the newsroom was of barely controlled chaos, which was normal. The desks, he noted idly, were covered by three layers, like an archaeological bisection of an ancient city. On the bottom were scattered newspapers and files; atop these, telephone books, dictionaries, and AP stylebooks spilled over onto vacant chairs and the scarred linoleum floor; and, on the very top, half-empty coffee cups tilted precariously beside carelessly discarded wirephotos and crumpled slips of paper scribbled with phone numbers. Mottos and favorite photos had been stuck to sides of desks and every other available vertical space. One sign taped to the back of a reporter's chair said, IF YOU DON'T WANT IT PRINTED, DON'T LET IT HAPPEN.

Barry refrained from staring as Diane strode somewhat lopsidedly to her desk and replaced one of the mismatched shoes. He knew Guy Chang was watching him.

3

By the time the bell rang, dismissing classes for the day, he was ready.

He had never planned anything like this before. They had happened, spontaneously. But then, he had never had a reason to plan it before.

The trick was fixing it so you got the right girl at the right time. Exactly the right time. Monday. Which gave him enough time to carry the whole thing off. He had until Sunday. No, Saturday, to be on the safe side.

He swallowed, feeling the dryness in his throat. A film of moisture coated his palms. He reached into his pocket and drew out a roll of Certs. Everything had been planned. Even the sweetness of the wolf's breath.

Leaning against a bike rack, he watched the students clatter down the steps of the high school. Would she see him right away? Maybe he should walk up to the front hall. No one would think anything of it. He'd arranged it so cleverly, being on campus this afternoon; no one even questioned it. Especially not her.

When they'd spoken earlier, made eye contact, he'd seen that spark. A bit of luck he hadn't expected, that sexual tension between a man and a woman. She would come with him without needing to be persuaded. All the better.

Hard tension between his legs. He half-dreaded, half-longed for that nightly ritual, the nursery rhyme, the probing hand, the inevitable slap. Sometimes she surprised him with the pain—fingernails clawing into his arm, high up so the sleeve would cover it, or a brutal twist of his little finger, hard enough to sprain it. ''Bad boy!'' Laughter, the smell of whiskey breezing across his face. And then, without warning, the nightly visits stopped.

He strolled up the steps and, from the top, surveyed the campus. Maybe the girl had come out from the back, by the playing field. The crowd was thinning, no longer rushing but ambling as the students exited the double doors and brushed past him.

From where he stood, without turning his head, he could see all the way to the library on his left and past the parking lot to the row of stores on his right. Great peripheral vision. Great depth perception.

She must have come out the back of the school. She was standing to his left, on the edge of the park strip that separated the high school from the library. Standing with a boy and another girl, a golden bracelet glistening in the sun as she gestured animatedly.

He hesitated. Should he go back down the steps? But he felt so powerful up here, like a god, dangling the world on marionette strings. If he stared at her long enough, called her to him, she would come.

4

As she darted out the side door of the newspaper, Diane glanced at her watch. She was going to be late to pick up Lara.

She shuffled into a half-run, not daring to go any faster in her uncomfortable shoes. Diane couldn't count the number of times she'd gone sprawling, or dropped her notes, or broken a heel. She liked to blame it on mental distraction; it sounded better than admitting she was clumsy.

Why had she agreed to have lunch with Barry tomorrow? Or why hadn't she just gone ahead and slept with him Saturday? She'd certainly wanted to. Millions of women jumped in and out of beds all the time and thought nothing of it. Millions of women moved in with men and thought nothing of it. Millions of women . . . well, never mind about that.

She yanked open the door of the aging green Volvo and tossed her junk into the back seat. He'd approved the story! Reluctantly, sure, but a yes was a yes.

Diane slid behind the wheel and started the car. The engine groaned, turned over once, and wheezed into silence.

She looked around the parking lot. Jimmy could usually get the clunker going, but he was out somewhere taking pictures. And she'd rather push the thing all the way to Citrus Beach High School than ask Barry for help.

Lara might give up and go off with that creep she was dating. No, probably not, but you couldn't tell. In the three years they'd known each other, Lara had changed from an eager child to a teenager with a brittle shell. But it was only a shell. Diane knew her well enough to recognize that.

A flick of the key and the engine turned over, hesitated, and caught. The entire car vibrated, like a dog shaking itself awake.

It was as she was shifting into reverse that the memory caught Diane off guard.

Four years. Four fucking agonized years and she still couldn't drive a car without a twinge—and sometimes, like now, a blow full in the face, as if a great black bird had struck her with its wing. Coming around the corner, seeing the delivery truck bearing down . . .

Diane shifted into neutral, put the brake on and got out to look around.

There was no one there, no little boy running into danger. *If only the truck driver had been more alert. If only I'd come home a minute sooner, just one goddamn minute.* How many times had she replayed that moment in her mind, like a videotape that you could view endlessly but never change? "Mommy! Hi, Mommy!" Mark running toward her, so chunky and alive, so glad to see her . . .

Across the parking lot, the guard glanced at Diane curiously. She took a deep breath, got back in the Volvo, and went to pick up Lara.

5

The footsteps whispered across the grass so swiftly that Lara didn't even have time to turn before she heard a metallic snick and felt the point of a knife at her back.

She noticed everything around her with startling clarity: the crisp March sunlight filtering through the pepper trees, the smell of exhaust from the street, the tilting of the earth. She felt a little dizzy, as if she'd forgotten to eat, but she never did that; the doctor was very strict. She wondered what effect adrenaline had, in combination with insulin, and it occurred to her that she ought to scream, but she couldn't.

"I am go-eeng to take you away from all thees, señorita," said a masculine voice with a badly faked Hispanic accent.

"Kris! That isn't funny!" She whirled around to face him, tossing her bangs out of her eyes. "What is that, anyway?" She looked down at the knife. The blade was a dull gray in the afternoon sunlight. "That's a switchblade, isn't it?"

"Yeah, my brother had it." He flicked the blade back into the sheath. "Carrying it around makes me feel like I'm really Bernardo, you know?"

"You're really an asshole, that's what you are." A good-looking asshole, all right, but she wasn't going to say it. Lara held out her hand, palm up.

"Aw, come on."

"Give it here," she said.

"Since when did you start bossing me around?" He was wearing his macho look. He did that a lot, especially since he got cast as the leader of the Sharks in the school's production of *West Side Story*. He'd probably showed the knife to half the school already. He was going to get in trouble again.

"Let's just say I need some protection, okay?" Lara heard her voice soften. He really was good-looking, and he was a senior, and he got to drive his mother's Mercedes a lot. Maybe those things shouldn't mean so much, she admitted silently, but when you came from a poor family in a snobbish town like Citrus Beach, you needed all the help you could get. Besides, there were moments when she sensed something vulnerable about him, a hurt to match her own, and then she almost loved him.

"Yeah, well, maybe you do, that neighborhood of yours." He handed her the knife. "You waiting for somebody or you wanna go for something to eat?"

They were standing in the strip park that separated the high school from the library.

"Waiting for my big sister."

"Sister? Oh, you mean in 'Big Sisters.' Why do you bother with her, anyway? Who needs another grownup looking over your shoulder?"

"I like her. Maybe it's because my mom split three years ago. Who knows?" Lara couldn't really tell him how she felt about Diane; it went too deep. It was part of a big, aching need that swept through her sometimes, a kind of desperation. She would feel as if she couldn't breathe, leaning against the wheezing washing machine in the back of that cramped house, hearing the kids crying, smelling the hot dogs and baked beans from dinner overlying the stale odor of sausage and sauerkraut from the night before. "Anyway, I'm gonna practice singing Anita. She bought me the new recording, you know, of *West Side Story* and we play it on her stereo."

"Maybe I'll come," Kris said, not meaning it. He was already looking around for his buddies. If she wasn't careful, she was going to lose him, Lara thought with a tug of fear. If only she were older and had better clothes. The only things

13

going for her were her looks and her contralto voice. They were, to use a phrase she'd heard in an old movie, her ticket out of Citrus Beach. With maybe a little help from Diane.

They strolled back together toward the front of the school where the other kids were hanging out. Lara tried not to keep glancing up at the open double doors to the administration building. She didn't want Kris to figure out who she was hoping to see. He got jealous easily.

"Hey, guys, guess what?" Jeanette Tracy glided up beside them. She was wearing a white blouse unbuttoned down to where you could see the lace from her bra. "I'm going to have my picture in the newspaper."

"Oh, yeah?" Kris wasn't missing a bit of the exposure. "For playing Maria? How about me, too?"

"No, it's the, you know, Man-in-the-Street interview they do different places." Jeanette flashed Kris her brightest smile, ignoring Lara. It was a very expensive smile; the Tracys never bought anything cheap.

Lara wasn't sure what made her turn just then to look at the head of the steps, but she did, and she saw him coming out of the front hall.

From this angle, you noticed his legs first, very long, and the slim hips. He was wearing a three-piece wool suit, like a businessman; Lara could almost smell the musk after-shave. She'd been surprised how potent it was, earlier, when he called her up on the auditorium stage during the demonstration.

He paused as if looking for something with those pale-blue eyes. They were—what was the word?—hooded, almost sinister. Then he saw Lara and smiled, and he didn't look frightening anymore.

"Oh, there's Mr. Ranier. Wasn't he terrific? He picked up all about Lara's family." Jeanette was still speaking directly to Kris. "He knew there were four kids and that Lara was the only girl, too. Isn't that weird?"

"Yeah," Kris muttered. He wasn't paying so much attention to Jeanette now; he was watching Lara watch Mr. Ranier.

"And he guessed about me, too, but he probably recog-

14

nized my name," Jeanette rattled on. "Like my dad being mayor pro tem on the city council . . ."

Lara knew Kris was angry about her reaction to Eduardo Ranier, but she couldn't help herself. She'd felt something earlier, when he picked her out of the whole auditorium. She knew he was waiting for her now.

She walked across the lawn and up the steps.

6

S he didn't sit straight in the bucket seat; she was turned sideways, facing him, her body radiating energy, the cells and platelets humming, the heart and liver and kidneys whirring along, the lungs breathing in and out, the pupils of her eyes adjusting to the slightly reduced light in the interior of the car.

All the spatial relationships had changed because of her, he noticed as he slid behind the steering wheel. The seats were more cramped, the floor space foreshortened, the colors dimmed.

"This is some car." She turned in her seat. Writhing. He could see her writhing. "Really terrific. Must have cost you a bundle, huh?"

Something stuck in his throat for a minute. He was so excited. She'd gotten in the car without needing any encouragement, almost suggested it herself. His hands felt cold and then hot. He wanted to touch her now. He wanted it to start.

She was waiting for his answer. "Anything worth having is worth paying for," he said, and then, deciding that sounded too stiff, added, "As a matter of fact, I inherited some money a few months ago. This was part of what I bought."

"I'd like to see the rest of it." She grinned.

"You weren't waiting for anyone, were you?" he asked as he eased the car out of the parking lot onto Citrus Avenue.

16

The traffic jam of departing students had left already, and he was almost certain no one saw them.

"Why should you think that?" She tossed back her blonde hair. The combs or clips or whatever they were had come off sometime during the day, or maybe she'd taken them off. Left free, the hair swayed tantalizingly around her neck.

"A pretty girl like you, I should think you'd have a boyfriend," he said.

"Oh, I've got several." A suggestion of a pout. She'd probably picked it up from some Hollywood vamp in a teenage movie. "But they're just children, you know?"

"I know." He paused at a stoplight. A police car was halted, facing them. The officer was gazing at someone on the sidewalk, a man walking unsteadily, maybe drunk. Suppose he looked up and noticed them?

The light changed and they moved through the intersection unobserved.

She was fiddling with her blouse, pretending to find a speck on it but actually drawing his attention to her breasts. He could read her like a book, knew everything she was thinking. He had so much power over her, he almost hated to see it end.

"Your parents might worry if you don't come right home from school," he said. He felt so strong now, he knew nothing could go wrong, but he had thought everything out and he would take no chances. If someone called the police too soon . . .

Sunday. By Sunday, they would all know who he was and what he had done and why. But not before then.

"Naw. I'm really independent." The girl slid down in her seat, looking for the moment like a stubborn child. "Nobody can tie me down, you know?"

"Sounds like fun." He flashed her his warmest smile, to let her know it was a joke.

She caught the innuendo. "Kinky stuff, huh?" She moved her body around. It was hard to concentrate on his driving. "I do what I want. Hitchhike, go out with older guys." Some of this was bravado, but it suited him perfectly. If she got scared at any point, he could manipulate her easily. Call her a kid, a mama's girl, and she'd do anything to prove you wrong.

The first time, he hadn't known he was going to do it. The girl had short bleached hair, a halter top, white short-shorts. Young for a hooker. She was chewing gum as she got in the car, and her speech was too fast, her movements choppy; she needed a fix.

"It's dark enough; let's do it here," she'd said, finding the lever that laid her seat flat and already starting to undo her top while he was still driving. Nice taut little breasts. His breath came rapidly. Her shorts slid onto the floor; nothing underneath but a springy bush. He stopped the car in an alley and fumbled with his jeans; she tried to help, but her hands were shaking.

Then he was on top of her, smelling the strawberry flavor of her chewing gum, poking around to get inside her. "Yeah, yeah," she muttered, faking desire. "You're terrific. Hot stuff." He could smell his own sweat, the familiar scent of hunger in the dark as he pumped himself into her, but it wasn't working. Something wasn't there. The little bitch was cheating him.

"Come on," he heard himself growl, and she pretended to moan, but it wasn't right. "You little shit!" His hands closed around her throat. As her eyes flew open and she began to struggle, the waves of pleasure rolled over him. Yeah, that was it. Harder, harder. "Bad girl. Bad girl." He crooned it lovingly, letting the tide of ecstasy flow away before he realized she'd gone limp.

It wasn't hard, finding a place to dump her in a ditch outside town. The tough part was fighting the urge to do it again too soon. He knew instinctively the cops wouldn't care too much about one dead prostitute, but they'd notice two or three. He had to be careful.

All these years, he'd watched himself. But this time it was going to be different.

They were cutting through Old Town, past the park where children scrambled over monkey bars and a bag lady dozed on a bench. He'd done one of them in Berkeley. As far as he knew, no one had even noticed she was gone.

"You live around here?" The girl was studying the succession of neatly manicured California bungalows on the side streets. "You own a house or what?"

"Renting," he said. "I own a place up in La Habra

18

Heights—that's one of the things I inherited—but I'm not ready to buy down here yet."

"It's really different from where I live," she said.

Turning down his street, he decided to leave the car in front of the house. That would make it easier to get the van out of the garage, later.

Although it was only midafternoon, the house was already in shadow. It resembled every other home in the neighborhood except that the paint was peeling and the cypress tree needed pruning. The squat palms looked scraggly, too, since that last storm. He'd meant to knock down the damaged fronds. Well, that was going to be somebody else's problem.

"This one?" She wiggled in delight as she surveyed the property. "It sure does look like a bachelor pad!"

"Needs a woman's touch," he said.

She brushed against him as he helped her out of the car. She must have dabbed on some kind of perfume after school, because it was really strong. He'd have to remember to air out the house afterwards, in case anyone came by.

They walked up the steps together and he held the door for her.

7

Diane checked her watch again as she pulled up in front of the high school. She was later than she'd thought, almost an hour overdue.

There was no sign of Lara or any of her friends.

Damn! Diane wished she could have gone in to see Barry earlier, but he'd been out of his office most of the day and then he'd had visitors. It was odd, the urgency she felt about the story on Eduardo Ranier, as if she were facing some kind of deadline. She half-wished that woman hadn't called this morning, the one with the runaway daughter.

Now, where is Lara?

Usually she understood about Diane's unpredictable schedule. Maybe she'd just gone across to McDonald's to get a Coke. That had happened before.

Diane pulled around to the parking lot and got out of the car, trying to ignore the pinching shoe on her left foot. The March air had a trace of a nip to it. There was no smog today; she could see all the way to the mountains ringing the Los Angeles basin.

Cars and an occasional truck rumbled past on the four lanes of Citrus Avenue. Diane tried to peer across to the hamburger stand, but it was impossible to see who was inside.

She sometimes wondered how she'd come to get this involved with a headstrong fifteen-year-old girl. The problem

20

was that Lara had almost no supervision. Her father meant well, but when he wasn't struggling to support his four children, he was out drinking with his buddies. And Lara naturally tried to escape whenever she could from the premature burden of being mother to her own three brothers. Which meant she ran around a lot, and Diane worried.

That was just what Diane needed. Something else to worry about.

Before she joined the *Record* staff two years ago, Diane had worked for a large public relations firm in nearby Santa Ana. As a public service project, they'd taken on a benefit for Big Sisters and she'd gotten interested in the program.

The idea of helping a young, motherless girl had appealed to Diane. Maybe it was egotism, wanting to feel important. Or maybe she'd needed the contact desperately, without wanting a deep commitment. Going out once a week to a movie or a museum had sounded like just about what she could handle.

Only it hadn't turned out that way. Bonding, that was what the psychologists called it. People flowed through your life like dollars through your fingers, and then one day you looked at one of them with a blink of astonishment and realized she'd taken over your gut.

Where the hell is Lara?

Diane stretched her shoulders and took another look around the campus. A few teenagers were sitting in the park strip smoking cigarettes. Maybe they'd seen Lara. It wasn't like her to just take off. Maybe she'd left some kind of message.

As she crossed the lawn toward them, Diane saw a woman come out of the library and turn in her direction. They recognized each other at the same moment.

"Diane! Diane Hanson!" The booming voice must have been audible all the way to the beach.

"Hello, Mrs. Belster," Diane called. She'd almost said Mrs. Bluster, which was Jimmy's nickname for her.

"Well! And how are you?" The large woman bustled toward her, clutching a stack of two records, three books, and a

21

videotape. She had a pretty face, but for some reason you hardly noticed it.

"Actually . . ."

"I called Friday but you weren't in so I didn't leave a message." Mrs. Belster drew to a stop slightly closer than felt comfortable to Diane. "It was about the grapes in the supermarket." She began chattering, something about confusing signs in the produce department and how she'd ended up with grapes full of seeds instead of seedless ones, and how that was false advertising, especially at a dollar fifty-nine a pound.

"I'm sure you're right." Being cornered by Mrs. Belster gave Diane a sudden, unexpected surge of claustrophobia, as if she were trapped in a great web. Trying to claw her way free, trying to get to the child in time, trying to make time go backwards, to undo that irrefutable moment, that crumpled still figure . . .

No, no, that was Mark, not Lara. Mark had been dead for more than four years. Lara was alive. She'd just gone somewhere with that adolescent boyfriend of hers. Right now she was laughing with him, absent-mindedly rubbing her wrist in that way she had.

"Well, I knew you'd look into it," Mrs. Belster was saying. "That was really helpful, when I called you about the sticking jar lids, that little device you recommended in your column, I can't tell you how much that's helped. Of course things aren't the same since my husband died, he used to take care of those things for me, but . . ."

The teenagers on the grass flicked out their cigarettes and stood up, stretching, stumbling into each other on purpose and making wisecracks as they wandered off.

Where the hell has Lara got to?

Mrs. Belster wasn't going to go away. She wanted to talk. Diane tried to force down her rising panic. This was another human being in need. She knew how that felt. Talk to her. Ask her something.

"Mrs. Belster, you know a lot of people in town." She was, Diane reflected, one of those people who turns up almost everywhere; impossible even to remember the first time Diane had heard that stentorian voice. "Do you know anything about a psychic named Eduardo Ranier?"

"Why, I've listened to his radio show a time or two and I've seen him around." The woman nodded to herself. "You might try Cissy Greenspon. You know her? She runs the Mystic Lights bookstore over on Cypress Street. Kind of a peculiar person, but she has a good heart, I'll say that for her."

"I'll give her a call. Thank you."

"Well, I've got to be running. Much as I'd like to stand here and chat with you, I have an awful lot to do. I'll look forward to seeing the grapes in your column. Good-bye now." Mrs. Belster shifted her books to get a better grip and hurried away.

The teenagers were gone. Diane bit her lip in frustration. She didn't really believe Lara had given up on her; their shared afternoons meant too much to both of them. And she'd told Lara there would be a surprise today. The surprise was probably pretty darn hungry by now, too; Diane had left plenty of food this morning, but she wasn't sure whether kittens regulated their eating the way grown cats did.

Maybe she would just take a walk across the street and have a look inside McDonald's.

8

He had drawn the curtains and they were sitting on the worn couch sharing a smoke, pure gold from Colombia. She was sprawled against the arm of the sofa, one leg brushing against him and her skirt draped suggestively up on her thigh. Dim light filtered over the old flowered carpet, the scratched pine coffee table, and the dusty TV set, its cord unplugged on the carpet as a precaution against the house's aged, erratic wiring.

"I like this place," she said. "I mean, it's kind of a dump, but it's a nice dump, you know?"

"Let me show you something." He leaned over and fished through the stack of magazines under the end table, pulling out an *Architectural Digest.* "See this place?" He flipped it open to the dog-ear and showed her the split-level design, high on a hill with a Jacuzzi in the back yard. "I'll bet you could build something like this in South America, for, oh, a hundred thousand. Maybe less."

"Who'd want to live in South America?" She lifted the joint and put it to her lips. It was already smeared with her lipstick, cherry red. Something else to dispose of later.

"Who knows?" He shrugged and moved closer. Damn, he wanted to prolong this. Get her clothes off. Have some fun first, but she kept kind of squirming away. Goddamn cock tease.

He could do it from behind, catch her unaware. The trick

with women was to make it sudden, before they had a chance to scream. But it was more fun when you were inside them first and you could look in their face.

There was a sheen of sweat between her breasts, where her blouse exposed the cleavage. He reached over and traced a finger along the soft curves.

"Wow," the girl said. "Hey." Her eyes half-closed. That was more like it.

"I'm going to give you a present." He kept his voice low and sexy. He could hear and see everything he did, as if he were standing over his own left shoulder, watching. "Something really special."

"Yeah." And then her eyes flew open. "Oh, my God! Presents! I forgot! It's my sister's birthday! I promised . . . Oh, shit! She's going to kill me!"

No, she isn't, he thought.

"Hold on." He handed the cigarette back to her. "What's the hurry? I'll take you home in a minute. Let's finish this."

"Well . . ." She chewed on her lower lip. "I feel like such an idiot!"

"You're really pretty." His voice was husky, dangerous.

"Yeah?" She focused on him again as she drew in a deep breath of smoke.

"Mm-hm." He leaned over and kissed her neck. She let out a long sigh and arched her back, letting him nuzzle her.

He wanted this to go on for a while, but it was too risky. If she started jumping around again, insisting he take her home, he'd have to force her down and she might scream. Or scratch him where somebody could see it.

"That's why I picked you," he whispered. "Because you're so beautiful." His thumbs traced up her chest toward the pulse point.

"Yeah, I could tell." She was still smoking, playing it cool. "I knew you were watching me. A girl can tell, you know?"

His fingers explored the hollows of her collar bone, closing in, not hurrying. "And you noticed me too, didn't you?"

"Yeah, sure." Her breath was coming faster. "But you know—I gotta go—I mean, my sister . . ."

"Your sister will be fine," he said.

9

"We have almost two hundred confirmed reservations for Sunday night," Lucille said from the doorway.

Mack looked up from behind his desk, startled. "What are you doing here? I didn't even hear you come in."

"I just dropped by to tell you the good news." She smiled and sat down in a fake leather swivel chair. "At a hundred dollars a head, that's a pretty good kick in the campaign fund, wouldn't you say?"

"I would." He mastered his instinctive irritation, replacing it with a look of what he hoped passed for admiration. Damn it, he did admire her; it was just that he hoped he hadn't made a mistake, letting his wife take over as his campaign manager. "By the way, did you see my secretary around anywhere as you came in?" He picked up a sheaf of signed reports.

"Michele's down in records flirting with Harry." Lucille could walk into a building and by some kind of osmosis immediately know where everybody was and what they were doing, especially if they were doing something they shouldn't.

She was a good-looking woman, alert and tanned, not sallow and half-sloshed all the time like his first wife. Lucille was fifty-one—only three years younger than he was—but she didn't look a day over forty. Her hair was permed or coiffed or whatever they called it these days, but anyway, it

26

looked damn classy. She dressed rich for a police chief's wife, too, but then she had her own money. And she brought out the best in him. Sometimes he'd almost forgotten there was a best.

"And we've got one TV station and a couple of print reporters coming to cover Assemblyman Gorwin's talk at the dinner," Lucille went on. "The Republican Women have really helped me out on this. Even if the sheriff's race *is* supposed to be nonpartisan, I've made sure they're all aware that your opponent is a Democrat."

"A Democrat?" Mack growled. "Tony Arroyo's so far left he's a goddamn pinko."

"I thought I warned you about that kind of talk." Lucille's voice took on the schoolmarm tone that she used when she caught him wearing brown shoes with a charcoal suit.

"All right. All right." He stood up and walked over to the window. From the second floor of the police building you had a great view of Citrus Beach's rambling old City Hall. He was going to like the Orange County Hall of Administration a lot better.

They'd hashed this out before he decided to run for sheriff. Lucille was right. You had to be smooth to make it in politics in a county with more than two million people. Maybe a lot of them were poor and spoke with an accent, but the ones who went to the polls had college degrees and bought their suits at South Coast Plaza.

"Actually, I did have another reason for coming by," Lucille said.

He'd suspected that. Lucille never did just one thing at a time. "Shoot." Mack turned away from the window. He caught her glance on his suit jacket and reached down to fleck away a spot of dust.

"Saturday night is the chili cook-off at the yacht club," Lucille said. "You know how people drink. You remember that time someone wandered out in the middle of Coast Highway and got killed?"

"You're damn right I do," Mack growled. "I'll have patrols all over the place."

"Well, that could be a problem." Lucille tapped a forefinger against her snakeskin purse. "Some of your best supporters are going to be there. I'd hate to see one of them end up in jail for drunk driving."

"You don't expect—"

"Now, Mack, let me finish." Her chin came up, and he subsided. "I'm merely suggesting that you put the word out in advance—perhaps ask the club to post signs—that the police will be enforcing the law very strictly. That will look good for you, and it should warn them off. Now, there's nothing un-ethical about that, is there?"

"No, of course not," he said.

"We just don't want any problems in Citrus Beach before Sunday." Lucille stood up. "You've made some enemies in the past, and we have to prove you're a viable candidate."

"Arroyo . . ."

"Is a deputy D.A. with a law degree from Stanford," his wife pointed out. "The fact that he's somewhere to the left of Jerry Brown doesn't mean he's going to be easy to beat. He's done his homework."

Mack's shoulders sagged. What the hell was he doing, run-ning for sheriff? He liked being a police chief. But damn it, this county needed a sheriff like him.

"What time are you planning to be home?" Lucille asked. "I thought we could have dinner at the club tonight."

"Fine." He hated eating at the yacht club. They never got through a meal without half a dozen interruptions, standing up, shaking hands, mouthing polite crap. Couldn't a man go home to a steak and a baked potato after he'd worked his butt off all day?

The phone rang. Lucille glanced out at Michele's desk and shook her head.

Mack picked it up. "Ferguson," he said.

"Chief? Sorry to bother you." The voice of the great Lt. Mario De Anda of the Detective Division. Another one cast in Arroyo's mold. Well, maybe not quite so bad. At least De Anda was a working cop, not a lawyer. "We've just got a missing persons report on a girl I thought you'd want to know about."

"Why? It sound like anything you can't handle?"

He could picture De Anda straightening up in his battered wooden chair in his cubicle of an office downstairs. "I've got Chenowski working on it." Sally Chenowski was in Juvenile. "The girl will probably turn up by dinnertime. Her family says she was supposed to come home directly after school to help her sister decorate for a birthday party, and she's over an hour late."

"An hour? And they called the goddamn police?" Mack made a face for Lucille's benefit. "She's probably rolling around with her boyfriend in the back seat of a car."

"Probably," De Anda admitted.

"Well? Why did you think I'd want to know about this little tootsie who took the long way home from school?"

"Because," De Anda said, "it's Jeanette Tracy. Councilman Tracy's daughter. You know he wanted a patrolman stationed in front of the high school after we picked up that Chino State Prison escapee . . ."

"Yeah, I remember," Mack said, feeling a black cloud start to form over his head. "Hank Tracy's daughter. Wouldn't you know it?"

He looked at Lucille.

"Shit," she said.

10

Diane was waiting for the signal to cross Citrus Avenue when she saw Lara come out of the McDonald's just ahead of Kris. Lara waved to Diane, turned and said something to her boyfriend, then darted across the street without waiting for the light.

"Hey, I'm really sorry," she called, breathless, as she drew up. "Kris and I had sort of a fight and we needed to hash a few things out. Were you waiting long?"

"Only a few minutes," Diane said. Amazingly, that's all it had been.

"You didn't think I'd skipped, did you?" Lara led the way to the Volvo. "You promised me a surprise!"

"And I intend to deliver." Diane still felt keyed up. She almost wanted to scold Lara, but where was the sense in that?

"Jeanette said she'd tell you where I was." Lara surveyed the now-empty campus. "She said she'd be hanging around for a while. You didn't see her, did you? Boy, I should know better than to trust her."

They got in the car and moved into the thickening flow of early rush-hour traffic. "You're awfully quiet," Lara said a block later. "Are you mad at me?"

"Not mad exactly." Diane sighed. "Worried, I guess. Maybe I overdo it."

"Because of your little boy?"

30

She nodded, tears pricking her eyes. Damn. You never knew when they were going to come, as if there were a great reservoir of them and her usual calmness was a thin covering of ice, easily cracked.

"Hey, I'm sorry," Lara said. "I didn't mean to bring that up."

"It wasn't really anything you did." Diane signaled and turned off the avenue toward the west side of town. "It's just . . . always there."

"I know." Lara remembered about her seat belt and buckled it. "After my mom left, for a long time, I would think of her at the oddest times. It hurt really bad, and then I'd get mad. Do you get mad?"

"Yes." She started to say more, but stopped. "Tell me what you and Kris were fighting about."

Lara shrugged. "He gets jealous. It's really stupid. I just went up to talk to Mr. Ranier."

"Mr. Ranier?"

"You know, the psychic." Lara's face took on a new animation. "He spoke at assembly this afternoon. He called some of us up on stage, me and Jeanette and some of the others. He figured out all about our families."

"That's called research." Diane turned the car into a drive-through dairy, an old 1950s one with a giant plastic statue of a cow on the roof, and pulled up to the service counter. "A half-gallon of low-fat milk and a loaf of rye bread, please."

"You pay a lot more at these places," Lara advised.

"I haven't got much money, but I've got less time. Now tell me about Mr. Ranier."

"Well, anyway, I saw him after school and I went over to talk to him. I thought maybe he could give me some advice about my career. Kris got all pissed off and came over and grabbed me and practically dragged me down the stairs. It was humiliating. Who does he think he is?"

Diane pulled a couple of creased dollar bills from her purse and fingered them absent-mindedly. "I'm going to be writing a story about Eduardo Ranier. He's a fake, Lara."

"Who says?"

Diane told her about the woman with the missing daughter.

"Well, maybe she *did* run away to Los Angeles!" Lara said. "What's he supposed to do, make something up?"

"There's no such thing as a real psychic." The heavyset clerk handed Diane a sack through the window. She gave it to Lara, paid the bill, and waited while the clerk shuffled back to the register for change.

"You're wrong." Lara radiated indignation. "Diane, he couldn't have learned all those things about me."

"Anyone could have told him. Kris, for instance. Or Jeanette."

"But they didn't! And I felt something, like a vibration, like he was looking into my soul! The principal said Mr. Ranier helped the police find a murder victim two years ago, a young girl. Now how could he have done that if he wasn't psychic?"

"Luck." Diane said. "Maybe he just stumbled across the body. Lara, don't be naive."

"I'm not." She sat back with her arms folded around the grocery sack as Diane tossed the change into her purse and pulled out onto the street. "He's not a fake. And there's something about him I really like, and I think he likes me too."

"Do me a favor," Diane said. "If you decide to talk to him again, let me know, will you? I'd like to come along. I promise to keep my mouth shut the whole time."

"We'll see." Lara unbuckled her belt as they halted in the apartment carport. "Now where's my surprise?"

11

The girl sprawled limp under him, her tongue protruding, her face turning purple. The cells and platelets lay silent, the heart and lungs no longer pumping and wheezing. With one twist of his hands, he'd emptied a universe.

His heart thudded with excitement and his body throbbed with release. Everything had gone exactly as he'd planned. No one had seen, no one suspected anything. She wouldn't be missed for hours.

He finished cleaning himself in the bathroom and went back to the girl. From under the couch, he pulled out a black plastic garbage bag and rolled her down onto it. A glance at the clock on the end table showed it was almost four-thirty. He wouldn't be able to dispose of the body until around midnight. That was all right. He had things to do this evening.

The Nikon was on the kitchen table where he'd left it. He rewound the film, took it out, and put in a fresh roll of black and white. He would have preferred glorious color, but you had to play by the rules if you intended to put out a press release.

Back in the living room, he studied the body in the filtered afternoon light. Maybe he should take some arty shots with natural light.

The hell with it. Get it over and done with. He looked at

the clock again. He'd have to be gone for a couple of hours. There was no time for fooling around.

He arranged the body so the face and the ravaged throat were clearly visible, then shot half a dozen pictures in quick succession, using the strobe. Good. They'd be able to recognize her without any trouble. Oh, how they'd scurry around, the police, the reporters. The ones before had been nobodies; this was different. He'd captured one of their own.

The doorbell rang.

He froze, but his brain was racing. Postman—no, he'd seen the mail already in the box when they came in. Door-to-door missionaries. Kids selling magazine subscriptions. Hell, nobody ever visited him here.

Someone pounded on the door. "Hey!" A girl's voice. "I know you're in there! Oh, come on!"

Rita Beth Tuohy, from next door. Damn skinny little twelve-year-old with a crush on him. Oh, shit. He ought to take her next, but he didn't dare. Someone would get suspicious; her parents could probably hear her yelling at his door, for one thing.

What if she'd seen him come in with the girl? But Rita Beth wasn't that nervy; she wouldn't have come over if she thought he had a date. Now how the hell was he going to get rid of her?

"Are you in the darkroom?" She was really shouting up a storm. "Can I come in and watch? Pull-eeeze?"

Cursing silently, he looked around for somewhere to hide the body. No, she'd hear the thumping; besides, it would take too long. Instead, he set the camera aside and tiptoed through the kitchen to the side door.

Stepping outside, he called, "Around here!"

"Oh, hi." She bounced up the side walkway. "Were you in the darkroom?"

"Yeah, but I'm done." He wiped the sweat off his forehead with the back of his sleeve. Dammit, why did the little brat have to come over *now*? "Aren't you supposed to help your mother with dinner or something?"

"She hasn't started yet." Rita Beth had a jaw that was al-

34

ways working on a wad of gum. "Are you trying to get rid of me?"

"Right." With Rita Beth, subtlety didn't pay, he'd learned. He would have ordered her off the property long ago, but then, the Tuohys *did* own the place.

"What'sa matter? You got a girl in there or something?" She giggled and feinted past him toward the kitchen. "I'm gonna go see."

He grabbed her around the waist and jerked her back. "You stay out of my house unless you're invited, Rita Beth."

"Ow!" She shrieked and twisted away. "I'm gonna tell the police you molested me!"

Oh, Jesus, why me? he wondered. "I'll tell you what." His brain seemed to be functioning again. "There's a concert Sunday in the park. Bluegrass music. How about if I take you?"

"Just me? No other girls or anything?" she asked suspiciously.

"That's right. It's just that I've got a lot of work to do this evening and I don't have time to fool around. All right?"

She stood storklike on one bare foot and rubbed the other one against the back of her jeans leg. "Well, okay. What time?"

"Noon."

"I'll be here." She grinned up at him. "Is this a date?"

"Your first date, Rita Beth." He smiled, and saw an answering joy flicker in her eyes. The little shit really believed he was going to take her out on Sunday. If he was still in town, he'd give her a taste of what blackmailers deserved.

"Okay. You promise?"

"Promise. Scout's honor."

"See you!" She darted off, then paused, hopping on one leg again. "Hey, is it okay if I bring our new video camera? Dad'll let me take it if you're along. We could get some great pictures!"

"Fine with me." He went back into the house and was closing the door when the idea hit him. Videotape. Now, that would be something. A lot more exciting than just a photograph of a girl after she was dead . . .

12

L ara nearly dropped the sack of groceries when the kitten pounced on her just inside the door. "Oh, it's darling! Is this the surprise?"

Diane nodded and removed the sack, watching the girl kneel and tousle the eager white ball of fur. "I haven't named her yet. Got any brilliant ideas?" She put the bread and milk in the refrigerator. "You hungry or anything?"

"No." Lara picked up the kitten and plopped onto the couch. "Hey! Don't nip me, little rascal!"

Putting water on to boil, Diane went into the living room and kicked off her shoes. The apartment was tiny; this close to the beach, rents were prohibitive for anything larger. The frayed velour sofa opened into a queen-size bed, and the kitchen was barely big enough to turn around in. The only thing that saved the place from claustrophobia was that Diane had gotten rid of most of her possessions after the divorce and hadn't been able to buy many new ones, except for the stereo.

There was no need to ask what Lara wanted to hear. Diane lifted the first disc of *West Side Story* out of its jacket and carefully set it on the turntable. As the jazzy overture blotted out the sounds of cars and voices drifting in from the street, Lara underwent a transformation. Her eyes widened, her expression softened, and a slight smile played around her mouth.

She really was a remarkably pretty girl, Diane reflected,

sinking into a cracked beanbag chair. The brown hair was badly cut, but it couldn't dim the sharply defined bone structure or the radiance of Lara's hazel eyes.

Lara began to sing along with the record. She took whichever part she favored at the moment, except that she always sang Anita, because that was the part she was playing at school. The cast had been practicing the music since the beginning of the semester and would be starting rehearsals on the stage soon. So far, they'd used only their chorus class time. Diane hoped the rehearsals wouldn't cut into her afternoons with Lara. Well, she supposed she could always go sit in the school auditorium and watch.

Lara's voice was throaty and promising. She still had to work at the high notes, but the school had an excellent music program and the training was helping.

Diane fetched her coffee. Lara took charge of turning and changing the records, still in her semitrance. Suddenly, in the middle of a song, she give a little jump, surprising a whimper from the kitten. "Officer Krupke!"

"What about it?"

"Not the song! The kitten!" Lara grinned. "Isn't that a great name? This silly little kitten with a big long name like that! Don't you think it's cute?"

Diane nodded. "Officer Krupke it is."

They finished the album. As usual, Diane chimed in as Maria—slightly off-key—for the duet "A Boy Like That." "That was really fun," Lara said afterwards. She hesitated for a moment before adding, "I've been thinking about, you know, my career. I mean, look at the movies. There are actresses who are little kids, for God's sake. I'm practically too old already."

"I wouldn't say that." Diane went to fix herself another cup of coffee. She knew she ought to cut down on her caffeine; Barry had been giving her a hard time since he quit smoking. Well, if he lasted his full month, maybe she'd switch to decaf. "Besides, there are laws restricting how much you can work until you're eighteen."

"It's not fair!" Lara's eyes narrowed. "But they wouldn't

have to know how old I am, would they? Kris says I could pass for eighteen. I could go to Hollywood now. Dad would scream, but what could he do?"

Diane's chest squeezed with apprehension as she walked back into the living room. She understood only too well the frustrations of Lara's life. Running away. Lara had mentioned it before, and it always frightened Diane more than she dared to admit. She didn't want Lara to see her as just another grownup, another jailer. "Don't go anywhere without telling me, okay? I mean, I could help you."

"Then let's do something!" Lara sat up straighter, nearly dislodging Officer Krupke. "That Mr. Ranier, he understood about me wanting to act. Sometimes I feel like I'm going to burst!"

"But you wouldn't leave *West Side Story*, would you?" Diane reminded her.

"Well, no. I guess not." Lara ruffled the kitten's fur distractedly. The little creature curled back into a ball, eyes half-closed, purring.

"I'll tell you what. South Coast Rep has a summer program for young actors. I could look into it, maybe help out with the cost," Diane said. "I'll call them and find out. Why don't I pick you up after school Wednesday? We can go out for a Coke."

Lara nodded slowly. "Yeah, I'd like that. Kris won't, though; he gets jealous of other people. Sometimes he can be so sweet, and other times he's really weird. Look what I had to take off him." She pulled a knife from her purse and the blade sprang open.

"That's illegal." Diane tried to calculate the length of the blade. It was only about five inches, but sharp as a stiletto, and the sight of it in Lara's hand disturbed her. "You could be arrested for carrying that."

"Yeah?" Lara grimaced. "That's all I need. Remember when one of the teachers caught me injecting insulin and she was going to call the police and report me for drugs? People are crazy in this town. Here, you take it." She closed the knife

38

and dropped it in Diane's purse. "Now you can get arrested instead of me."

"Thanks a lot." Diane stood up. She'd have to dispose of the knife later. The bottom of a trash bag seemed as good a place as any. "Now I'd better get you home before the entire Ryan clan starves to death."

"I should be so lucky," Lara said.

13

He took the roll of black-and-white film out of the camera and was about to go into the darkroom when he decided he ought to hide the body first, until he was ready to get rid of it.

It hadn't been part of his plan; no one ever came in here. But after Rita Beth's unexpected intrusion, he didn't want to take any chances. Suppose Mr. Tuohy decided to drop over and inspect the wiring? Not that he'd bothered to do it in ten months of complaints, but you could never tell.

He lifted the girl with a grunt. Damn, she felt heavy. Her arms and legs flopped and the gold chain around her neck dangled as he carted her through the narrow den into the bedroom in back. Damn pain-in-the-ass little rich bitch. Making trouble for him even after she was dead. How did she like it, there under the bed with the cockroaches?

Satisfied that even a busybody like Rita Beth wouldn't detect anything, he returned to the front of the house. It only took a minute to get rid of the cigarette and spritz some air freshener around. Oh, damn, the purse. He picked it up, stood there indecisively, and then went back to the bedroom and stuck it under the bed with her. The sea water would take care of the fingerprints.

Her purse. He'd come home early from school that day when he was seven and seen her purse in the living room. She never left it there. Then he heard a noise in her bedroom, gasping sounds, and a man's voice.

He got a knife from the kitchen like he'd seen someone do in a horror film, and then he walked to where he could look in. His mother was lying naked on the bed and this big man was hunched over her, putting his big thing in and out of her, and she cried, "Oh, God, that feels wonderful! Oh, God!" It was sick, disgusting.

He didn't know which one of them to stab. His arms and knees felt weak, and he realized he wouldn't really be able to hurt them, not before the big man caught him.

Well, fuck her. Fuck all of them.

He went out and got the afternoon edition of the *Record* off the lawn. Flipping through it, he scanned the ads. There it was. Portable VHS videocassette recorder and color video camera with electronic viewfinder and power focus lens. $864.83 after rebate—no, screw the rebate—$964.83. Weighed 5.7 pounds without battery.

Have to remember to get a battery, he told himself. Over a thousand dollars by the time you added tax and everything. That was a lot of money for something you'd only use twice.

There was another problem, too. He'd want to take longer to videotape a murder, draw it out so it really looked like something. He couldn't risk doing that in this house, where Rita Beth was likely to come pounding on the door. Of course, there was the place in the Heights. He'd let it run down the last few months, since he threw the party there, and it had never been fancy, but it was isolated enough. On the other hand, it was a forty-minute drive away—if you didn't want to get stopped for speeding, and he certainly didn't— and how was he going to get some girl to ride all that way with him? Maybe the video camera wasn't such a great idea.

Tossing the paper aside, he went into the darkroom, which was, in fact, the bathroom with a shelf added across the back to hold his enlarger and trays. From a cabinet under the counter, he fetched the developing tank and chemicals and set them out, then bent under the shelf to plug in the enlarger.

Without warning, as his hand touched the plate, a jolt of electricity zapped through him. Sparks crackled and he jerked backwards, hands flying up to protect his face. His shoulder smashed into the shelf, half-lifting it off its brackets, and with a sickening sense of futility he felt the enlarger shift into a short, painfully certain slide until it smashed onto the bathroom floor.

Goddamn the Tuoys and their frigging rotten wiring! If he got Rita Beth alone on Sunday, he'd pay them back in spades!

He crawled out from under the shelf, being careful not to cut himself on the broken glass, and stood up to survey his darkroom.

The place was a mess. At that moment, he thought he'd rather pee out the window than walk in here again.

He clutched the edge of the counter for support. Sweat collected on his forehead, under his arms, on his lower back. Omens. This was a bad omen. Why hadn't he remembered to be more careful about the outlet?

And what about the film? He had to print it tonight . . .

Maybe things weren't so bad, he told himself, beginning to steady his nerves. Maybe it was a different kind of omen. Maybe it was telling him to get the video camera and forget about the darkroom. A thousand dollars—shit, he'd inherited a lot more than that from the insurance. Enough to live like a king in South America.

As for who would ride all the way to the Heights with him . . . it would have to be someone who thought she knew him, who trusted him, who would come along without a lot of questions. And he knew exactly who that would be.

14

The shin splints started about Juniper Street. By the time Barry turned onto Serra, the new jogging shoes were raising blisters on the back of his heels, his lungs were pumping like a pair of old bellows, and his heart was thudding loud enough to drown out the rock music blaring from a parked car.

Oh, hell, he wasn't doing badly for a forty-one-year-old recently reformed smoker who jogged only when he got around to it, which was maybe twice a week.

A police car drove by, cruising Old Town at about twenty miles per hour. In the twilight, the cop looked much too young to be out of school.

At Serra Elementary, two couples were playing a desultory game on the lighted tennis courts. There'd been a whale of an argument in the city council about paying for those lights, but in the end they'd sprung for it. That was nine years ago, soon after Barry joined the *Record*, when tennis was the latest fad and people had to make appointments to use the courts. Then had come racquetball and then—what *were* people playing these days? Anyway, you sure didn't have to stand in line for a court anymore.

Well, you couldn't fault the city council. They weren't prophets, and they had a lot to take care of.

Actually, Citrus Beach wasn't much different from any

other Orange County beach town, he reflected. North toward the freeway clustered rundown apartments filled with Indochinese refugees, undocumented Mexicans, and just plain poor people. Going south toward the beach, you ran into the bland 1960s middle-class apartments and houses like the one Barry lived in, and then, here on the eastern side of Citrus Avenue, you hit Old Town—funky, with irregular winding streets and the perpetual aroma of marijuana drifting down to mingle with the sea breezes at Pacific Coast Highway.

He paused for a signal light, decided to push himself further, and turned south on El Portal toward the park.

This was a good place to jog. He was just as glad, all things considered, that he didn't live on The Other Side of The Boulevard. So what if the beach here on the east side did attract more than its share of tattooed hangers-on? If they ever got around to tearing down the old pier, things might get cleaned up a bit—but Citrus Beach would lose a lot of its flavor.

"The Boulevard" was Citrus Avenue, haven of car dealers, auto repair shops, and mammoth discount houses. To the west of it, fancy shops and restaurants overlooked the manicured beach and the new pier. Then, at the far west side of town, an enterprising developer had dug out a harbor—oh, sorry, they actually spelled it "harbour," if you please.

He came to the park and with relief turned off the sidewalk onto the yielding lawn. There was hardly anyone around at this hour of the evening, just a bag lady rummaging through some take-out fried-chicken boxes in a trash container.

Which reminded him. He had asked Celia in Lifestyles a month ago for a story on the homeless of Citrus Beach. He made a mental note to ask her how it was going.

He connected with San Cristobal, letting it lead him northward again. The shin splints had disappeared, but he realized as soon as he hit the sidewalk that the separate aches in his body had merged into one great misery.

No pain, no gain.

The patrol car cruised by again. No, it was a different one; this cop looked older. From the loose jowls, Barry guessed the officer had a beer belly to match. A man after his own heart.

44

Were there a lot of cop cars out tonight, or had he just happened to run into two in a row? He made another mental note to ask Chang to check on it tomorrow.

Sarah had said Barry never stopped thinking about his work. Well, how could you? A newspaper editor was supposed to know everything that went on in his town. Sarah had even accused him of taking up jogging so he could spy on the neighborhood. Spy? That's what journalists were paid to do—watch people. Especially the ones who didn't want to be watched.

Sometimes he missed Sarah, like at Christmas. She'd always baked cookies from scratch. He'd taken her for granted; he could admit, now, that he'd been partly at fault. But where had all that rage come from? He still hadn't figured it out five years later.

He stayed on San Cristobal north to Valencia. Another black-and-white came by. The driver was talking on his radio. Barry thought about flagging him down, but you never knew with young cops. They didn't have the congenial feeling toward newspapermen that older cops had.

Not that Barry particularly liked Mack Ferguson either; he'd always considered the chief a half-assed redneck bigot, until the man's first wife kicked off last year and he married up. Since Lucille had persuaded him to run for sheriff, Mack had turned into a half-assed hypocritical bigot, which is less interesting and a lot more common.

Maybe there'd been another minimart holdup. Citrus Beach had been hit with a string of them recently, mostly along the freeway. So had neighboring towns. The robbers were armed, and a clerk in Huntington Beach had been shot in the shoulder when he tried to set off an alarm. But the robbers always hopped right back on the freeway; that wouldn't explain the cop cars in Old Town.

Ah, the home stretch—Alicante Avenue, coming up. What smartass had named these dull suburban streets after fabled Spanish cities? On the other hand, he preferred Alicante and Valencia to Somerset Lane and Hyde Park Drive over in Citrus Harbour. And Grosvenor Avenue, for God's sake. They'd once

45

done a "Man-on-the-Street" asking six people how to pronounce Grosvenor, and every one had done it differently.

When he saw a fourth patrol car pull slowly past, Barry knew something was up. He had the familiar reaction: a newsman's fascination with the Big Story, mixed with dread that this time disaster was striking too close to home.

Was Diane all right?

He chugged to a halt in front of his one-story ranch house and fished in his pocket for the key. Damn it, he'd never meant to get involved with a woman, not after that last hellish year with Sarah. Not after the pain he'd seen in Elizabeth's eyes. She'd been fourteen then, old enough to understand the words but not the reasons. Hell, he didn't understand them either.

When Diane came to the *Record* two years ago, he'd felt the chemistry right away, but they'd both worked hard at ignoring it, especially her. Then about six months ago he'd had free tickets to a musical and she'd accepted his invitation, because it was a show she wanted to see. Since then, well, they were officially just friends, but they both knew it was more than that. He hoped she'd start trusting him, one of these days. One of these days real soon.

Barry let himself in, still panting, and flicked on the police radio. Crackling, blurred sounds spilled out, and then he caught something. A description of a girl. A name—Jeanette Tracy.

Tracy, Tracy. Hank Tracy's daughter?

Barry glanced at the digital clock on the videocassette recorder. It was after six o'clock. The news desk would have gone home for the day. Except, most likely, for Guy Chang, who had the obsession of a born reporter. One night a few months ago, when the coastal storms were whipping up big news, Barry had come in early and found Guy sleeping on his desk.

And Meyer Krantz, the head of photo, might be in, or one of his minions.

Although an afternoon paper wasn't on deadline until morning, Barry had never lost the instincts developed on a

46

wire service years ago. Always on deadline. It went against the grain to wait until tomorrow, even though anything they learned tonight would probably be old news by then.

He called Photo's direct line.

"Photo, Owens." It was Jimmy, the *Recorder*'s whiz-kid photographer, frequently referred to as Jimmy Olsen. Diane stood in for Lois Lane, and Chang, Barry suspected, pictured himself as Superman.

"Barry here. Listen, have you heard anything about a missing girl named Jeanette Tracy?"

"Name's familiar," Jimmy said.

"Has Chang got the radio on?"

A brief pause. "No. Methinks I hear the click of VDT keys, though. You want to talk to him?"

"Yeah. Wait. Would you check and see if we've got a picture of her?"

"Hey!" Snapping fingers. "As a matter of fact, we do. Jesus, I took one today for Man-on-the-Street. I knew I'd heard her name somewhere. What happened to her?"

"I don't know yet," Barry said. "Switch me over to Chang."

"You got it."

Chang came on the phone. "What's up, boss?"

"I hear via the airwaves that Councilman Tracy's daughter Jeanette is missing."

There was a brief pause while Chang searched his encyclopedic memory. "She's been in trouble before. Got busted at a pot party last summer. The judge is a pal of her father's; he sentenced her to six months lounging around the family swimming pool."

Barry ignored the resentful undertone; it was par for the course with Guy. "Mack Ferguson ought to love this. The timing is fershtunken as far as he's concerned."

Guy chuckled. He was working on an analysis piece about Mack's campaign for sheriff and had been complaining to Barry how hard it was to shake the guy's new yuppie image. "I'll see what I can do."

"I don't want us to miss anything," Barry said. "You or Jimmy keep an ear to the radio, in case she turns up."

"Or pieces of her turn up," Chang said.

Barry shook his head. Kid reporters had all the delicacy of a sledge-hammer. "Let's hope that doesn't happen."

But he realized as he hung up the phone that he had a funny feeling about this one.

15

Spoiled brats like Jeanette Tracy were a pain in the ass, Lt. Mario De Anda reflected as he glanced up. He saw that the hour hand had edged past eight o'clock, which meant that Cheryl would be putting the kids to bed. One more bedtime story without daddy.

Of course, it was a slight consolation that Chief Ferguson was sweating this one.

The phone rang. Emma had gone home an hour ago—staying late, as she often did, was a real act of dedication considering the lousy pay secretaries got—so he answered it himself.

"I'm sorry to keep bothering you, Lieutenant." The tear-streaked voice belonged to Mrs. Tracy. "Have you heard anything?"

"I'm afraid not." What if it were Skeeter or Billy lost out there? He tried to sound more sympathetic. "She's probably gone off with some friends for the evening, if I know anything about teenagers."

"Yes, but her sister's birthday party—I can't believe she'd break her promise. Jeanette is kind of wild, I know, but she does keep her word."

"Maybe she forgot. Kids do that," he pointed out. "We're on the lookout for her, Mrs. Tracy. I'm sure she'll turn up."

"Thanks, Lieutenant. Is it . . . all right if I call back?"

"I'll probably be leaving soon, but the watch commander will let you know if she's been found," he said. They exchanged good-nights and hung up.

De Anda hoped he could have five minutes alone with Jeanette Tracy when they found her, to tell the little snot what kind of anguish she'd caused her mother. Not that it was likely to do any good.

On the other hand, to be perfectly fair, it wasn't entirely Jeanette's fault that he was pulling another late one. It was because of Ferguson and his damn politics.

Not the politics of running for sheriff. That wasn't De Anda's problem, although he hoped like hell Tony Arroyo was going to get it. But the politics within the department.

It boiled down to a game of musical chairs. If Ferguson got elected sheriff, that left the chief's office wide open. Of course, the city council could and probably would consider candidates from outside, but they had a longstanding preference for promoting from within.

Only they weren't bloody likely to boost a mere lieutenant all the way up to chief. The plum would go to one of the captains.

He ticked them off in his head. Keith Llewellyn, Patrol. Age: sixty-two. Way past the usual retirement for a cop, and planning to take it come September. He and his wife had already bought the motor home.

Then there was Jed Rollins in Traffic. Too ornery. He had scathing things to say about the city traffic engineers, sometimes at city council meetings, and he let his superiors feel the rough edge of his tongue a bit too often.

That left the chief's buddy Harry Pyne in Records. He was in his early fifties and distinguished-looking, but there was nothing distinguished about his career. Nothing embarrassing about it either, and he'd have Ferguson's recommendation.

Which was why, when Detective Capt. Bert Kraus had departed two weeks ago to take over as police chief in a town up north of Sacramento, Ferguson had stalled about appointing a replacement. Everybody knew De Anda was the obvious choice; he had more seniority than the other lieutenants, he lectured to classes in police science, and he just plain worked his ass off.

Even the dicks were grumbling about it. For one thing, De Anda was doing the work of two men, without the pay or the credit. For another, it was clear to everybody what was going on: Ferguson didn't want Pyne to have to compete with a fifteen-year veteran of the force who at thirty-nine had a degree in criminal justice behind him and was only a couple of credits away from an M.B.A.

De Anda rested his elbows on the stack of reports and grinned. Boy, I sound pretty good, the way I describe myself, he thought. Real hot stuff.

For Jeanette's parents' sakes, he hoped she got her tail home real soon. For Chief Ferguson's sake, he hoped she'd gone fishing at Yosemite and wouldn't be back for a week.

16

"**Y**ou going to be here much longer?" Jimmy Owens perched on the edge of Guy's desk. "It's after nine o'clock. I'm about to pack it in."

Chang flexed his shoulders. He'd been staring at the screen for five hours straight, with time off to stick a Le Menu in the company microwave. "I can't get a handle on this damn profile. You sure you won't give me some real dope on Mack Ferguson? Off the record, even. I could check it out."

"Sorry. Family loyalty and all that crap. I mean, the guy *is* my stepfather, which kind of makes us related. More or less." Jimmy grinned, stretching his freckles. Chang sometimes thought Jimmy had been invented in Hollywood. He had red hair and dimples like Ron Howard on *Happy Days* reruns. "Hey, anything new on that missing girl?"

"No." Guy began systematically cracking his fingers.

"Give you big knuckles."

"When you're half Vietnamese and half Chinese, you can use 'em."

"Good line," Jimmy said. "You know, it kind of gives me the creeps. I took a picture of her today, that girl, Jeanette. Real cute kid—a little stuck on herself, but who wouldn't be, with her looks?"

"And her money," Chang added. "She's probably shacked up somewhere with a surfer."

seeing her in Old Town? Or were they just checking on general principles, because a lot of druggies lived around here?

Then had come the stroke of luck—a robbery-homicide at a minimart up by the freeway. He'd breathed a sigh of relief, hearing it on his police radio, knowing the black-and-whites would be swarming up there like flies to carrion. They'd probably given up on the girl by now anyway, figured she'd run off to Hollywood or something.

This was the best time to dump her, now while the cops were tied up. Besides, rigor mortis hadn't yet set in, so she was still fairly easy to carry, but she wouldn't be for long.

Of course, it would be a hell of a lot simpler just to get on the freeway and toss her out in an orange grove or a canyon somewhere. But he wanted this body found tomorrow. And he wanted it found in Citrus Beach.

The garage door slid up at the touch of a button and closed again obediently as he eased the van away into the night.

From the bungalows along El Portal, lights glowed and televisions flickered through thin curtains. A dog gave out a high-pitched bark; a baby wailed. He was the fox, slipped into their midst to pluck the fattest chicken and then escape before they knew he'd been there.

He paused at the stop sign at La Vida and smiled to himself. So far, everything had gone smoothly. The photograph was ready, here beside him in its manila envelope. When he got home, he'd put the note together. He kept rewording it in his mind, trying to find the perfect phrasing. No point in tipping his hand too soon. Yet it had to be threatening enough to draw media attention from beyond Citrus Beach. It wasn't the number of people you killed; it was how you did it that counted, and how you made the public quiver and shake in their flimsy houses.

He used to lie awake at night, listening, after the man moved in, hearing his mother cry out in ecstasy. His hand would move down the way hers used to. Once she'd come in to say good-night and seen what he was doing. She started to turn away, but he grabbed her wrist and squeezed it so hard she gasped. His whole body jerked with orgasm, and when he looked at her again, she was smiling.

In the park, a balding man was walking a white poodle. A dark shape behind a bench might have been the bag lady sleeping, but more likely it was just some trash.

Not a cop car in sight on San Cristobal. At Citrus Avenue he spotted one, but it was headed north, away from the beach.

"You having a good time?" he asked the corpse in the back. "Wanna go hang around the beach for a while? Sure you do."

The night was crisp, very clear here by the ocean, crackling with negative ions and salt spray. Citrus Avenue dwindled as soon as it crossed Coast Highway, veering sharply left to become a narrow beach-front lane. Old cottages, many of them boarded up and vacant after the ravages of the winter's storms, gazed eyeless over the beach and the crumbling pier.

He halted in a parking space alongside the pier and climbed out to reconnoiter.

No one stirred on the beach. The lifeguard tower was shuttered now. Away off to his right glittered the lights of the New Pier restaurants, still open at this hour but too far away for anyone to see him. Dead ahead, the Pacific Ocean stretched to Catalina Island and beyond, the water choppy and treacherous with late-winter rip tides.

His heart began to pound. This was the most dangerous moment. His body hummed. He was going to mount this town and fuck it.

Sliding open the side doors, he slid the girl's purse over his shoulder, then lifted her out of the van, swinging her up into a fireman's carry.

Another check down the beach. No one around.

The light was too dim to read the signs at the foot of the pier, but he knew them by heart. KEEP OUT—UNSAFE. THIS PIER IS CONDEMNED. NO TRESPASSING.

You had to watch your footing. Some of the boards were missing, and others had rotted through so they looked sturdy enough until you walked on them. Test each step, keeping the corpse in balance. Jesus, she seemed to have gained fifty pounds. Maybe it was just the damn awkwardness of carrying a limp body with the arms flopping.

Water lapped against the pilings down below. Cold, very cold. But then, the girl wouldn't mind.

It was the perfect spot. The sea water would rinse away any evidence he'd overlooked. And the thick muck of seaweed and trash would keep the tide at bay, holding her body right where he dumped it.

Her hair blew up against his neck, smelling of jasmine-scented shampoo. It would look nice, floating in the water like spun-gold seaweed. Somebody was going to get quite a surprise tomorrow morning.

A snapping sound warned him just in time to shift his weight. He'd better keep his mind on business.

He kept going until he couldn't find a safe board to walk on. Beyond, most of the pier had been sheered away by heavy seas. A rough winter, and not over yet, despite the warm days. But with any luck, he'd be gone before the next storm hit.

Kneeling, he eased the body over the pier's edge and listened to it slide down the pilings. It hit the water with a faint splash, almost lost in the steady thrum of the waves breaking farther out. The purse tumbled in after her.

Good-bye, Jeanette.

He straightened up and picked his way back to the beach, then halted abruptly. A Volkswagen bug was turning off Coast Highway, chugging toward him. A Tina Turner song shimmied through the open windows, accompanied by drunken laughter from the four kids crammed inside. The car rolled past. He started breathing again. He could have sworn they hadn't even noticed him.

Everything was working out just the way he wanted.

18

O fficer Krupke hopped up onto the rim of the bathtub. "Hi, fella." Diane lifted her hands, dripping, from the water and spread them apologetically. "No can pat."

The kitten meowed and peered over the edge, teetering.

"You look clean enough to me," Diane said.

The kitten reached toward the water with one paw, thought the better of it, swiveled, and paced down the rim to sniff at the half-empty glass of sherry resting in one corner.

"Not for cats!" Diane snatched the glass away. "Down, Krup."

The kitten watched her curiously, making no effort to leave.

"I'm getting out," Diane warned. "Drip drip."

Officer Krupke cocked its head.

"Here goes." Diane stood up, spraying water over the kitten, which hissed a protest and beat a hasty retreat. She dried herself quickly and slipped into a terry-cloth robe.

She'd taken the bath and the sherry to relax herself. It hadn't worked.

If only she could stop thinking about the things Lara had said. There wasn't any danger of her running away from home, not until *West Side Story* was over at least; but the fact that Lara imagined some kind of mystic connection with Eduardo Ranier was more than a little disturbing.

What the hell had the principal been thinking of, to let a fake like that appear at the high school in front of a bunch of gullible kids?

Taking her sherry to drink at the kitchen table, Diane wished she knew more about the man. What he looked like, for instance. She'd been imagining someone short, dark, and oily, but that didn't sound like the type to appeal to Lara. Maybe he was handsome. An unsettling thought.

What *had* happened to that woman's daughter? Had Eduardo Ranier been involved in her running away? Diane frowned at her own imaginings. White slaving was a bit beyond the scope of the average psychic, wasn't it? Impulsively, she reached for the telephone.

It rang five times before Jimmy answered it, and he sounded a little out of breath.

"Sorry. I guess it is kind of late." Diane rested an elbow on the table. "I needed your sage advice."

"That's okay." She could hear him settling down, and the creak of what might be a bed. "I had to work late, so I was up. Besides, it's only a quarter to eleven."

She told him about Barry's approving the story on Ranier, and about Lara's meeting him. "You grew up around here, right?"

"Pretty much."

"Did you know him?"

"Slightly." He exhaled deeply, shifting gears. She could picture his eyes narrowing as he searched his memory, the way they did when he poked around under the hood of her Volvo. "His uncle used to own a camera store, so I saw him hanging around."

"What does he look like?"

"Pale and tall and sort of intense. Like a ghost." Jimmy's tone lightened. "We used to all pretend to be scared of him. He hated it. You know, some people are just outsiders no matter what they do, and he was one of them."

"Family?" Diane finished her sherry and weighed the merits of a late-night cup of coffee. The caffeine might keep her awake, but she'd skipped her after-dinner cup and her head was aching a little. Withdrawal.

"Father split when he was a kid, I guess. His mother was weird too." She could almost see Jimmy shaking his head. "I think she finally married an ambulance-chaser from San Diego. He used to get in trouble a lot—Eduardo—that isn't his real name, you know. It's Theodore Raines."

"I'll bet he hated that." Diane couldn't help feeling a tug of sympathy for the kid everybody made fun of, especially being stuck with a name like Theodore. She wished she didn't have such a soft heart. "What did he get in trouble for?"

"Petty stuff. He told some girl he owned a Lincoln and was necking in the front seat with her when the real owner showed up. Served the guy right for leaving it unlocked."

"No high crimes and misdemeanors?"

"I don't think so." Jimmy's voice stretched into a yawn. "I mean, Ted's about eight years older than me, so I didn't know him too well."

"I'll let you get some sleep." Diane stretched. "I'd better hit the sack myself before I make another pot of coffee."

"Bad for the liver, or something like that." Jimmy yawned again. "Not that you're boring me or anything . . ."

"Thanks for the help, pal," she said. "I owe you one."

"A home-cooked meal would be nice."

"You're on." She was too tired herself to think straight. "Let me know what night is good."

"Will do."

They hung up, and she went to bed, visualizing a thin teenager trying to impress a girl at his uncle's camera shop; then her mind interwove the image with a faint picture of another girl, a runaway, disappearing into someone's car and never coming home.

19

The homicide victim had been the market owner, a forty-seven-year-old Vietnamese man with five children and a grandmother to support. His wife, who'd been working in the back of the store, had heard the whole thing and was too upset to talk to police tonight, a situation De Anda found understandable but frustrating.

One witness had seen a Toyota of unknown color speeding away with two men in the front seat. He hadn't been able to read the license number. That was as much as De Anda had found out at the scene.

Now he wiped his forehead with his shirt sleeve and watched the hands on his office clock edge past eleven. Damn. He'd have Detective Amboise handle the follow-up. She'd covered most of the holdups before; besides, Sergeant Hewett was due in court the rest of the week to testify in a drug rip-off slaying from last fall.

No one had found Jeanette Tracy yet, but under the circumstances, that wasn't surprising. They'd sent most of the patrol cars cruising the north end of town on the slim hope that the robbers were still around.

Jesus. A forty-seven-year-old man. He'd probably left everything behind in the fall of Saigon, fleeing to a better life in America. A goddamn shame.

The phone rang, not his private line but the general detectives' number. He considered not answering it but gave in on the fifth ring.

"Lieutenant, I'm sorry to disturb you at this hour." The man's voice sounded vaguely familiar. "There's been something bothering me all evening I felt I should discuss with you."

This is some kind of weirdo, he thought. "Who is this?"

"My name is Eduardo Ranier. I'm—"

"Yes, I know who you are." Cheryl collected horoscopes, read the *National Enquirer* devotedly, and always listened to *Ranier Reflects* on the radio Wednesday nights.

"Today I was speaking at the high school and I had a chance to do readings on several of the students." The voice had a detached, flat sound to it, not the fake warmth projected on the radio. "I picked up some flashes of danger."

De Anda reached for his cup of coffee and drank the cold dregs. "Oh?"

"I wish I could be specific. It was a very strong feeling, but you know, there's no way to control these things. It's not like a camera that you can bring into focus."

Something nagged at the back of De Anda's mind. Ranier had found a girl's body two years ago down in Dana Point. The man had located it psychically—or had claimed to. "Was there one particular student you felt this about?" he asked, hoping he didn't already know the answer.

"Well . . ." Maybe that wasn't flatness in the voice, but tension. Why? "The truth is, I felt it about two of the girls."

"You wouldn't happen to remember their names?"

"One of them, yes, Jeanette Tracy, Councilman Tracy's daughter."

Had Ranier been listening to the police radio? For all De Anda knew, KCIT might have picked it up for their news broadcast. "Anything specific? You wouldn't happen to know where she is right now, for instance, would you, Mr. Ranier?"

There was a pause on the other end of the line. "I'm not a complete fool, Lieutenant." Ah, a trace of emotion—anger. "It did occur to me how it might look, calling you, particularly if something had happened to either of the girls, but I felt it was my duty . . ."

"Yes, of course." De Anda tapped a ball-point pen against his scarred blotter. "Who was the other girl, by the way?"

"I believe her name was Lara something. Ryan or Rowen."

Ferguson was going to have a fit about Ranier butting into this Jeanette Tracy business. The chief was touchy enough about it already, and he hated fortunetellers with an old-style lawman's raw contempt. "Give me your phone number, Mr. Ranier. We may be getting back in touch with you later."

Ranier provided it. "I take it the Tracy girl is missing?"

"That's right." He waited.

"I knew I should have called you sooner."

De Anda said good night and hung up. Jesus, surely the guy wouldn't have set the whole thing up. . . ? It was like a plot out of a movie, or maybe half a dozen old movies. The guy had to know he'd get caught.

No, most likely Ranier had heard the whole thing on the radio and just decided to capitalize on it. There was no point in telling the chief and getting him mad at De Anda for paying attention to the creep.

Nuts. God, the world was full of 'em, just waiting to make hay out of somebody else's misery.

TUESDAY

20

Diane woke up at two-thirty in the morning, thinking she'd heard Mark call out for a glass of water. The illusion was so real that she'd thrown on her robe and made it halfway into the living room before she realized where she was.

It was almost too much, coming back on her all at once. Moments before, Sol had been her husband, and they'd lived in a house in Irvine, and she'd had a precious two-and-a-half-year-old son, the one she'd gone through three years of fertility treatments for.

Now she was Diane Hanson, not Berk any more, thirty-four instead of thirty, not a mother, not a wife. Her head ached and her throat felt scratchy.

She went into the kitchen and fixed herself a cup of coffee. To hell with being sensible.

Even the faintest noises echoed eerily at this hour. Diane flicked on the radio, tuned to KCIT. Soft forgettable music surrounded her, tinny and disembodied. She had the impression of riding forever in a sterile elevator with Muzak wafting overhead.

Diane sank down at the table with her coffee. Oh, Mark. Oh, God, Mark, isn't it ever going to stop hurting?

She'd tried to ignore Sol's drinking, tried to hold things together, even though she knew she was doing too much—tak-

69

ing care of a toddler, working part-time, cleaning, cooking, calling in sick for Sol when he was hung over.

I used to say, *At least he's supportive.* She squeezed her eyes shut and felt the sting of tears. What the hell did that mean? He couldn't even stay sober when he was watching his own son.

That day had been some obscure holiday—for him, not for her—and the baby-sitter had the flu, so he'd offered to watch Mark while she worked. The funny thing was, she'd had a comfortable feeling about it all day at work, imagining Mark and Sol playing together, glad the boy was getting more of a chance to know his father.

She'd stopped off for some milk and bread on the way home. Someone ahead of her in line was hassling over the price of a sale item. *A few minutes. Just a few goddamn minutes. I should have known. I should have sensed something was wrong.*

But she hadn't. Not until she turned the corner onto their block and saw the panel truck heading toward her. And a little figure running across the lawn, chubby legs pumping over the grass and into the street, calling, "Mommy! Hi, Mommy!"

She could still hear her own voice, screaming, "Go back! Mark, go back!" but it was too late. That horrible thud—had she really heard it, or just felt it down to her soul? And then Mark, lying there limp, blood all over his head. Mark. Mark. It couldn't be Mark.

The delivery truck screeched to a halt and Sol came running out, and then a few minutes later the paramedics arrived, and the police. All she registered was how light Mark felt in her arms and the way Sol kept saying, "I could swear he was in his room." She could smell the gin on his breath.

Diane pressed her forehead against the table and cried.

A commercial came on the radio pushing used cars. And then the announcer, late-night mellow, saying, "If Jeanette Tracy is out there listening to this, your mother asks you to please call home. Your family is very worried."

Her head came up. Jeanette Tracy—wasn't that Lara's friend? So she'd run away, or disappeared; that explained why she hadn't given Diane the message that Lara was in McDonald's.

Right now, the pain that had become old and familiar to Diane was fresh and razor-sharp for Jeanette's mother. Please let her little girl be all right, Diane prayed silently. God, how many children do you have to take? Do you get some kick out of making people suffer?

Just a runaway, she told herself. Please, God, let that be all.

She turned off the radio and went to sit on the sofa. After a while, her eyelids felt heavy. She could see Lara quite clearly. The girl was smiling and walking toward her across the high school campus. A shadow fell over her.

Now Diane was farther away, driving to pick up Lara. The motor ran and the wheels turned and the buildings along Citrus Avenue rolled past, but it was taking a long time to get to the school. Much too long. There was something dark and horrible on the campus, closing like a fist around Lara. Diane stepped on the gas and the car shot backwards. She jerked at the gears but that damn thing wouldn't shift into forward.

The shadow deepened and spread like a storm cloud, blotting out half of the city. Lara was at the center, visible even from so far away, a faint golden glow. Something reached toward her, something cold and evil, and Diane couldn't get her damn car to work right, and she was screaming for help but no sounds came out . . .

She woke up with tears in her eyes, not for Mark this time but for Lara. It took a minute before Diane could swallow. It was just a dream, just a dream.

She remembered about the knife in her purse. For some reason, she felt better, knowing it was there.

Diane went into the bedroom, burrowed under the covers, and slept dreamlessly until dawn.

21

The toaster oven had just popped open when the phone began to ring. Kris heard his mother answer it in the kitchen as he reached for the English muffins, and then she came into the breakfast room and said, "It's for you."

"Me or the runt?" Leaning back and tilting his Danish Modern chair onto the back of its runners, Arnie grinned at her cockily. Kris wanted to put a fist through that smile.

"It's for your brother, Champ." Brigitte Lender smiled down at her oldest son.

"Must be somebody selling magazine subscriptions," Arnie said.

Kris jerked his chair away from the table and stamped across the tiled expanse into the kitchen. He didn't even have to look to know Arnie was already buttering the muffins for himself.

"Yeah?" he grumbled into the phone.

"Kris?" It was a woman's voice, high-pitched with strain. "This is Mrs. Tracy, Jeanette's mother."

"You sure you don't want to talk to my mom?" he asked, slouching against the butcher-block counter. Vaguely, he recalled meeting Mrs. Tracy once, playing bridge with his mother at the yacht club. She had nervous little eyes like a bird's.

"No. Jeanette didn't come home last night. I've been calling everybody I could think of who might have seen her. Do you know where she went after school yesterday?"

He couldn't remember if she'd said anything; he didn't think so. "She was just hanging around, you know. I guess I saw her about, oh, three-thirty maybe." He shifted position and glanced out the window. By the swimming pool, a black bird was pecking at crumbs.

"You don't remember who she was talking to, do you?" Mrs. Tracy's voice broke. Jesus, he didn't need this, not first thing in the morning. Besides, Jeanette was okay. That girl knew how to take care of herself.

"Well, she was talking to us—Lara Ryan and me—and then Lara and I kind of had a fight and we ended up in McDonald's," Kris said. "Jeanette was gone by the time we came out. As far as I could see, anyway. I didn't really look."

A dull silence on the other end of the phone told him Mrs. Tracy had run out of ideas. Oh, God, she wasn't going to cry, was she? "I'm sure she's around somewhere," he said lamely. "She was kind of keyed up, I guess. She'll probably be at school this morning."

Mrs. Tracy drew a ragged breath. "Yes . . . yes, that's probably right. Well, if you think of anything, or hear anything—I mean, kids seem to have their own network. You might run into her before I do."

"I'll give you a call first thing," he promised and then, for good measure, gave her Lara's phone number.

"Thank you, Kris," she said.

As he hung up, he turned to see his father standing in the doorway looping his tie through the knot. "Now what kind of trouble are you in?"

Kris's jaw tensed up but he didn't want a fight. "Nothing. That was Mrs. Tracy. She's trying to find Jeanette."

He returned to the table and stuck another muffin in the toaster. Arnie was wearing his USC football sweatshirt. "Girl trouble?" he asked. "You need any advice, just come to me."

Kris stabbed his knife into the butter. He could hear their

parents talking in the kitchen, running over their routines for the day.

"That reminds me," Arnie said. "You've got something of mine."

"What?" Kris said.

Arnie nodded at the knife.

Shit. He'd forgotten about the damn thing. "I gave it to Lara."

"Well, you just get it back from her." Arnie leaned forward. He had big shoulders and muscled arms.

"Yeah, okay, if she still has it," Kris said, staring through the little glass door at the slowly browning muffin halves.

"She'd better have it."

What was taking the damn toaster so long? "I'll buy you another one. What's the big deal?"

Arnie raised his voice. "When I lend you something, I expect to get it back. Not some cheap substitute."

Their father moved toward them. "What's going on here?"

Arnie shot Kris a warning look. "Just something I lent my brother and he gave away."

A look of annoyance flashed over Erik Lender's face. "What does it take to teach you responsibility, Kris?"

His face hurt from holding back the angry words. "I'm gonna be late for school," Kris muttered and dodged past his father out of the room. Behind him, the toaster oven popped open.

He dashed down the hallway and grabbed his books, then went out by the side door, skirting the jade hedge and hurrying across the small, manicured lawn. He nearly stumbled over the curb as he dashed around the corner onto Somerset Lane before slowing to a walk.

At the corner of Somerset and Grosvenor, he stopped and took a deep breath. Christ, you couldn't win with them, could you? He didn't even know why. It wasn't really because he wasn't a football star like Arnie, or because once he'd cut class and gotten caught smoking dope behind the lockers. Other kids did that kind of stuff all the time. It was something else, like he'd disturbed some perfect triangle when he'd been born and he couldn't ever make it right.

He wished he could walk out of there and never go back. Maybe that was how Jeanette felt.

He began walking east on Grosvenor toward Orange Avenue. He supposed he could catch a bus there, but he wasn't ready to go to school yet. Instead, he decided to skirt the harbor and head down to the ocean. What he needed was a walk along the beach. Then he'd take a bus to school. If he felt like it.

In the morning light, the marina lay at peace off to the right, sailboats and yachts bobbing at their moorings, the small docks damp and empty except for a few scattered pelicans. Gulls mewed to each other as they wheeled overhead, and, as he walked down the sloping street, he could hear the distant whine of a saw.

The shops were closed now and so were most of the restaurants, except for a small coffee shop. Through the window as he passed, Kris could see an old man reading a newspaper spread out on the table and a young couple drinking coffee and looking at each other.

He hoped Lara still had the goddamn knife. Not that he really wanted to give it back, but he hated being put in the wrong. Arnie already had four years on him and about twenty pounds, not to mention a caseful of trophies. Why couldn't the guy go live in an apartment like any normal college student? But then, why should he, when he could be king of the roost?

Kris crossed Coast Highway at the light near the New Pier and turned east, leaving the harbor behind him and walking at the edge of the beach. A pear-shaped woman in pedal pushers was combing the sand with a metal detector. She stooped and picked something up, turning it over in her hand before tossing it back.

You'd think a guy's parents would get excited about him being cast as practically the lead in a musical, wouldn't you? Well, not the lead, maybe, but it was an important part. That guy George Chakiris won an Oscar for it, so somebody thought it was a big deal. Sure, his mother had said something about how nice it was, and she'd told a few people at the club, but his father didn't care. He probably wouldn't even come and see it.

Kris peered upwards at the thick clouds rolling in from the sea. Their darkness answered his mood better than the shafts of sunlight at the marina, yet it made him vaguely uncomfortable, too.

He passed the T-shaped intersection with Cypress Street. Traffic wasn't too heavy and the cars were moving fast on Coast Highway. There wasn't much rush hour along this strip. Further south, in Newport, they'd be bumper to bumper.

He shifted the books to his other arm. Christ, he wished he had the nerve to toss them in the ocean.

When he reached Citrus Avenue, he turned south instead of north and walked toward the old pier. So he'd be late for class. Maybe he wouldn't go at all. That would fit in just right with the way his parents thought about him anyway.

Dropping his books onto the sand, he bent and untied his Nikes, pulling them and his socks off together. The sand felt cool underfoot. The ocean breeze smelled of fish, and his stomach growled. Oh, yeah, he hadn't eaten, had he? Kris hesitated. Maybe he should go on to school. He could run over and get a hamburger before it started. But he wasn't ready to face all those people yet.

He stood for a moment, staring out to sea, and then he saw something stirring in the water, way out near the end of the pier. Some kind of seaweed, maybe. No, it looked like a wig. A blonde wig somebody had tossed in the water.

Kris walked to the edge of the sand, in the shadow of the pier. It continued out over the ocean for a ways on its thick dark pilings. All sorts of junk had collected there—seaweed and soft-drink cans and cellophane wrappers. And blonde hair, and a sodden white blouse and something metallic, like jewelry.

Oh, Jesus. Oh, sweet Jesus. His heart turned over and his

skin felt clammy. Shit. He wasn't really seeing this. Mrs. Tracy was sitting by her telephone, waiting for Jeanette to call home. Right now the other kids were getting out of their cars at school, tossing friendly insults at each other. The water looked so damn cold.

Kris sat down on the wet sand and started to cry.

22

Mack Ferguson took the news over the telephone. He was standing in the bedroom wearing his jockey shorts and an undershirt and had been trying to decide between the gray pin-striped suit from Nordstrom and the dark blue one from Neiman-Marcus.

"Jesus H. Christ," he said into the receiver.

Lucille poked her head in from the dressing room and watched him. She had one false eyelash on and the other one in her hand.

"What about the guy who found her?" Mack asked. "Somebody she knew?"

The watch commander filled him in. One of the county's rent-a-coroners was on the way and Lieutenant De Anda had been notified, he said.

He didn't need to remind Mack that they had two murders going at one time in this city and they didn't even have a damn captain of detectives. Maybe he could shift Jed Rollins out of Traffic. No, not with that mouth. God knows what he'd tell the press. As for Pyne or Llewellyn, hell, they'd just get in De Anda's way.

Mack hung up with a sinking feeling.

"Well?" He'd forgotten about Lucille. "Aren't you going to tell me what happened?"

"Somebody killed Jeanette Tracy. Or maybe she OD'd." It

78

was an encouraging thought, but unlikely. People didn't overdose with drugs and then throw themselves off the end of a pier.

Lucille ran through a few swear words he'd forgotten. Then she sank onto the edge of the bed. "You've got to take care of it, Mack. The robbery, well, that could happen anywhere. But this . . ."

Automatically, Mack began putting on the dark blue suit. "The kid who found her goes to the high school. Apparently he knew her. Might be some kind of boyfriend."

Lucille brightened. "You think he did it?"

"Cases like this, it's usually somebody they know." Mack began to feel more hopeful. "He'd better have a damn airtight alibi for yesterday afternoon. Anyway, it's a place to start."

"I can't fix this one for you." It seemed like a peculiar thing for Lucille to say, but people said strange things when they were upset. "You've got to get this resolved before the dinner, Mack. If it weren't Hank Tracy . . . Christ, the poor guy, and Lena. She'll be hysterical. I'll go over there myself and see what I can do. If it's the boyfriend, you know, putting a patrolman in front of the high school wouldn't have done any good."

He nodded, but the way things were going, he had a feeling it wasn't going to be that easy.

23

Lara was going to be late for school again. Dave and Sammy had gotten themselves off for the bus on time but Gerry, the seven-year-old, was working on a temper tantrum and their father was hulking in his chair at the breakfast table nursing a hangover and a bad temper.

Every time she tried to make Gerry get up and go dress himself, he began to scream, which set their father off cursing.

"Well, all right then!" Lara pushed damp bangs out of her eyes and glared at Gerry. "Stay home! I don't care! I'll call the truant officer on you, you little brat!"

"That's enough!" Brendan Ryan slammed his glass of tomato juice-with-a-dash-of-vodka onto the table. "Shut up, both of you."

"Yeah," muttered Gerry. "Shut up." He poured some more of the tomato juice from the can into his jelly glass and gulped it down just like his father. Then he thumped the glass onto the table so hard drops sprayed across Lara's T-shirt.

"You little creep!" She grabbed Gerry under the arms and dragged him out of his chair. He shrieked, ear-piercing yelps that made the whole house vibrate, as she hauled him out of the kitchen and let his leg bang against the edge of the door.

"You're not my mother!" he wailed. "You cut it out, Lara. Dad! Dad! Help me! She's hurting me!"

There was no response from the kitchen.

Clothes were heaped on the floor of the bedroom Gerry shared with Dave, along with broken toys, records, torn books, and copies of *Mad* magazine. "Get dressed!" Lara shouted, pushing him inside and slamming the door in his face.

She ran into her cubbyhole of a room and slammed that door too. This was her last clean top and besides, the tomato juice would never come out.

Angrily, she jerked the hangers across the rod in the doorless closet, pawing through Sammy's misshapen garments—he slept in the living room, which didn't have a closet—until she found a wrinkled blue shirt that would have to do. It was clean, but everything smelled from one of Dave's stray cats that had wandered in here last week and left its mark.

Lara scraped the hangers back and forth one more time as loudly as possible just to set her father's teeth on edge. Why should he enjoy his breakfast? He was the one who'd had four kids, not her.

She thought about calling Mrs. Tracy back and offering to let them adopt her. If she had a nice home like that, she wouldn't act the way Jeanette did. Maybe she could offer to switch. One week in this madhouse and Jeanette would never make her mother worry again.

By the time she'd changed tops and brushed her hair, Lara felt calmer. Calm enough to know she couldn't take two more years of this. She would have to come up with some kind of a plan.

It had been nice of Diane to suggest the acting conservatory, but that wasn't enough. Lara turned toward the poster on the wall, of Vivien Leigh in *Gone With the Wind*. *She* wouldn't have sat around waiting for something to happen.

She walked out into the hall. Splashing noises came from the bathroom. "Aren't you ready yet?"

"No!" Gerry shouted from inside.

Brendan Ryan loomed in the doorway from the kitchen. "You quit raising a racket, Lara. You're not too big to be whipped."

"But Gerry—"

"He's just a little kid," her father said.

"Oh, yeah?" Lara yelled. "And what am I? An old woman?"

She ran into her bedroom and turned on the radio, full blast, as a song ended and a promo blared. "This is KCIT-FM, Citrus Beach's hometown radio station. Rock and pop and our own resident psychic . . ."

The moment she heard his name, Lara could see him again in her head; no, feel him—it was like in the movies, that funny tingling you got, an awareness even when you weren't looking at each other.

She tried to remember exactly what he'd told her. Not the stuff about her family, but about her future. "You're a very complex young woman." That's what he'd said—not girl, but woman. "I see many things for you. Are you interested in acting?" It was amazing how he'd picked that up. "Yes, there are definitely strong possibilities. But something else, much sooner." Then he'd frowned, and in the audience some smartass had yelled, "You saw the poster for *West Side Story*, huh?" and the mood was broken.

Lara stuck her head out in the hall. Her father had gone into his room.

She darted out to the living room and found the phone book on the floor under the coffee table. It took a while to look up KCIT because the radio stations were at the beginning of the Ks instead of being alphabetical.

The switchboard operator put her through to a man who said, "I'm sorry, Mr. Ranier only comes in on Wednesday afternoons to tape his show."

"Could you give me his home number, please?" Lara said. "It's really important. I mean—I need a consultation. I have to make this important decision."

"I'm sorry," the man said. "You'll have to call back tomorrow."

"Tomorrow?" It seemed such a long time away. "But . . ."

"Good-bye," the man said, and hung up without waiting for an answer.

82

"Well, up yours, too!" Lara snapped into the buzzing phone.

As she walked back toward her room, she heard the familiar tinny music that ushered in the KCIT newscast and then the announcer's voice said, "The body of a young woman was found today off the old Citrus Beach pier. Police declined to comment on the cause of death or to say whether there is any link between the body and the reported disappearance of Jeanette Tracy, the daughter of Councilman Hank Tracy . . ."

It couldn't be Jeanette, Lara thought with a flash of resentment against the know-it-all announcer. God wouldn't be that cruel, to make somebody die before they'd even had a chance to live.

24

When Diane walked into the newsroom, she knew immediately that something had happened.

First of all, Barry wasn't in his office but sitting at a desk next to Rand Franklin, the news editor. Usually Barry didn't emerge until after ten o'clock, when the copy desk was on deadline.

The second thing she noticed was the knot of photographers standing just outside the door of the photo lab, drinking coffee and talking. Photographers almost never stood up if they could lean or sit on something.

But they weren't all there. "Where's Jimmy?" she asked.

Meyer Krantz, his thin, unevenly bearded face poised above a coffee mug that read "Head Honcho," said, "We sent him out to the pier."

"What's going on?"

He told her about Jeanette Tracy.

"Oh, God." For a moment, Diane had trouble breathing. Last night's dream came back full force, the darkness reaching out for Lara, the evil thing at the high school. Jeanette had been right there on the campus yesterday afternoon. Maybe the killer had been too.

Meyer told her Jimmy had radioed in that it might be a strangulation but nobody was saying anything. Too soon to know whether she'd been raped, and anyway the sea water had probably messed things up.

Diane glanced over at Guy Chang. He had a telephone propped on his shoulder and was typing furiously at his terminal. A field day for a police reporter.

"And somebody blew away a store owner up by the freeway last night," Meyer said. "Chief Ferguson must be tearing out what's left of his hair."

Diane went over to her desk, looked up the police detective number, dialed it, and told the secretary she'd been at the high school about the time Jeanette must have disappeared.

"The detectives are out, but they'll get back to you as soon as possible," the woman said, taking her name and number. "Is there anyone else you think might have seen something?"

Diane gave her Lara's and Kris's names and added, "There were some kids sitting on the grass too but I don't know who they are."

After hanging up, she sat at her desk trying to calm her thoughts. They kept shooting off in different directions. What if it had been Lara? A matter of a few minutes . . . but no, Lara had been with Kris, so she'd been safe. Jeanette's parents—what they must be going through . . .

"Are you all right?" Barry slid onto the edge of her desk. "You look pale."

"I'm sorry." Diane swallowed hard. "Meyer told me about the Tracy girl."

He shook his head and when he spoke, his voice was tight with anger. "I hope they kill the goddamn bastard when they catch him."

He touched her hand lightly. Just having him close by comforted her. A horrible thing had happened, but this time, it hadn't happened to her. She was letting the fears of the past overwhelm her, that terrifying sense of vulnerability that follows tragedy. "I guess I'd better get to work," she said.

Barry glanced away, then back again. "About lunch . . ."

"Late is okay," Diane said, "Or would you rather do dinner?"

85

"Sounds good." The tension lines around his mouth eased. "The House of Fishes? Or we could broil some steaks at your place."

The idea of being alone with him sounded wonderful, safe and protective. "My place," Diane said.

As soon as he moved away, she turned to the computer, first typing in her log-on—her last name—and then her secret code, which was Cin. Because her father lived in Cincinnati.

At the top of the screen, the words "Message Pending" flashed. She pressed control and the MSG key. There was only one message, saying one of her readers had called with a question and would call back. The log-on at the bottom, added automatically by the computer, read HERTZ. That would be Ginny, the newsroom secretary.

Diane turned to the stack of papers on her desk.

Her column came out Mondays, Wednesdays, and Fridays. She'd already finished enough of them to last until mid-April. Of course, there was always the matter of Mrs. Belster's grapes, and half a dozen letters, the usual complaints about stores that wouldn't replace defective merchandise promptly and mail-order houses that didn't deliver. Nothing urgent.

Diane flipped open her notebook. It was almost new. The only thing she'd written on the first page was the phone number of KCIT and the questions, How get show? Background? References?

Eduardo Ranier. Somehow, after the news about Jeanette, exposing him didn't seem so important. Maybe he made people feel better, who knows?

On the other hand, he hadn't made that mother feel any better, the one who'd called Diane yesterday. Besides, she felt too restless to sit behind a desk all day. An interview would give her an excuse to get out.

Mrs. Belster had said something about a bookstore owner. Cissy Green—no, Greenberg—no, Greenspon, that was it. At the Mystic Lights bookstore.

Diane looked up the number in the phone book.

25

Mornings were normally a busy but predictable time for Lt. Mario De Anda. There was the morning report to look over, the briefing to get through, the reports to be read and sent back with omissions noted, the routine telephone calls from reporters, and three or four cups of Emma's drip-brewed Colombian coffee to wash the whole thing down with.

This morning had been a nightmare. You never got used to it, seeing a body with all the life squeezed out of it. Especially a kid like that, a seventeen-year-old girl tossed into the ocean like a sack of garbage.

And this wasn't one of those obvious husband-wife things or a dope burn where you might get a break from one of your informants. It might have been some transient passing through town; it might never be solved.

The murder couldn't have come at a worse time. He had one detective tied up in court and one working on the mini-mart murder. Chief Ferguson had begun making noises about moving Capt. Harry Pyne over from Records to Detectives, even though they both knew Harry's brain was mildly pickled and he'd be more likely to slow things down than anything else. So the Tracy murder had fallen to Sally Chenowski from Juvenile, who'd gone out to the high school to see what she could find out, and De Anda himself, who'd talked to the people who'd called in.

There were two young couples who thought they might have seen a van near the pier last night but they weren't sure what time and they didn't remember the color of the license plates or what the driver looked like, or even if they'd actually seen him. The consumer columnist over at the newspaper had picked up one of Jeanette's friends about four and the girl was gone by then, which helped fix the time of her disappearance, but the woman hadn't seen anyone suspicious.

Which brought him to the best suspect at hand: the boy who'd found the body, who was waiting right now with a lawyer on one side of him and an aggravated father on the other. He'd decided to handle the kid himself; Chenowski would be busy most of the day at the high school, and they were spread pretty thin around here now.

De Anda got up, poured himself another cup of coffee, and went into the hall.

They were sitting on a padded bench three abreast. The boy's head came up when he saw De Anda. The kid didn't have a record, although the high school principal said he'd been caught once smoking marijuana on campus and he'd nearly been suspended after a fistfight with another student last fall. Right now he looked a little scared and a little defiant.

"Look, I don't have anything to hide." The boy's voice came out squeaky and his cheeks flamed. "I don't want a lawyer or anything. Like I told the cop at the pier, I happened to see her, that's all."

"I'd just like to go over everything with you again," De Anda said.

The lawyer cleared his throat. "I'd like to get one thing clear, Lieutenant. Is my client a suspect?"

"Not at the present time," De Anda said.

"Then I have no objection to your questioning him, as long as I'm present."

"But I don't want you!" the boy snapped.

"Shut up, Kris." The father was looking at De Anda.

"Well, let's go. I'd rather you waited here, sir, if you don't mind." A touchy situation. De Anda kept his tone neutral. He didn't want to get into a power struggle with the father in front of the boy.

The father—Erik Lender, that was his name, owned a clothing import business—glanced at the lawyer, shrugged, and said, "Then I'll be getting back to work." Finally he looked at the boy. "Just tell him everything, Kris. We know you didn't do it."

An hour and a half later, De Anda was pretty sure of that too.

There were two damning factors: Kris had been one of the last people to see Jeanette Tracy alive, and he'd found her body. On the other hand, he named two witnesses who'd seen him at the high school after Jeanette vanished. The girlfriend, Lara Ryan, might lie for him, but Kris said the newspaper columnist, Diane Hanson, had seen him too.

And he'd been home most of the evening. Not that he couldn't have sneaked out and disposed of the body, but it would have been difficult. Furthermore, the boy said the Lenders didn't own a van, which would be easy enough to check.

Also, the kid didn't have a motive, at least not as far as De Anda could figure out, and he had no history of violence. Plus he was bright enough to have realized he'd come under suspicion for finding the body.

Ferguson wasn't going to be happy about this one, De Anda reflected as he switched off the tape recorder.

"I may need to talk to you again," he said. "But for the time being, you can go."

The boy nodded. The lawyer, who had earned his no-doubt hefty fee by requiring that several questions be reworded, collected his briefcase and headed for the door.

"Lieutenant," Kris said as they walked out of the windowless interrogation cubicle into the hall, "I didn't kill Jeanette. I wish I knew who did. I keep thinking that maybe if I'd stuck around, if I hadn't gotten into a dumb argument with Lara, this whole thing might not have happened."

"I know," De Anda said. "Sometimes we all feel that way."

"You don't have any idea who did it, do you?" Kris stuck his hands in his pockets. "I mean, I know you probably couldn't tell me, but—well, do you think the other kids might be in danger?"

"I think everyone should be very careful until we get this thing solved," De Anda said. "No hitchhiking, for one thing." Mrs. Tracy had told him last night that Jeanette sometimes hitchhiked. Yes, the transient theory had a lot going for it. They were already checking for any similar unsolved murders around the state.

"I can drop you off at the high school," the lawyer told Kris.

"Okay. Yeah. I want to talk to Lara," the boy said, and went out with the lawyer.

The coroner would be checking the body, of course, for any stray hairs, fingerprints, whatever clues the sea water might have spared. But De Anda suspected that whatever they came up with, it wouldn't belong to Kris Lender.

26

The news conference was to be held in the city council chambers, a dark, cool room with rows of padded seats and, on the low platform, a scythe-shaped counter behind which the council men and women usually sat.

As he and Jimmy came in, their eyes adjusting gradually to the dim interior, Chang's gaze swept the room, taking in two television crews, a couple of radio people he recognized, maybe half a dozen print reporters. He wondered if there was anyone here from the wire services.

"It's almost eleven now. I wish to hell they'd get started," Jimmy muttered. Unlike Guy, he couldn't phone his story in, and the *Daily Record*'s deadline was twelve-thirty.

"Meyer have anything cute to say about you sending that picture to AP?" Chang asked as they took seats on the aisle for a quick exit.

"Nope," Jimmy said. "They didn't put it out until the news broke this morning, so it was too late for the A.M. papers anyway."

As he listened, Chang mentally reviewed their surroundings. The telephones were in the foyer through which they'd entered. Maybe he should go back and hang an "Out of Order" sign on one, but he hadn't brought any tape. Besides, there was another bank of pay phones around the corner in front of the main City Hall entrance.

A door opened at the rear of the platform and the mayor, Patricia Reilly, came out, followed by Mack Ferguson and Lester Logan, president of the Chamber of Commerce. The murmured conversations among the press ended abruptly and the room flooded with light for the TV cameras.

It was all pretty standard stuff. Mrs. Reilly expressed condolences for Mayor Pro Tem Tracy and his family. Mack Ferguson read a prepared statement saying that an investigation was under way and police were pursuing several leads. He declined, in response to questions, to be more specific.

Finally, Lester Logan, a big bear of a man who seemed to have trouble reading his notes, announced that several corporate members of the Chamber had agreed to offer a ten thousand dollar reward for information leading to the arrest and conviction of the killer.

Jimmy spent the entire time angling around the room, no doubt trying to get an interesting shot of three decidedly uninteresting people. Well, fair was fair, Chang told himself; he'd just spent half an hour getting what was essentially going to be a one-paragraph drop-in into the story he'd written earlier.

The most interesting person, Hank Tracy, hadn't come. That was to be expected, under the circumstances, but Guy would have liked to see the fireworks between him and Mack Ferguson. Maybe old Mack's facade was about to crack, after all. But not, unfortunately, this morning.

The TV lights went out. Chang stood up and strolled for a phone. No one was rushing on this one.

He rang through to Rand Franklin. "Nothing much happened here. The Chamber's offering a ten thousand dollar reward."

"I want you back here right now." Rand's usually low-key voice snapped over the phone wires. "We've been contacted by the killer."

27

Lucille Ferguson sat in the lunchroom just off the corridor that led to the council chambers, drinking machine coffee out of a paper cup and wondering what the hell was happening to her careful plans.

She kept one ear perked for the sounds of the press conference breaking up, but it was impossible to hear anything through the thick walls.

A janitor came in, his pail clanking on its rollers, a mop handle sticking straight up. Pushing it to one side, he lit a cigarette and began to puff deeply, the foul-smelling smoke filling the poorly ventilated room.

It was lunchtime. At the club, the ladies would be gathering for bridge. *I could be there right now without a worry in the world. Except for dying of boredom.*

A door scraped open down the hall and Lucille jumped up. Leaving her cup on the table, she hurried out.

Patricia Reilly gave Lucille a barely perceptible nod and strode past to her office. Lester looked uncomfortable as he shambled past.

Mack followed, his skin gray under the tan. Or maybe it was the damn fluorescent lights, Lucille thought. He shrugged and answered her unasked question. "The usual. Nothing terribly embarrassing. Not yet."

He was a stocky man, not fat but powerfully built. There

was an animal sensuality about him that roused an elemental response in Lucille. She'd felt it the first time they met, when they were both still married to other people, and had seen it reflected in his face. Raw, naked sex, that was what it was, and in the forty-odd years before she'd met him, she'd never experienced it once.

They walked side by side out to the parking lot. He was staying at work, she was going home. She wasn't sure why she'd come this morning except that she had to be here. She'd never understood before why women did things like that, married men who were socially and financially beneath them; but then, she'd been so certain of the route to salvation, the elevation of her street cop to the higher echelons of politics. She could almost smell the scent of power in the hall of administration, mixed with the feral reek of musk in her Laura Ashley bedroom.

"We'll work it out." His voice was hoarse. "Shit, it's not my fault the little brat got herself killed."

"If Hank Tracy makes a statement—" She thought rapidly as she wiped a spot of blue ink off his chin—"Your answer is going to be that the mayor pro tem is understandably in shock from his daughter's death, and it would be pointless for you to respond to his accusations until he's recovered."

"What would I do without you?"

His body pressed hers into the door of the Cadillac and his hands gripped her forearms. Lucille felt the throbbing heat of him and she wanted him to take her, roughly. "We could go home . . ."

"Shit. I can't. How would it look?" He pulled away reluctantly. "This whole damn mess—"

"We'll work it out." She wished she felt as confident as she sounded. "By Sunday you'll have that son-of-a-bitch locked up. It could even work for you, you know."

"Yeah." He rubbed the side of his nose. With those big, callused hands, it looked crude.

She slid into the car and drove home, thinking about the things she wanted him to do with those hands.

28

The envelope must have lain buried under a stack of newspapers on the front counter for over an hour before a classified advertising clerk saw the manila corner peeping out, and then she didn't get around to carrying it back to the newsroom for another half-hour.

By that time, no one could remember seeing anyone leave the envelope. Scores of people must have walked past that counter, including advertisers, subscribers, and half the staff of the *Daily Record*.

The packet was addressed to "Editor," in letters cut from the newspaper. Inside were two things: a photograph of Jeanette Tracy, dead with her neck bent oddly, and a note, also with cut-out letters, that read: "There will be 2 more dead by Sunday. You cant stop me."

Barry stared at it, hardly believing what he held in his hands. A confession, and a threat. Jeanette's murder was no crime of passion, no fluke. The note, the photograph felt un-real to him, yet he knew they weren't. Somebody out there wanted to kill women and wanted to tell the world about it, and it made him sick and frightened and angry.

Rand Franklin took a look at the package, and so did Meyer Krantz and about a dozen other people before they remembered about fingerprints.

Barry carried the photograph and the note carefully back to

the cameraman to have him shoot veloxes, the dot-screened pictures needed for newspaper reproduction, then put the material back in the envelope and called the police. They said they'd send someone over right away.

He took the veloxes down to the publisher's office and laid them in front of Ardrey Glenn. The publisher, whose background was in business rather than editing, turned several shades of pale before he said, "Jesus Christ."

"Do we run them?" Barry asked.

Ardrey shrugged. "It's a good story, isn't it?"

"Yes, but that photograph's not going to do much for her family, is it?" Barry said. "And the note might give somebody else an idea."

"It might also warn somebody to be careful," Ardrey said. He was about fifty, rather heavy, with an intelligent face and a sense of decency, Barry knew.

"How about if we run the note but hold the picture?" Barry said. "We've got shots from the pier, and a mug of the girl. That ought to hold us."

"Sounds good to me," Ardrey said. "But maybe you'd better check with the cops first."

Barry went upstairs. As he passed the clerks, he could hear them twittering to each other about the killer having been right there, close enough to breathe on them. "Chang's on his way back," Rand told him when he reached the newsroom.

"Good." Barry put in a call to Mack Ferguson and told him about the envelope.

"Yeah, I just heard from downstairs." The chief coughed. "That note—it's evidence—" He ran through the same points Barry and Ardrey had already come up with, pro and con, plus, "It might help us identify the killer, if nobody else knows about this. Shit, why Sunday? That isn't much time." A long pause. Barry decided to let the chief keep arguing with himself, so he didn't say anything. Finally: "If somebody else gets killed, you guys will say I didn't warn the public. I'll tell you what. Run the contents of the note but don't show a picture of it, the way it's lettered. We'll keep that a secret."

"Right." Barry hung up and swung around to his screen

96

and wrote a new deck headline, so that now it read, "Councilman Tracy's Daughter Murdered," and then, "Slayer Threatens to Kill 2 More by Sunday."

God, he wanted a cigarette right now.

It ticked him off, to know that bastard was going to be reading this and grinning to himself, delighted with all the ruckus he was stirring up.

Who the hell was it, anyway? Citrus Beach was a small town. Sure, it could be a transient, but a transient with a darkroom? The guy was taking one hell of a chance. Why hadn't anybody noticed him at the high school, or this morning at the paper? Was he that bland looking, or was he somebody familiar, somebody no one would suspect? A damn cool son-of-a-bitch.

Barry was glad he wasn't a cop. The frustration of trying to solve this one would drive him crazy. He decided not to bum a cigarette. If he could survive this without one, he could survive anything.

He sent the new headline to composing. There was nothing to do now. Almost noon. Chang would be back and he'd have to rewrite his story, but that shouldn't take long, and the typesetting only took a minute or so. Thank God for computers.

Barry took the veloxes in their plastic envelopes over to Meyer Krantz. "Hang onto these for me, will you? We're not running them now, but we might need them later."

"Right." Meyer stuck them into his desk drawer, and Barry went back to his computer, checking through the wire queues to see whether AP or UPI had any new angles on the murder. They didn't.

Diane stopped by. Like everyone else, she'd seen the picture and the note. "I can't believe it," she said. "This is the kind of thing you see on television. I knew that girl. Not very well, but I knew her."

Barry thought about his daughter. "I'm glad Elizabeth's at Stanford right now."

"Well, Lara isn't." Diane's voice sounded shaky. "Barry, I was right there. Lara was, too. Anything might have happened. And Kris—him finding the body gives me the creeps. You don't think he could have done it, do you?"

"I have a strong suspicion he was with the police when that note was delivered," Barry told her.

She tapped a finger on top of the computer monitor. She looked vulnerable and young, dark-blonde hair wispy around her delicate face. "I keep trying to act like everything's normal. I called for some information I promised Lara about an acting conservatory. And I set up an appointment this afternoon with a bookstore owner about Eduardo Ranier. And all the time I felt useless. Why can't somebody do something?"

Guy Chang and Jimmy Owens hustled into the newsroom. "Got to go," Barry said. "Tonight. I'll bring the steaks. Six o'clock?"

Diane nodded, but he could see her thoughts were elsewhere. Worried about Lara. Reliving the tragedy with her son, probably, too. Hell, she didn't need any more anxiety in her life. "And try not to worry."

"Right," she said.

Now if he could just manage to follow his own advice.

29

The principal, Mr. Gfeller, had called an assembly for noon, which normally would have raised protests among the students, but today nobody had done anything but talk about Jeanette Tracy anyway.

To Lara, nothing at school looked the same today. She felt as if she were seeing everyone from years in the future, looking back and noticing how unfinished they were.

How had Jeanette felt? Had she known, even for a moment, that she was going to die? Just thinking about it sent tremors through Lara's stomach, and yet she couldn't turn her mind off. What would it be like if she died? Not so much the act of dying—she couldn't really focus on that—but, well, what would her life have meant?

People were talking about Jeanette everywhere, in the girls' room, in the hall, in their seats as they plopped down in the auditorium. "She hitchhiked sometimes . . . She was really wild . . . I don't know, I kind of liked her . . . Do you think it was some older guy she was seeing that nobody knew about? . . ."

What would they say about Lara? "She had kind of a nice voice . . . All those creepy little brothers to look after . . . Did you notice how shabby her clothes always were?"

I'm not ready to die! Two more years to get through before she could even start to live. What were the odds? Last year a whole carful of seniors were killed on Coast Highway the night after graduation when they ran head-on into a transport truck from Camp Pendleton. And Jeanette . . .

Kris slid into the seat beside her, three-quarters of the way back in the auditorium. "Hi."

Heads turned all around them. Whispers. "I thought you'd be there all day," Lara said.

He shrugged. "They let me go. I think the lieutenant's pretty sure I didn't do it."

"Yeah." Lara had watched a lot of cop shows on TV, but the reality of Kris being questioned in a police station was hard to imagine. "I talked to a detective today too, but I guess I wasn't able to help much. She's the one up there on the stage with Mr. Gfeller."

"Hey," he said. "Remember that knife . . ."

Mr. Gfeller tapped on the microphone and the room silenced. Kris scrunched down on his chair, shoving hands into pockets.

"Pledge of Allegiance," the principal said. They all stood up, making as much noise as possible, then mumbled the pledge and sat down again.

"I expect you've all heard of the tragic death of one of our seniors, Jeanette Tracy." Mr. Gfeller adjusted his glasses. "We've called this assembly at the request of the police department."

The woman detective took her cue by standing up and walking forward. "My name is Detective Chenowski. I won't go into the details of the murder, but we're almost certain it *was* a murder, although the preliminary autopsy report hasn't come back yet."

"Think she has a scriptwriter for the dialogue?" Kris muttered. "Autopsy report. Jeez."

"First of all, we will have a patrolman on duty at the high school from seven A.M. until five P.M. daily, for the time being," Ms. Chenowski went on. She was kind of chunky and no-nonsense, and Lara liked her. "However, he can't be everywhere at once. We have to count on all of you to be our eyes and ears."

"Eyes and ears," Kris grumbled. "And other parts of the anatomy." Lara ignored him.

"We also urge extreme caution," the detective said. "We have to assume that whoever killed Jeanette Tracy is still at large."

Kris started to say something but Lara kicked him in the ankle.

"We suggest that you avoid hitchhiking or walking alone to or from school, or being alone in any secluded place. Please notify the authorities at once if you notice any suspicious activity. Miss Tracy may have met her slayer almost anywhere—at a store, on the beach, in a restaurant. Don't try to be a hero; this man is dangerous. If you suspect anything, call us." Ms. Chenowski gave them a phone number and turned away. The students started to talk and some of them stood up.

"Sit down," Mr. Gfeller said from the stage. "I have another announcement to make."

There was some groaning, but everybody subsided.

"The staff and I have had some serious discussions this morning and we've come to the conclusion that we will have to cancel this year's production of *West Side Story*," he said.

Lara's heart felt as if someone had just hit it with a hammer.

"What the hell?" Kris sputtered indignantly.

"We realize this comes as a severe disappointment to many of you," Mr. Gfeller continued. "But as you know, Jeanette had been cast in the leading role of Maria."

"Other people tried out!" someone called.

"That's right, and we considered that," Mr. Gfeller said. "We're not canceling the show for lack of talent. But we feel it would be inappropriate to replace her and go on as if nothing had happened. Think of her family and how they must feel."

I can't bear it, Lara thought. How am I going to get through the rest of the year?

"Instead, we're going to have a concert in her memory. The cast will sing some of the songs from the show as well as other music as seems appropriate." "Appropriate" was one of Mr. Gfeller's favorite words.

"Well, whoop-de-doo." Kris's jaw jutted forward.

"Those of you who are scheduled for lunch now may take an extra fifteen minutes," Mr. Gfeller said. "The rest of you, please return to your classes."

As they scuffed out of the auditorium, the students seemed more upset about the show's being canceled than about Jeanette's death. "What a rotten deal," somebody said. "I mean, it isn't our fault, is it?"

Lara hardly listened. She had to figure out what she was going to do.

30

M r. Gfeller had just come back from the assembly and walked into his office when the phone rang. Mrs. Arbor picked it up, rubbed her nose where the new glasses pinched, and said, "Citrus Beach High School."

"I'm trying to reach a student there." The voice was masculine, slightly clipped and oddly familiar. "Her name is Lara—Lara Ryan, I believe."

Mrs. Arbor flipped through her cards. "Yes, she's a sophomore here. Is this a member of her family?"

"Well, no." Why couldn't she remember where she'd heard that voice before?

"Just a minute." She put him on hold and picked up the other call. "Citrus Beach High School. Yes, that's correct, the production is canceled." She put the call through to Mr. Gfeller, then returned to the first call. "Go ahead, please."

"I have some information for her," the man said. "For Lara Ryan. A business matter. Is it possible to speak to her?"

This was strange, Mrs. Arbor thought, and then she remembered that Lara was the one who'd sung "Silent Night" at the Christmas concert so beautifully. A pretty girl, too. It might have something to do with show business. There'd been a student here a few years ago who'd won a role on a TV show, although it didn't last long.

"You could leave your number," she said. "Frankly, we

103

don't have any system for giving messages to students except in an emergency." She wished she could help. It would be nice to have some good news for a change, after what happened to that poor Tracy girl. A Citrus High student landing an acting job, or a recording contract, now, that would be a shot in the arm. Of course, she couldn't actually give out the girl's phone number, but if they were listed, didn't that mean they wanted people to call them? "I'll tell you what," she said. "Her father's first name is Brendan. They might be in the book."

He didn't respond immediately, as if he were thinking it over, and then he said, "Well, I suppose that will do. Thank you very much."

"My pleasure," Mrs. Arbor said.

It was about twenty minutes later, as she was filing yesterday's attendance forms, that she remembered where she'd heard that voice before.

Why, of course! The man sounded just like Eduardo Ranier, that fascinating psychic. He'd been so kind to donate his time to come to the high school. And so good-looking!

Well, he was certainly in show business, of a sort. Perhaps he was planning some kind of television show, and he wanted Lara to be on it. Now, wouldn't that be kind of him?

31

Diane's appointment with Cissy Greenspon wasn't until three o'clock. The bookstore owner had revealed that she was casting a horoscope at two and "wanted to give the dear enough time to ask all her questions."

What a bunch of cuckoos, Diane thought.

While she was still at her desk, she also put through a call to the manager of KCIT Radio. He said their publicity director would be happy to give her information about Eduardo Ranier. When she pressed further, he said he might be able to work her into his schedule tomorrow and transferred her to his secretary, who said the best she could do was to pencil Diane in for nine o'clock. "First thing in the morning, sometimes he's not so rushed."

Briefly, Diane weighed asking to watch Eduardo tape his show but decided against it. In fact, she would ask the manager not to mention their discussion just yet. She wanted to catch Eduardo off guard when she finally set up an interview, coming in with facts and figures and embarrassing details from his past. At the very least, she didn't want him to have time to do any background research on her own life. If he pretended to "see" Mark's death . . . She burned with anger just thinking about it.

"Boy, do you ever look like somebody I wouldn't want to meet in a dark alley." Jimmy pulled up a chair and straddled it backwards. "Somebody must have really ripped off the consumers this week."

Diane had to laugh. "I'm just borrowing trouble," she said. "How did your pictures come out?"

"Nothing likely to win me a Pulitzer," he admitted. "That press conference was a waste of time. I was hoping Mr. Tracy would show up so we'd get some real fireworks."

That was probably the right way for a reporter to react, but it bothered Diane. "Don't you have any feelings at all?"

"If I did, Chang would eat me alive." Jimmy crossed his arms atop the back of the chair. The only thing lacking was a sprig of hay sticking out between his teeth and he'd look like a Norman Rockwell painting. "Come on, Diane. What's really eating you?"

"I'm worried about Lara." Why did she feel embarrassed to mention it? She wasn't Lara's mother; maybe that was it. She shouldn't care so much. Or maybe she didn't want to over-react because of Mark. Damn it, Diane thought. I've always worried about her; she's so vulnerable, and so headstrong, and there's a killer out there.

"You mean because of this murder?" Jimmy shot her a skeptical look. "It was probably a pickup. I hear Jeanette Tracy was always looking for action."

"That doesn't make me any less anxious," Diane said. "Lara does dumb things too, sometimes. And I'm not too crazy about that boyfriend of hers."

"Wasn't he the one who found the body? You don't think . . ."

Diane had been trying not to think that all day. "Oh, Jimmy, what if he is? I can't be there to protect her; she'd probably resent it if I even tried. No, I don't think it's Kris, but I wish I were sure."

Across the newsroom, the copy desk was emptying out as the rimrats went to lunch. Barry and Rand stayed at their desks, waiting for the final Page Two proofs.

"I wish there were some way I could help." Jimmy's eyes took on a faraway look, as if he were seeing beyond her. Sometimes Diane wondered what went on beneath that cheerful, easygoing surface, what secret wounds and dark fears stabbed at his dreams. Or maybe there weren't any. Maybe he was just what he seemed. "You're right; I get so caught up seeing things through the lens that I forget it's a real world out there. You think Lara would listen to me, if I told her not to be alone with Kris?"

Lara had met Jimmy a couple of times, dropping by the paper with Diane, and had seemed suitably impressed by the sophisticated older man of twenty-five. "It's possible, but I don't know," Diane said.

"Hmm." Jimmy scuffed the toe of a tennis shoe against the linoleum floor. Watching, Diane remembered that she'd meant to buy herself a new pair of shoes today. She was wearing an old canvas pair that felt all right but looked like hell. "Let me give it some thought, okay? Is she listed in the phone book, in case I need to reach her?"

"Brendan Ryan." It was funny how much better Diane felt, knowing Jimmy was going to help. He'd only been at the paper a little under a year but they'd struck up a friendship. Most of the time he seemed self-absorbed, a typical young hotshot photographer, but he could be surprisingly kind, like getting her car started any number of times. Maybe that was what made her suspect he had hidden depths.

What would happen if a kid like him stumbled into the murderer? she wondered suddenly. "Hey," she said. "Be careful yourself, Jimmy. This guy's dangerous."

The response was a cocky grin. "Don't worry about me. I'm tougher than I look."

Diane sighed. Maybe he wasn't the coolest head to advise Lara. But on the other hand, she might listen to him.

According to the wall clock, which usually ran two or three minutes fast, it was a quarter to three. Diane stood up to go meet Cissy Greenspon.

32

"I think we ought to get out of here before we turn into zombies like our parents." Kris had been muttering all afternoon since the assembly, and for a moment what he was saying didn't sink in. Then Lara pivoted on the school steps and stared at him excitedly, ignoring the unfriendly glares of a pair of freshman girls who had to swerve around her.

"Like where?" she said.

"Well . . ." He guided her over to the park strip, where they found an empty bench. "I was thinking maybe somewhere in the mountains. My folks have a cabin they don't use much."

Lara could have kicked him. "I thought you meant, you know, Hollywood, someplace we could get a start in show business and have a chance at earning a living. How long do you think we could stand it, stuck off somewhere in the mountains? What am I supposed to do when I run out of insulin?"

He pulled his arm away from her waist. "You sure have been a pain in the ass today. What the hell's wrong with you? Anybody'd think you were the one who stumbled over a dead body."

"A cabin in the mountains!" Lara snapped. "What a dumb idea. People would think you killed her and decided to hide out. Or did you? Huh?" She didn't know what devil made her keep needling him. "Am I supposed to be the next victim?"

108

"Oh, shut up." He stood up. "And by the way, I want my knife back."

"I gave it to Diane. She said I could get in trouble for carrying it. Thanks for not telling me those things are illegal."

"You gave it away? Terrific!" He tossed his head back. When he did that, he looked a little like Michael J. Fox, and she had to remind herself that he'd just disappointed her in the worst way. For one splendid moment she'd thought they were really going somewhere, that she could have Hollywood and Kris too, and instead it had turned out to be another one of his half-baked ideas.

"You said I could keep it."

"I wanted you to be safe. I didn't mean for you to give it away!" When he scolded like this, he sounded like her father. "It happens to belong to my brother. How about showing a little responsibility, Lara?"

"When I need lessons, I'll let you know!" She jerked to her feet and grabbed her purse. "You're just mad because you can't play Bernardo and you're taking it out on me. Well, I'm upset too!"

"You wanna get a Coke?" he asked, more calmly.

"No." Right now, Lara didn't know what she wanted. Her skin prickled with irritation and her chest hurt with unwept tears, and she wasn't even sure whether they were for Jeanette or herself. Or even for Gerry, poor little munchkin without a mother. She felt bad, remembering how she'd jerked him around this morning. "Look, I'd better go home. I don't have any clean tops left and the place is a mess. I'll see you tomorrow, okay?"

"Yeah." He didn't look pleased. "Yeah, sure."

By the time she'd walked half a dozen steps, the tears were threatening to burst out. Now she'd gone and ticked off Kris. Why was she so short-tempered? Lara considered going back to apologize, but she was afraid she'd start crabbing at him again.

School was letting out as his car cruised along Citrus Avenue. He'd heard there was going to be a patrolman stationed, but the man was nowhere in sight. Probably poking around the athletic field, or getting it on with one of the girls.

Lara was standing with her boyfriend, and then as he watched she broke away and walked toward him. It was magnetism; he was drawing her this way, without her even knowing it.

He'd treasured and discarded half a dozen plans for capturing her. It was exciting, being the hunter. Especially now that the quarry was getting more difficult to chase to ground. Jeanette hadn't had any reason to be wary. Lara, now, she'd be watching out for strangers. Strangers. But not him.

Finally he'd abandoned his attempts to figure out a scheme. This hunt would have to be calculated on the spur of the moment, testing his wits to the limit.

The video equipment was in his trunk, still packed in the manufacturer's boxes. He wished he had time to fool around with it. Maybe he would. He might lure her up to the Heights on the pretext of helping him make a home movie. He could practice with her, and then make the real video. She might even let him tie her up before she figured out it wasn't a game. He'd have to position the camera just right on its tripod. Too bad he wouldn't have time to make a copy of the tape before Sunday. He'd like to keep one.

He could feel her neck under his hands, feel the thrill cresting in his groin. Hard, yeah, he was going to do it hard, but slow. He'd never tried to pace it before. A new experience. Special for the video.

Right now, Lara wasn't even watching where she was going along the sidewalk. He eased the car toward her, glad of the cover of slow-moving traffic along the curb, mostly parents who'd driven down specially to pick up their kids today because they were afraid of him. Oh, God, it was great. All of them, shitting in their pants. And that newspaper, that headline. Too bad they hadn't run the photograph. It was such a good shot.

Lara came to a crosswalk and halted. He gave the car a spurt of gas and moved toward her.

33

The Mystic Lights bookstore was located in a converted California bungalow-style house, circa 1920, on Cypress Street near Fuchsia, just down the street from City Hall. Three concrete steps led up to a sagging front porch shaded by giant camellia bushes. A patchy dog that looked to be at least half basset hound lifted its head, thumped its tail twice against the porch, and went back to sleep.

For a moment, Diane felt displaced and disoriented as she stepped inside and the door set off a shimmer of wind chimes. The scent of incense and the quaint spaces of the interior carried her back into a more innocent time, a different world than the one that held the vicious killer of Jeanette Tracy.

What had once been the living room was now lined with floor-to-ceiling bookcases crammed with much-used hardcover books. In front of the windows, a low rack held some new paperbacks. She scanned them, noting that the topics ranged from reincarnation to nutrition.

It was hard to believe anyone made a living off this place, judging by the dust that lay thick on some of the books and floated in the air. It must be the horoscopes that kept Cissy Greenspon in business. *You will meet a dark man—or a pale one silhouetted against darkness.*

"Is anyone here?" Diane called. She felt as if she were trespassing in somebody's home.

111

"Oh, I'm in the back, dear," came the slightly dry voice she'd heard on the telephone.

Diane walked through the living room into the hall. Four doors opened off it, and at the rear she came to the brightly lit kitchen.

"Come in, come in." The small, ruddy-faced woman sitting at a table piled with charts and books didn't look anything like Diane would have supposed—no sunken rouged cheeks, no piercing eyes. Cissy Greenspon wore a jogging suit and, although she must have been at least fifty-five, looked as if she probably worked out at the racquet club three times a week.

Diane introduced herself, and Cissy pushed back the stack of papers. "Would you like some coffee?"

"Yes, thank you." Diane glanced around the jumbled kitchen. Every inch of counter space seemed to be covered with something—books, pans, a box of Hamburger Helper, cat food, dog chow, rusty appliances, telephone directories. There was a smell of sour milk and orange-herbal tea in the air. Nothing occult or sinister, or particularly hygienic, either.

"Instant all right?" Cissy opened the cupboard and fetched a jar that contained a caked brown powder. Diane nodded uncertainly. "I'm thrilled that you're doing a story on Eduardo. He's never gotten the recognition he deserves. He's quite a man, although he's hard to get to know. We drive in to lectures in LA together sometimes, and we've given each other a few referrals, but I still don't feel I know him all that well. Have you talked to him yet?"

"As a matter of fact, no." Diane cleared her throat. "I prefer to get background information before I interview someone for a profile." It sounded plausible; at least Cissy was nodding as she measured a cupful of tap water into a frying pan and set it on one of the burners. "I'd rather you didn't say anything until I'm ready to talk with him. Sometimes people get nervous and start rehearsing in their head, and by the time I interview them, everything sounds stale."

"Oh, I can imagine." Cissy tossed a spoonful of brown

112

powder into the water and stirred it vigorously. "Do you take cream, dear?"

Diane was almost afraid to answer. "Uh, yes."

Cissy reached back into the counter and pulled out a jar, this time of caked white powder. A spoonful of that went into the frying pan too. "Be done in a jiff."

"No hurry." Diane nudged a calico cat off a wooden chair and sat down. "Tell me about your business. I can't imagine there's enough demand for occult books to keep you going."

"Oh, you'd be surprised." Cissy bent down to pet the cat. "Poor prettikins, would you like some milk?" Receiving a meow, she fetched a carton of fresh milk from the refrigerator and poured some in a bowl. Diane looked wistfully at the coffee, which was beginning to boil. "People come from as far away as Long Beach," Cissy said, straightening. "How long do you like your coffee cooked, dear?"

"I think that will be fine," Diane said.

Cissy poured it into a mug and set it out with a bowl of sugar lumps. Diane added two and stirred the mixture for a long time. "Yes, we get quite a clientele. Of course, I do horoscopes too, you know."

"When did you first discover you were psychic?" Diane took out her notebook.

"Psychic? Oh, my dear, I'm not!" Cissy sat down on the other side of the table. "Not many of us are so gifted. Now, Eduardo, there's a psychic. But me? I've made a study of horoscopes, and I piddle a bit with tea leaves and the Tarot, but I haven't got the second sight. No, not me, I'm afraid."

"Have you ever actually seen Eduardo do anything . . . psychic?" The coffee tasted sweet and metallic. If Diane didn't think of it as coffee but as some exotic high-tech drink, she could get down a few mouthfuls.

"Oh, all the time." Cissy leaned one elbow on a book, not seeming to notice as she creased the page. "That man, why, he knows the oddest things—who's calling on the telephone, whether a friend is in trouble. Of course, it's not often a person has a chance to witness something truly momentous, what the public would call 'proof.' If you've ever thought about it, most of the things in our lives could be predicted by anyone using a little common sense.''

"So you've never actually seen him do anything—extraordinary?'' Cissy's unflagging defense of an obvious fraud disturbed Diane. The woman seemed normal, logical. But you could never tell what lay underneath.

"Well, no, but then, I've only known him for about a year and a half.'' The cat jumped up on Cissy's lap and began to purr. "You know about the girl's body he found, down in Dana Point? That was maybe two years ago, I guess.''

"But surely that wasn't the first incident.'' Diane tried to disguise her skepticism. "I mean, a person doesn't suddenly become psychic, does he?''

"That depends.'' Cissy fondled the cat. "It's a talent. A person can be artistic, for instance, but it isn't until a certain point in his life that he becomes an artist. Eduardo told me that he's always had flashes, but, like most of us, he discounted them. Figured they were just guesses.''

"What did he do before he . . . became a psychic?'' Diane asked. "For a living, I mean.''

"I think he was in some kind of real estate.'' Cissy reached into the sugar bowl, took out a lump, and fed it to the cat, which licked it thoughtfully before crunching it sideways between small sharp teeth. "If you ask me, he's never received the credit he should.''

"But he does have a radio show.''

"Oh, but my dear, there was talk of television—not cable, either, a segment on a syndicated talk show—why, you wouldn't believe the offers he got after the *National Enquirer* wrote him up. But none of it came to anything.''

"Why not?'' If he was so damn psychic, why hadn't Eduardo foreseen all this and found a way around it?

Cissy leaned across the table and lowered her voice confidingly. "If you ask me, it was that police chief. Mack Ferguson. The one who's running for sheriff.''

"Why?''

"He was some high muckamuck in the Police Chiefs Asso-

114

ciation at the time," Cissy said. "You know how people hate what they don't understand—foreigners, homosexuals, what-have-you. Well, he hates psychics. Just as things were really heating up, he put out some statement to the press about what a disgrace it all was, and how could a self-respecting TV show legitimize such nonsense. He even started raising questions about how Eduardo came to find the body, as if that sweet man would have done anything wrong! It just makes me sick, the whole thing. Anyway, that was the end of most of it, except for the radio station, and Eduardo writes a column for a gossip magazine—insight into the stars, and so forth. And then there are the public appearances, of course. And the private consultations. That's what pays the bills."

"Does he seem bitter about it?"

"About the police chief? Oh, no, dear. Never mentions it." Cissy let the cat jump down and folded her hands in her lap. "He's not the type to hold a grudge. He's a very kind man, really, not entirely comfortable with his gift, if you ask me."

"Then why doesn't he do something else for a living?"

Cissy shrugged. "I suppose he may give it up one of these days. He did rather well in real estate, so I hear, but then there were some problems, I don't know exactly what, and he got out of it. Perhaps he's hoping something else will come along."

Diane thanked her and stood up. The telephone rang, startlingly close. Cissy picked it up and waved good-bye at the same time. The conversation had something to do with a new book about Edgar Cayce, Diane noticed as she slipped out of the kitchen.

As she left, she saw a young couple, both with long straight hair, leafing through books in the front room. They wore tie-dyed clothes and sandals. Born twenty years too late, she thought.

A transistor radio dangled from the girl's hand, sputtering with a newscast. The words "police" and "no suspect" buzzed in Diane's ears.

Out in her car, she tossed the notebook on the front seat and stared out the windshield for a moment. Eduardo Ranier.

Was he involved with Jeanette? All right, he was a con man, but what else? Citrus Beach, like every other town, had its dark underbelly of drug pushers, thieves, and prostitutes. How well did Eduardo Ranier know them, and what had he picked up that the police hadn't found?

Maybe this was going to be his big break—he'd find the killer "psychically" and become a hero. Diane thought about the girl who'd died two years ago in Dana Point. She'd have to dig out the clips on that.

34

The northbound bus pulled up on the other side of Citrus Avenue and Lara darted out without waiting for the light. It was a good thing the car closest to the curb was moving so slowly, or it might have hit her.

She ignored the blare of horns, racing across and scooting up the bus steps just as the door started to close.

Settling onto one of the benches in front, she wondered why she'd been in such a hurry. She often killed half an hour waiting for the next bus; there were lots of shops to look in. Her whole body felt keyed up, like a car idling too fast, eager to get on the move. But to where? The only place she was going was home.

She couldn't believe they'd canceled *West Side Story*. God, that really hurt. Part of her could understand why they wanted to show respect for Jeanette, but it wasn't as if the show was built around her. In fact, she'd barely beaten out a junior who would have been glad to step in. The principal just didn't understand how much it meant to the other kids. Lara had been living with the music, dreaming about playing Anita for so long now. And there was nothing to take its place. A concert? Fourth-graders gave concerts!

Diane had offered to help if push came to shove, but Lara knew instinctively that she didn't really mean it. Oh, sure, she'd help in her own way, getting Lara into acting classes, but that wasn't what she needed. Except that Lara wasn't exactly sure what it was that she did need.

Mr. Ranier could figure it out. There was an aura about him, a kind of power, a seeing through things. He would know what to do.

She wondered what it was like to be psychic. Did Mr. Ranier know how she was feeling right now? Had she meant something special to him? She'd gotten that feeling from the way he looked at her, not casual the way he'd treated some of the others, but kind of—startled. As if he'd found something he wasn't expecting.

Mr. Ranier wasn't the type she usually went for. He was slim and almost—otherworldly, that was a good word. Light blue eyes, almost white-blond hair. It looked soft; how would it feel to touch it? She wondered how old he was. Late twenties? Early thirties? No. Nobody that handsome could be over thirty.

The bus stopped at Palm Street and she got out and began walking to their house. It wasn't even really a house, but a crummy unit. Back in the fifties, somebody had built these little cabins, six of them with a common walkway, kind of like an old motel. Maybe it had been pretty once, but now, as she turned in at the driveway, she noticed how sparse the grass was and that the adobe was laced with cracks.

Nearing the little house, her lungs began to strain for breath, as if she were walking into a huge trap that was about to shut off the light and air. God, how could she go on living here for weeks and months and years?

Lara forced herself to take a deep breath. She reached for the door and found it was unlocked.

From the back, she could hear Dave and Sammy quarreling. The whole house smelled musty. Lara threw open a couple of windows and walked to the tiny laundry room. Towels and underwear and shirts and pants overflowed. She ought to do the sheets too, but you didn't need to wear those to school.

It took a while to sort everything and get the cranky washing machine started. It was going to break any day now, and

118

they couldn't afford a new one. The nearest laundromat was four blocks away. Maybe if she screamed a lot, Dad would make Sammy do some of it. After all, he was twelve.

She walked into the kitchen and took a can of diet root beer out of the refrigerator. Dinner. She couldn't bear to think about it yet. Maybe an omelet. She and Gerry were the only ones who liked them. Well, if anybody complained, she'd offer to let them cook tomorrow night.

Sammy and Dave came banging in through the rear screen door, with Gerry in pursuit.

"Hey!" Dave called as they rushed through. "Some guy called you."

She lunged over and grabbed onto the waistline of his pants, bringing him to an abrupt halt and nearly pulling her arm out of her socket. "Who? Kris?"

"Naw. Some older guy." He squirmed. "Mister something. Reindeer, I think."

"Ranier?" She was practically shrieking. "Mr. Ranier called me?"

"Yeah, right." Dave tried to pull away again. "Hey, let go, willya? We're gonna go over to the video arcade."

"Did he leave a phone number?"

"Yeah, but I forgot it." Dave must have realized he was in danger of a thrashing, because he gave a harder jerk and got free. He vanished out the front door in the wake of his brothers.

"You little creep!" Lara yelled after him.

Mr. Ranier had called her! He'd figured out that she needed him, and he was trying to reach her. It was so unjust that she had to live with three obnoxious little brats who didn't bother to write the number down or even ask Mr. Ranier to call back.

Now what was she going to do?

35

Mack's gut had been kicking up acid since before the press conference, and the rest of the day hadn't made things any better. De Anda seemed damn certain that Lender kid wasn't the killer. Well, maybe he was right. The guy came from a good family, and he looked All-American. Still, you couldn't rely on that any more.

The shit was flying from every direction. Mack had to put out a new press release every couple of hours. Like the one on the autopsy report. Cause of death: strangulation. No indication of sexual molestation. Time of death: sometime between 3 and 6 P.M. Monday.

There'd been another release that said the boys at the sheriff's department were going over the girl's purse with a fancy laser device, checking for fingerprints. Not that the ocean was likely to have left any.

But he could handle the press. He could handle the public hysteria; he'd worked on two serial killers during his years on the LAPD, and, although this man had only claimed one victim so far that they knew of, the public was already reacting as if he were the latest Hillside Strangler. Well, that was to be expected, he supposed.

What was new this time was the politics.

Hank Tracy was still in seclusion. But Mayor Reilly wasn't. She didn't like Mack much, didn't like the old school of coun-

120

cil members who'd hired him and didn't like the way he ran his department. But up till now, there hadn't been a damn thing she could do.

There still wasn't. Not yet. And wouldn't be if he had anything to say about it.

Mack popped another antacid tablet as he came out of the police station and descended the steps to the parking lot. He'd promised to meet Lucille for dinner. Then he might be coming back here tonight. Not that there was a hell of a lot he could do, but it would look good. Besides, De Anda and his crew would be working overtime, and he wanted to encourage them in any way he could.

He kept trying not to think about the girl. Jesus. He'd met her a couple of times, a pretty young thing, nice body, bright eyes, a mouth that wouldn't stop talking. A normal kid, nothing unusual maybe, but you expected her to live long enough to grow up.

A slim dark-haired young man was leaning against Mack's white city-issue car. Damn. It was that Chink reporter from the *Record*.

"Hi, Mack." Guy Chang flipped his notebook open. "Got a few questions for you."

"I'm afraid I'm late for an appointment." He opened the door.

"Let's see—yacht club again tonight?" Hell, how did that bastard know where he'd had dinner last night? "I'll just ride over with you and take a cab back." Chang slid into the passenger seat and buckled his seat belt. Nervy bastard.

Mack knew better than to quarrel with the press. It was their job to be antagonistic to authority, Lucille would say, using that jacked-up sociology of hers. You had to honor their role in the power structure. Which, translated into English, meant you couldn't throw them out of your car onto their heinies.

"Let's see." Chang drew out a pen as the chief screeched out of the lot, venting his irritation on his driving. "Don't the note and the photograph make this an unusual case?"

"Everything makes this an unusual case." Mack slammed

121

on the brakes as a light turned red. The damn reporter would probably write it down if he ran a light.

"Like what?"

"Who the victim is. The fact that she disappeared from in front of a high school. Being dumped in a public place where anybody might have come by. The note. You name it."

"Would you say we're dealing with a dangerous psychopath here?"

"That would be a fair assumption." Keep a hold on yourself, Mack commanded, feeling the acid creep slowly up his stomach walls into the esophagus.

"He's threatened to kill again. Why do you suppose he'd send a note like that?"

Mack cursed silently as he hit another red light on Cypress Street. Couldn't the engineers do anything right? "He's probably getting off on a power trip; he enjoys taunting us because it gives him a sense of power."

There. He'd given Chang a straight answer. Now maybe the son-of-a-bitch would get off his back.

"How is this going to affect your campaign for sheriff?"

Jesus. The bastard went straight for the jugular. "I don't see why it should affect it in any way." Mack struggled to keep his voice calm, but he knew the annoyance showed.

"What about the fact that Councilman Tracy had asked that a patrolman be stationed in front of the school?"

"We couldn't put a man in front of every school in town." Mack had his answer to that one carefully prepared. "What about the elementary schools? There've been a lot more cases around the region of small children being abducted than teenagers."

Chang didn't look pleased. Mack was familiar with the tactic—they needled you, hoping to make you lose your temper and say something you'd regret.

"Getting back to your campaign, would you say the timing was bad?" the reporter continued.

"I can't think of a good time for somebody's daughter to be murdered." With a prayer of relief, he turned east on Coast Highway and saw the harbor straight ahead.

122

"What's going to happen to your campaign if this guy carries out his threat, if he kills two more women?" Chang's jaw was working in frustration. Mack began to feel better.

"I'm an officer of the law," he said. "I treat this case as I would any other, regardless of how it affects me personally. We want to catch this guy. We want to prevent any further tragedies, and we want to see justice done." He pulled up at the entrance to the yacht club parking lot. "Now from here it's members and guests only, Mr. Chang, and I don't recall you being invited."

The reporter opened the car door. "Thanks for answering my questions, Chief. I'll get back to you."

Mack barely waited until the door slammed before shooting forward into the safety of the lot

Chang stared at the retreating car and wondered what he'd accomplished. Oh, sure, he had a few quotes for tomorrow's story, but they were the standard public relations line. Somebody must coach cops, like athletes on TV, the ones who were trained to repeat the interviewer's question back to him while their sluggish brains chugged into first gear.

But he'd noticed things, things that wouldn't mean much on paper but which told him a lot. The way Mack was sweating. The undercurrent of anger in his voice.

The chief was running scared. Well, maybe not quite yet. But if they didn't catch the guy soon, and if somebody else disappeared . . .

Not that he wanted anybody else to die. But Chang couldn't wait to see that facade crack. Above all, he wanted to record it first.

36

L ara was on the phone with the radio station manager when her father came in the door. "But it's urgent," she was saying. "He tried to call me, but my brother didn't write the number down."

"Miss, I'm not allowed to give out his home phone number." The manager sounded as though he might hang up any minute.

"Lara, get off the phone," her father said.

She ignored him. "At least you could call him and ask him to phone me, now that I'm home. Couldn't you at least do that?"

Her father yanked the receiver from her hand and slammed it into the cradle. "When I say off, I mean off!"

Lara jumped up, knocking against the phone and sending it jangling to the floor. "Don't you ever do that to me!" She faced her father. He smelled as if he'd had a couple of beers, but then, that was his normal smell.

"Don't you dare talk back to me." He sounded tired and drained. "Go get dinner, Lara."

"I'm not your wife!"

"That's right. If you were, you could talk back."

"The hell I could!" She could feel sweat start to trickle down her back but she didn't care. "You treat me like some goddamn slave. Lara, do this! Lara, do that! And then when I

124

try to have one telephone conversation, you yank it right out of my hand. No wonder my mother left!"

She stopped, shocked at her own words, and they stared at each other.

"That does it." Her father broke the deadlock by grabbing her wrist, hard. "I told you this morning you're not too big to be whipped, and I meant it."

"You let go of me!"

He was dragging her into the hall. Hot red fury seared through her chest. She'd done everybody's laundry, had the phone ripped out of her hand, and now he was going to paddle her for nothing with that old Ping-Pong bat he used on the boys.

"Let go!" she screamed again, and twisted. The skin on her wrist flamed. "I'll never cook for you again! I'll never wash one more goddamn piece of laundry! I'm not your slave!"

"Lara . . . Look, I've had a hard day. I guess we both lost our tempers." He paused and let go of her arm.

She turned and ran, grabbing her purse on the way through the living room. He was too old and tired to catch her as she pelted across the walkway and onto Palm.

"Lara! Wait a minute!" His voice drifted after her.

"And I'm not coming back, either!" she shouted.

37

Broiling the steaks and making salad together eased some of the tensions of the day, but by the time Diane and Barry finished their wine and coffee and the little petits fours Diane had picked up earlier, they were back to talking about Jeanette. She couldn't seem to get her mind off the murder, and apparently neither could he.

"I keep thinking that he was right there at the paper." He sat on the couch, unlacing his shoes and propping his feet on the coffee table. "He just walked in there and dropped that envelope off and nobody noticed him. Can you believe it? Not one goddamn person remembers who left it. It's incredible. It's frightening."

"I know." After a moment's hesitation, Diane perched on the sofa next to him. She enjoyed being close, yet she knew where it was likely to lead. "When I went to pick her up yesterday, Lara wasn't anywhere in sight. Barry, that was before we even knew anything was wrong, and I was still terrified."

"But she was all right?"

"Yes, but—I never meant to get this close. Friends, yes, but not . . . Losing Mark taught me that you'd better not love someone unless you can face losing them." She twisted her hands together. She knew—they both knew—that she was talking about her and Barry as much as her and Lara.

"That's a bunch of bull, Diane." He reached over and began massaging her neck. The relaxation soothed all the way down her spine to the small of her back. "Life has always been random; you just had this middle-class illusion that if you did everything right, you'd be safe."

"I know."

"Sometimes you drive me crazy, woman. How much patience is a man supposed to have?" His hands slid down to her shoulders and he kissed the back of her neck.

"Oh, Barry!" She pulled away. "Let's talk about something else."

"What?"

"Well—how about Eduardo Ranier?"

"What about him?"

Diane described her interview with Cissy Greenspon. "Don't you think that's strange? That he used to be in real estate and apparently got involved in some kind of scandal, and suddenly he became a psychic?"

"I never doubted he was a fraud," Barry reminded her, his voice full of strained patience. "You're just after him because of that woman who called."

"There's something else." Diane plunged ahead. "Eduardo was at the high school yesterday. He talked to Jeanette and to some of the other kids. He was there after school. Lara talked to him for a few minutes, and that was before Jeanette disappeared."

Barry tilted his head slightly in his editor-evaluating-the-facts mode. "Did you tell the police?"

"I didn't actually see him, and that was all they wanted to know, what I'd observed myself." Diane's explanation sounded lame to her own ears. What had stopped her? Was it the sympathy she'd felt after talking to Jimmy, for the unloved ghost in a borrowed Lincoln?

"It's pretty circumstantial." Barry reached into his shirt pocket as if for a cigarette, and smiled ruefully when he didn't find one. "There were a lot of people at the high school other than kids. Janitors, teachers, secretaries."

"But he was different," Diane said. "He was a visitor."

"That's right. So everyone would have been aware of him. Not a very good disguise for a killer." Barry finger-combed his dark hair. "Would you please come over here and stop fidgeting, Diane?"

Relieved at having unloaded her fears, she snuggled closer.

"By the way." Barry pulled something small and round out of his pocket. "I forgot to give you this earlier."

"My button!" Diane cupped it in her hand with delight. "Thanks." She set it on the end table.

"This time, if you don't want me fooling with your buttons, just say so instead of jerking away, okay?" Barry's mouth twitched humorously.

"Smartass."

"Tease."

"Bully."

"Sexpot." His arms encircled her waist.

He smelled good, cologne and A-1 sauce and white wine. "You have such a poetic way of putting things," she murmured as their lips met and she sank against the back of the couch, wanting him so much she couldn't bear to let him go.

The phone rang.

"Shit," Barry said. "Let it ring."

Diane hesitated. "Nobody ever calls me at home except you. It might be an emergency." Her father and stepmother rarely called from Ohio, and then it was usually on Sundays. Lara, she thought, and reached for the phone.

It was Brendan Ryan. "I'm really sorry to bother you, Diane, but I wondered if Lara was over there."

"Why, no, she isn't." Diane sat upright. "Is something wrong?"

"We had an argument and she ran out of here about an hour ago." His voice was rough with worry. "I thought she'd be back before dark. And another thing. I don't know whether she took her insulin or not. It's—well, it's just not like her." He'd already called Kris, with no luck, he said. "Where would she go? I guess I don't know my own daughter very well, do I?"

"Probably a shopping mall." Diane was peripherally aware

128

of Barry straightening his tie and slipping on his shoes. "Did she have her purse with her?"

"Yes."

"Then she's got some money, anyway." Quickly, Diane began working out a plan. She would stay here, in case Lara called. They would round up everyone they could to search for Lara: Kris, for instance, and Barry—he nodded agreement—and, on a stroke of inspiration, she thought of Jimmy, too. If Lara wasn't back by eight o'clock, they'd call the police.

"Oh, and there's somebody else helping out," Brendan said. "Just a few minutes ago, a man called Lara. It was that psychic on the radio, Eduardo something. He said he'd be glad to look for her."

Diane's stomach tied itself into a knot. "Did he say what he was calling about?"

"No. No, he didn't."

After she hung up, she walked Barry to the door.

"You look terrified." He traced the line of her cheekbone. "She's all right, Diane. Kids do this all the time."

"Sure," she said. "Sure."

38

Lara caught a bus that ran down to Coast Highway and turned south toward Newport Beach. She knew she wasn't ready to go to Hollywood; she didn't even have any clothes. Right now, she just wanted to get away.

She ached all over with anger. Why had she put up with being a drudge for so long? And then her father slamming down the phone like that! Now she'd never dare call that radio station manager again.

The bus rumbled through the dimming light, passing the old pier. That's where Jeanette's body had been found. Had she been killed there? No, there'd been something on the radio saying police thought she died somewhere else. Did it really matter? Jeanette was dead. All these details had nothing to do with her.

Or me, Lara thought. I'm not dying like that. I'm going to get my living done now.

Maybe she should call Kris. She wanted to apologize for her bad temper this afternoon. But if she told him where she was, he might tell her father.

The bus turned onto the Balboa Peninsula. It was funny how in places you couldn't actually see the ocean on your right or Newport Harbor on your left, and yet the peninsula was only a few blocks wide. At least you could smell the brine, and feel the tingle in the air, and hear a couple of sea-gulls mewing overhead.

She began to feel better, studying the funky beach cottages and little shops. This wasn't like the snooty area around Citrus Harbour. Newport was older, more casual, a popular place for kids to hang out on weekends.

Several people got off at the Newport Pier, and she did too. Even this late, there were a handful of skinny guys just finishing up their surfing, most of them wearing black wetsuits that looked like something out of a James Bond movie.

Lara went into Charlie's Chili and got a chili-cheese omelette. She knew she shouldn't eat without taking her insulin, but one night couldn't make that much difference. Besides, she had milk with her meal, to help absorb the starch.

Skipping her usual predinner routine gave her a sense of freedom. She hated pricking her finger to test the blood-sugar level, the cold alcohol swab on her thigh, the sting of the needle. She hated diabetes. It meant she'd never be free from doctors.

After eating, Lara went back out. Most of the shops were closed, but she crossed the plaza in front of the pier until she reached the shop-lined walkway. Idly, she stared at the bikinis in the window of Far-Out Sportswear. There were some nightclubs around here. Would they ask for ID? She knew she could pass for eighteen, but probably not twenty-one.

If only she had Eduardo Ranier's phone number! Lara's hands clenched into fists, wanting to pound her brother. If it weren't for him, they might be together right now.

She could picture Eduardo sitting beside her in front of a fire, talking softly, his hand covering hers as the heat flickered against their faces. He would tell her how much talent she had, devise a strategy for her. There were ways to audition, she'd heard, and he probably knew about agents and show-cases and all that stuff.

Two girls came along the walkway, giggling. One of them stumbled against Lara and they both apologized before going

131

on. But her fantasy was shattered, and she couldn't summon it back.

A chilly wind picked up from the ocean. It had been cloudy all day, and Lara glanced apprehensively at the sky. Impossible to tell anything from the black-hearted clouds. Might rain. Might pass away to Baja or out over the desert.

She wondered what was going on at home. Who had fixed dinner, or had her father taken the boys out to eat? Had anyone thought to put the clothes in the dryer? Was everybody glad she was gone, or did they feel bad about how they'd treated her?

Maybe her father would call Kris, or Diane. The idea made Lara uncomfortable. She didn't want her friends worrying over her.

The wind stung against her cheeks, whispering of rain. There was a bank of pay phones back toward Balboa Boulevard. Lara started toward them, then remembered the only change she'd had after paying for her omelet was a nickel and some pennies.

She had almost reached Charlie's Chili to get change when a man came out and stopped in front of her. He looked like he might be in his late thirties, small-eyed with thick, choppy hair. "Need some help?" he asked.

"No, thank you." She tried to edge by him.

"I could give you a ride somewhere."

A pulse fluttered in her throat. Could this be the man who killed Jeanette? He looked so ordinary. "I'm meeting my boyfriend."

He shrugged. "Have it your way." Then he swung around and walked back into the restaurant. Lara just stood there for a minute, her heart pounding.

She hadn't meant to run away helter-skelter like this. She'd intended to plan everything carefully, to have a place to stay if the time ever came, and some friends to turn to. She'd thought maybe she could find a roommate through a newspaper ad or a college housing office, like UCLA. And she'd counted on having a hundred dollars or so to start off with, maybe borrowed from Kris or Diane.

She didn't want to go back into the restaurant. If the man saw her asking for change, he might follow her out. The base of the pier looked deserted now, and there were a lot of dark places where somebody could drag you.

Lara walked toward Balboa Boulevard. She'd just have to wait until the next bus came by. The ones for Citrus Beach only ran about once an hour, and there wasn't any shelter, and it was starting to rain. But it was better than hanging around here, that was for sure.

39

By seven-thirty, Diane was sure Lara wasn't going to call. She was too restless to concentrate on anything, and here in the apartment she felt cut off from the search. Finally she called Brendan Ryan.

"Please come over," he said. "I'd have gone out before now but I figured some adult ought to be here, in case she tries to run in and grab her clothes."

Diane arrived at the Ryan house ten minutes later. A steady drizzle was starting.

"Kris and some of the other kids are checking the malls," Brendan told her as she came inside. "Maybe she went inside to get out of the rain. Most of them close at nine o'clock."

"Do you think it's time we called the police?"

The little boy—Gerry, that was his name—came toward them out of the hall, dragging a teddy bear and wearing nothing but pajama bottoms. "Is Lara coming home soon?" he asked. "She didn't go away like Mommy, did she?"

"Sammy!" Brendan bellowed. "Put your little brother to bed." One of the older boys darted out and retrieved Gerry. Their father returned his attention to Diane. "If it weren't for that girl getting killed, I'd say, hell, let her get wet and scared enough to come home. But—sure, I think it's time."

He made the call. Afterwards, he said, "Some of the

searchers are fanning out, up and down Coast Highway. I'm going to drive around and see what I can see."

"I'll be here."

It didn't make Diane feel any better to know Eduardo Ranier was one of the men driving alone through the night, looking for Lara.

The call was immediately reported to Lieutenant De Anda. Chief Ferguson, who was sitting in the Lieutenant's office, looked grim when he heard the news.

"Jesus H. Christ," he said.

"Sounds like a runaway so far." Mario wondered why he bothered to reassure the man who was cheating him out of a major promotion. But until they caught the killer, they were in this together. So was the whole Detective Division.

Among them, they'd managed to empty Emma's coffee pot three times and fill out enough reports to leave De Anda and Ferguson bleary-eyed. There were a lot of leads, most of them useless. Half a dozen people reported seeing prowlers. A man resembling Vincent Price had been observed near the school athletic field. Three people suspected their neighbors.

Most of the work was drudgery. It was amazing how important organization, and filing, and checking, and cross-checking could be. New York's Son of Sam had been traced by a parking ticket.

Cops from some of the neighboring towns with minimart robberies were helping with the holdup-murder investigation. A good thing, because right now, Citrus Beach was stretched mighty thin.

On the Tracy killing, De Anda had his detectives grouping the clues into categories, giving priority to the ones that included enough concrete details to be checked easily. There had even been one phoned-in, anonymous confession. The man sounded weak and shaky and, although they were looking into it, De Anda couldn't imagine him luring Jeanette Tracy to a deserted place, strangling her, and then carrying her body along the pier. And the man hadn't known about

135

the trash bag found floating around her ankles, or the way the note was lettered. They were details he'd decided not to release to the media.

As for the computer, it had turned up a number of unsolved murders. Unfortunately, it wasn't unusual for girls and young women to be found stabbed, strangled, bludgeoned, or shot. But there was no case where similarities stood out.

Ferguson started to drink some cold coffee and then plopped the cup down with a grimace. "Why?" He shifted uncomfortably on the hard wooden chair. "Why the note? Why the photograph? Why the threat to kill two more this week? What kind of maniac have we got here?"

You could speculate all night about that one, De Anda reflected. But you couldn't let yourself worry about what the killer might do next. You just had to do the agonizingly slow, painstaking police work and hope you'd get a break.

Please don't let Lara Ryan be the next one, he prayed silently. Please don't let there be a next one.

40

It was almost eight-thirty by the time the bus came, and Lara was drenched. She climbed gratefully up the steep steps and sank onto the nearest seat, digging in her purse for her wallet.

The bus, which was almost empty, rolled away from the curb and headed toward Coast Highway. There were only a few people on board, a Hispanic woman with a baby, a seedy-looking old man, and three teenagers she'd never seen before, two boys and a girl, who were snickering together. But the interior was brightly lit, the advertising placards reassuringly normal.

She couldn't find her wallet.

"That'll be seventy-five cents, miss." The driver glanced at her. "Exact change."

"I don't have change," Lara said. "I'll have to give you a dollar." She began pulling things out—lipstick, comb, tissues, keys, a tampon left over from her last period. "My wallet! I had it—I can't imagine . . .''

Then she remembered. The two girls, giggling and stumbling into her. The bitches! They'd taken her wallet. It was only five dollars, but she needed it.

"Somebody stole my money," she told the driver.

Behind her, one of the boys called out, "Yeah, sure. We've heard that one before!"

137

Lara glared at him before turning back to the driver. "Look, I've got to get home. I'll mail the money in. Or you can call my father."

"I wouldn't trust her if I were you," the boy called, and the girl piped in, "She does this all the time," and burst into a fit of giggles. Lara wanted to strangle her.

"Honest, I—"

"Yeah, right." The driver sounded weary. "You're getting off at the next stop, miss."

"I can't!" She stuffed the junk furiously back into her purse. "It's dangerous!"

"Yeah, sure." He swung the big wheel as the bus curved onto the highway.

Angrily, Lara stared at his name plate posted near the door. "I'll report you for this. Somebody really did steal my wallet." She glanced back. The three teenagers wore looks of exaggerated innocence. If she ever saw them again, she'd make them sorry.

The bus groaned to a halt on Coast Highway. It was dark here, and there weren't any stores close by. She hated that bus driver. She wouldn't beg again. He probably got a kick out of this. She climbed down and restrained an impulse to hit the side of the bus as it lurched away in a cloud of exhaust fumes.

The rain had eased off but the air was cold and her clothes were damp. There wasn't even a bench to sit on, and Lara was beginning to feel lightheaded. She remembered that she hadn't taken her insulin.

A police car would probably come by eventually. No, that was too humiliating, to end up huddled on a chair at a police station, waiting for her father to pick her up. The boys would laugh at her. Lara the Runaway. Big joke.

She stood there staring as cars whizzed past, their lights blurred by the speed and the mist. She could always hitchhike. Yeah, sure. Like Jeanette? She bit her lip to keep back the tears. Well, there wasn't any other way to get home, was there? If she could just get to Citrus Beach, she could walk to Kris's house from the highway.

Lara stepped closer to the roadway and stuck out her thumb.

On the other side of the highway, a silver Mustang went by, slowed, and made a left turn into a parking lot beyond her. It was turning around. It was coming back to get her. Lara's throat clenched. She'd been hoping for a woman driver, or maybe a family, but this was a man . . .

The car pulled up and she looked inside. "Oh." Lara broke into a smile for the first time in hours. "Oh, thank goodness, it's you."

41

L eft alone, Diane took stock of the Ryans' house. It was
sparsely furnished, almost depressing, with weary furniture that looked like it had come from a Goodwill bin. A
torn comic book lay on the coffee table, and some toy trucks
were in the process of being ground into the carpet. Fraying
Vincent Van Gogh posters had been tacked onto the walls.

She walked down the hallway, noting that the boys had
retreated into one of the bedrooms. From their voices, she
gathered that they were playing some kind of board game.

In the laundry room, she noticed a pile of colored clothes
waiting to be washed. Lifting the lid on the machine, she
found a clean, damp load, which she moved into the dryer. A
few minutes later, the machines were clunking noisily about
their business.

Diane wandered into the kitchen. She considered making
herself a cup of coffee and thought about Cissy Greenspon.
What a naive woman—or was she cleverer than Diane had
suspected? The bookstore owner had provided quite a bit of
information, but how much of it could be trusted?

It was hard to concentrate on anything. Diane felt Lara's
presence everywhere, smelled the Ivory soap that Lara used.
Surely she would come bursting in the front door any minute,
laughing or maybe crabby, but healthy and alive.

Finally Diane turned the radio on. It made her feel better

when a newscast went by with no mention of Lara. At least that meant they hadn't found a body . . .

Someone rang the front doorbell.

Diane waited a moment for the boys to answer it, but they didn't, and the ring came again. It might be Barry or Jimmy, checking in. She went to the door and peered through the glass panes. In the dim porchlight, she could see a tall, light-haired man.

Cautiously, Diane opened the door. "Yes?"

Something about him transfixed her, an intensity in the eyes and in the way he stood, a restless energy like a naked electric wire sparking near tinder. "I'm Eduardo Ranier," he said.

She already knew that. "A sweet man," Cissy Greenspon had called him. Not the word Diane would have chosen.

"Come in." She moved back. "I'm Diane Hanson, a friend of Lara's."

He wiped his feet on the threshhold, since there was no mat, and stepped inside. "She hasn't turned up?" His words and movements seemed ordinary and yet, to Diane, not quite natural, as if he'd learned a role very carefully.

"No." She had a flash of disorientation, standing here in a strange house with this man.

"I drove up and down Coast Highway but I didn't have any luck." He gave her a shy smile, nice white teeth, a bit of a self-deprecating curl to the lips.

"Mr. Ranier," she began.

"Eduardo. Ted, actually."

"Why did you call Lara today?"

Some of the friendliness faded as he studied Diane. "You said you're a friend of hers?"

"Big sister. In the Big Sisters program." She felt awkward just standing there, so she sat on the sofa. A spring dug into her thigh.

"I see." He folded himself into a chair. He must be at least six two, she thought. "I met Lara at the high school on Monday."

"And Jeanette," Diane couldn't resist adding.

His lids flickered and then his face relaxed again, as if he were willing himself to look normal. "Yes, and Jeanette. I sensed danger, for both girls. I should have warned them, although perhaps it wouldn't have done any good. Things have a way of taking their own course. That's why I was calling Lara today. To tell her to be careful."

"I don't suppose you have any . . . flashes about where she is tonight?" Diane shifted away from the jutting spring and ran into another one.

Again that rather disarming smile. "I wish my gift were something I could control, but it isn't. It does what it wishes."

"I see." Why had he come to the house? Why not just phone in and keep searching? Maybe he knew exactly where Lara was. Maybe he had found her already and . . .

Masculine footsteps crunched outside on the walk, and Kris entered through the half-open door. "Hi, Diane. Oh, Mr. Ranier." He didn't look pleased to see Eduardo. "Lara hasn't showed up, huh?"

"No."

"All the kids have called in. She wasn't at any of the malls, and they're starting to close," he said.

It was going to be a long night.

42

L ara sank gratefully into the low, cushiony seat of the
  Mustang. "Boy, am I glad you came along. I was getting
scared."

"This place does look kind of deserted." Jimmy checked
the rearview mirror before pulling back onto the highway.
"Don't you know better than to hitchhike?"

"Somebody stole my wallet, and then the bus driver put
me off. I was scared stiff." Lara wallowed in relief. "I sure am
lucky you drove by."

"Actually, I was looking for you."

She turned to him in surprise. "You were?"

"There's a bunch of us out searching. Diane's been really
worried."

"I'm sorry." Lara sucked in a deep breath. "My dad was
impossible. He treats me like a servant—or a wife. Well, I'm
not either one, and I don't want to be."

They were skimming along the highway toward Citrus
Beach. Now that the rain had stopped, the clouds thinned and
Lara could see a few stars overhead.

"I didn't get along so well with my dad either," Jimmy
said. "I'll bet I could trade you horror stories."

"Maybe everybody feels that way. But none of the other
kids I know has to do all the cooking and cleaning." Lara

checked herself. She didn't want to sound like a whiner. "Oh, I guess it's not so bad. I just lost my temper."

"You feel ready to go back and face everybody?" Jimmy slowed down at Florencia, the beginning of town. She appreciated his being such a careful driver. Kris liked to screech around corners and gun the car through yellow lights. He had quite a collection of traffic tickets as a result.

"Oh, I don't know," she said. Lara was enjoying the smooth ride and the adult conversation. At the newspaper once, Jimmy had shown her some of his work, mostly shots of basketball and baseball players, but some more interesting stuff of beach scenes and oddball people around town. She was flattered that somebody like him would even care if she was missing.

A wave of guilt flushed over her. She'd put a lot of people to a lot of trouble tonight. Had her dad really been that concerned? He must have been, to call everybody.

Something red flashed in the mirror. "What the hell?" Jimmy pulled to the curb.

The police car pulled in behind them. The officer came around to the driver's side and checked his license.

"Was I doing something wrong, officer?" Although he must be irritated, Jimmy kept his tone polite. Not a hothead like Kris.

The policeman glanced across at Lara. "Do you have some identification, miss?"

"No, I don't. Somebody stole my wallet in Newport Beach." Suddenly she wanted to cry. "And it's the truth!"

"What's your name?" the man asked.

"Lara Ryan."

"That's what I thought." He gave Jimmy a hard look.

Jimmy pulled a press card out of his pocket. "I just found her down in Newport and I was taking her home."

The officer nodded, his expression friendlier. "Well, I'll radio in and have the dispatcher call your house, miss. They'll be real glad to know you're all right."

"Thank you," Lara said.

Jimmy hit the turn signal, then pulled slowly out into traf-

144

fic. He grinned at her. "I thought he was going to give me a ticket and I couldn't figure out what I'd done."

There were three unfamiliar cars in front of the Ryan house when they pulled into the drive. The door flew open and little Gerry ran out ahead of the grownups, his bare feet plop-plopping against the wet walkway. "Lara! Lara! I thought you went away like Mommy!"

She knelt down and hugged him, and then she started to cry for real. "I'm sorry," she said. "I won't ever do that again. I promise."

Her father reached her and put his arms around them both. "I'm just glad you're okay, honey."

She glanced up at Diane and Barry and Kris, and then behind them she saw someone else. Eduardo! He'd come, too. He'd cared that much about her.

Suddenly she didn't feel so bad.

Driving home, he cussed at a cat that darted into his path and swerved toward it, but it scampered under a parked car.

If his luck had been better tonight . . .

She liked him. He could see it in her eyes. Like Jeanette, she wouldn't give him any trouble. Tonight, she'd been defenseless out there. Luck just hadn't been with him. Well, that was the way you played the game. The real winners, the ones in control, they accepted that you couldn't have the dice fall your way every single time. Just most of the time.

Maybe it had been for the best. Everyone had been searching for her tonight. They'd even called the police right away. It could have made things difficult.

He thought of the boy who cried wolf. He liked the idea.

Tomorrow, nobody would be watching Lara Ryan.

WEDNESDAY

43

It was 9:25 A.M. when Diane finally got past the recep- tionist at KCIT Radio, after waiting in a cramped lobby where the only reading material was a dog-eared program guide. Early as it was, she already felt haggard from a night of bad dreams, the last—and only clearly remembered one—a haunting scene of Lara being sucked into a dark mist.

Following the receptionist's directions, Diane walked down the worn gray carpeting of a narrow corridor to the second door on the left. Overhead, a malfunctioning speaker sput- tered the morning cooking show. Through one open door- way, she glimpsed what appeared to be an oversize closet full of tapes.

The station manager's office turned out to be not much big- ger, a cubicle papered with glossy photographs and furnished with what looked like hand-me-downs.

"Bruce Jorgas." The tense man with thinning hair stood up to shake hands, then waved Diane into a chair. "You're doing some kind of story for the *Record*, is that it?" He had a thin face with a faint scar on the jaw line. Diane guessed his age at late forties, but he seemed stretched and worn, as if he'd lived too long.

"That's right." She pulled a steno pad out of her purse. "Tell me, how long has Eduardo Ranier been working for you?"

149

"Almost two years." He plucked a large envelope from among the loose papers on his desk. "Here's a press kit. Photograph, all that stuff. You know, our publicist . . ."

"Tell me, Mr. Jorgas, do you believe Eduardo Ranier can really predict the future?"

His mouth tightened. "Oh, *that* kind of story. Look here, Ms., er, Hanson, I frankly don't give a damn. You can't quote that. I'm being honest with you. Do I ask if the recording artists can sing? Do I care? The public wants it, the public gets it. We're a small station. We haven't violated our license."

"I'm not out to get your station." Diane could feel the man mentally pushing her out of the room, but she refused to budge. "Two years ago, Eduardo Ranier—or Theodore Raines—found the body of a girl in Dana Point. Do you believe he found her through some kind of psychic flash?"

"Like I told you, miss, that's not my concern." Jorgas fiddled with the tangles of his telephone cord. "It's like the horoscope in your newspaper. Do you believe in that?"

"You have a point." Time to ease off. "All right, then. I need some background information. I won't connect it to you or the station. I understand Mr. Ranier was involved in some real estate dealings that went sour a few years back. Who could I talk to about that?"

"Now look. Ted happens to be an old friend of mine. Well, his uncle was, actually. The kid was in and out of trouble, but nothing serious. I happen to like him. I wouldn't have hired him if I thought he was a schmuck."

"Thanks for being frank." Diane didn't like manipulating people, but she was about to use an interviewer's best trick—blackmail—and she hoped it would work. "Unfortunately, I can't write my story until I dig out the full information. I know Mr. Ranier has an uncle around here and a mother in San Diego. I'd hate to disturb them, but if that's the only way to find out what I need to know, I'll have to do it."

She held her breath, silently thanking Jimmy for telling her about Ranier's family.

"Yeah, okay, I don't suppose it was all that bad." Jorgas dug through a Rollodex crammed with smudged cards. "He had a partner—here it is—Artie Ballard. Santa Ana. No, I think that's old." He pulled out an Orange County phone book and flipped through it. "Ballard. Yeah. He's moved to Newport." He gave Diane the address and phone number. "He'd know all about it."

"Thanks." Diane considered whether to ask Jorgas not to mention their meeting to Ranier, but decided it wouldn't do any good. She stood up.

"Ms. Hanson." Jorgas slapped the phone book shut. "Mind if I ask why you're doing this?"

"I'm a consumer reporter and one of our readers complained." She hesitated. "Oh, hell. You want to know the real reason? Mr. Ranier was at the high school the day Jeanette Tracy disappeared."

"So?"

"He was one of the last people she spoke with."

"Then this is a matter for the police, wouldn't you say?" Jorgas lit a cigarette. There was a slight tremor in his hand.

"I'm sure they've already talked to him and learned nothing." Diane's anger boiled up unexpectedly. "Now he's getting friendly with someone I care about very much, a teenage girl who's a little wild and real vulnerable to somebody like him. If he hurts her in any way, Mr. Jorgas, I will crucify that man. Do you understand me?"

He let out a mouthful of smoke. "If Ted Raines ever hurts anybody, I'll be right behind you, lady. But he won't."

"Thanks for your help. I hope you're right."

Walking down the hall, she found herself picturing Eduardo as he'd stood in the porch light last night—the pale eyes, the tall self-possessed body, the impression of being slightly larger than life. A small part of her had yielded to him, not liking him exactly but feeling drawn to the man. Now, at the memory, her skin prickled as if she were a cat scenting danger.

When she got outside, Diane took a deep, shaky breath. She wasn't sure where the fury had come from, or whether she'd said too much. Suppose Jorgas repeated her words to Ranier?

Then maybe he'll leave Lara alone, she told herself, and started back to the car.

44

"The guy you want is Colin Bregman." The voice was a harsh whisper over the telephone. Chang wasn't even sure he'd heard the name right through the newsroom din.

"Who is this?"

"Never mind. Bregman. Graduated from Citrus High five years ago. Check it out." Click.

Chang shifted his shoulders, trying to get rid of a cramp. He'd thought maybe something would come of that Ryan girl's disappearance last night, but it had turned out to be a false alarm. Other than that, nothing new to write about. Oh, well, there were more than three hours yet to deadline. He dialed the number of the high school and got through to the principal.

"Colin Bregman?" The creak of a chair marked Roy Gfeller's course as he swung around to pull out a yearbook. "Sure, here he is. I remember him. Big guy, on the football team for a while, until he assaulted one of the cheerleaders."

"Sounds like a sweetheart."

"He hung around the high school the year after he graduated. We complained, and the police gave him the bum's rush." Creak creak. Gfeller must be leaning back, putting his feet up, enjoying the role of amateur detective. "You think he

152

could be the killer? I haven't seen him around, but something rings a bell."

As he waited, Chang glanced across the newsroom at Jimmy. Freckle-face was sitting on the corner of Diane Hanson's desk, looking seriously sympathetic. Was he flirting, or what? Chang tried to peer into Barry's office but the managing editor was bent over his desk, probably marking up yesterday's paper.

"Tustin. Or maybe it was Villa Park." Gfeller crackled back to life over the phone line. "Some kind of rape or attempted rape charge, I think about three years ago. That's right; I seem to recall Bregman got sent up for a while." A shift in tone to sorrowful righteousness. "You know, it always hurts me when one of ours goes bad, but there wasn't much anybody could do about Colin Bregman."

"Tustin or Villa Park." Chang made a note in the computer. "Thanks."

"Whoever it is, just help the cops catch him, okay?" There was another creak as Gfeller sat up and projected earnestness. "The safety of our kids . . ."

"Nothing I'd like better. I'll get right on it." Chang hung up and called the Tustin dicks. No luck. He did better in Villa Park; the detective in sex crimes remembered Bregman.

"I got an APB about a month ago." The voice sounded boyish, a nice Irish tenor. "Bregman escaped from a work-release program in Los Angeles. Just walked off. As far as I know, he hasn't been in contact with any of his relatives around here."

"You wouldn't happen to have a photo of the guy, would you?" The answer was no. Gfeller would lend the yearbook, though, Chang suspected. "Thanks for the information. I'll buy you a drink sometime."

The next call was to Lieutenant De Anda. No, Citrus Beach was not aware that a rapist named Colin Bregman was on the loose. They'd look into it.

Satisfied, Chang began to write. It was enough to keep the story alive, along with the inevitable sidebars about people

153

buying locks for their doors and carpooling the kids to and from school. Jimmy, to give him credit, had managed to get a photo this morning of some dumb redhead hitchhiking to school, and quoted her saying she wasn't worried about the killer. "Why should he pick on me?" A classic.

The main story, working the angle on Colin Bregman into the lead, was finished by ten-thirty, way early. The copy desk would have time to monkey around with the commas to their hearts' content.

"Guy!" Rand Franklin swung across the newsroom. "Hank Tracy is holding a press conference at City Hall. Right now."

"I'm on my way." Chang grabbed his pad, leaving the tape recorder behind. There wouldn't be time to listen to it; besides, he never trusted the damn thing in a pinch. With Jimmy on his heels, he dashed out the door.

45

L ucille Ferguson stood at the back of the city council chambers, twisting a Pierre Cardin scarf nervously in her hands. She'd insisted on coming; after all, it wouldn't look right for Mack to be here, and someone had to find out what was going on. But she hadn't been prepared for an anxiety attack.

Breathe deeply, Lucille. You'll be all right. Her mother's voice, echoing in her head. *You just need to suck the air in from your diaphragm.*

This was her man. It was odd, but with her first husband, she'd felt more as if she were making an alliance than a marriage, old Pasadena families on both sides. He'd never shown his disappointment when the children didn't come; maybe he hadn't really cared. They'd led twin lives, moving to Citrus Beach, going to the club; they'd slept in twin beds; and she'd cried a little at his funeral, not so much because he was gone but for so many years only half-lived.

Last night Mack had come in late, sweaty and tired, his tie askew, his face creased. She couldn't explain now what had come over her; she'd never been so aggressive before. He hadn't quite grasped what she was doing at first as she pulled down his pants and knelt, and then her mouth closed over him and she felt him swell and grow hard, and heard him

155

groan deep in his throat, and they'd done it on the floor like a pair of animals. God, she wanted him right now.

Lucille bit her lip hard, watching the cameramen adjust their lights on the podium. This wasn't his fault. They couldn't blame him for some maniac who just happened to pick the mayor pro tem's daughter.

From the side door, Patricia Reilly came out, and then Hank Tracy. He was wearing dark glasses and he looked pale, but maybe that was because of the sudden flood of lights.

The reporters sank into silence as Hank Tracy walked to the microphone. Lucille wondered if they really felt bad about the dead girl, or if they just wanted to be sure they didn't miss anything.

Hank took his sunglasses off. His eyes looked narrow and red around the edges.

"I want to thank my colleague, Mayor Reilly, and the other members of the council and the Chamber of Commerce for their support." He rubbed his cheek and swallowed before continuing. "I've given this a lot of thought over the last twenty-four hours. As you all probably know, there's been no love lost between Mack Ferguson and me, but I wanted to be fair. I didn't just want to lash out at him because I was in pain."

Lucille spotted Jimmy Owens, creeping closer and taking a rapid series of shots. He was, in a manner of speaking, her stepson, but she hardly knew him. She'd invited him for dinner a couple of times, but he'd been working. True, he'd always spoken to her pleasantly enough. But today he was part of that pack of wolves called the press. It didn't seem right.

"Several months ago, I asked that a police officer be stationed outside the high school. There'd been some incidents there from time to time, and I felt it was a natural magnet for trouble. Unfortunately, I've been proven right. Chief Ferguson disagreed with me. If he hadn't . . ."

Hank Tracy's voice caught, and it took him a minute to regain his composure. "That's what I keep coming back to. If he'd done as I asked, my little girl might still be alive. Chief Ferguson is running for sheriff as a law-and-order candidate. I don't believe him. I think, as I've always thought, that he's simply right wing. Yes, he supports the death penalty, and so do I, but he's also made derogatory statements over the years about homosexuals and the women's movement. Those issues have nothing to do with law and order."

Lucille could see his next statement coming. She brought the scarf up to her mouth as if to stifle a cry of protest.

"I've decided to announce my support of Tony Arroyo. His excellent record as a prosecutor speaks for itself. I realize that the timing of this announcement, coming right after my daughter's death, looks as if I'm blaming Chief Ferguson for it. I'm not, exactly, but I'm not exonerating him either."

Hank hesitated for a moment, and then stepped aside. Immediately, reporters began calling out questions. Did he have any suspicions as to the killer? Was he criticizing the handling of the murder investigation? Hank answered both questions with a shake of the head.

Then one of the cameras swung around and lights dashed into Lucille's eyes. She lowered the scarf quickly and tried to look assured. Blinking against the glare, she spotted Jimmy and shot him a pleading look, but he was regarding her as the others did, with the detached air of a spectator at a baseball game that was just beginning to liven up.

"Mrs. Ferguson!" A woman's voice, but she couldn't see who it was. "How do you feel about Councilman Tracy's remarks?"

Lucille cleared her throat as someone thrust a microphone in front of her. She'd prepared a statement for Mack. Now what the hell was it?

"Chief Ferguson and I would like to extend our deepest sympathies to Mr. and Mrs. Tracy." Did her voice sound too smooth? "I was never fortunate enough to have children myself, but I can imagine . . ."

"Yes, but what about the sheriff's race? You've got a big fund-raising dinner coming up Sunday night. Are you going to cancel it?"

That possibility hadn't even occurred to her. Should it have? Had she slipped up? The campaign treasury needed the money, but how would it look? There was no time to think about that now.

"We all hope the criminal who murdered Jeanette Tracy will be caught before then, especially in view of the threats quoted in yesterday's newspaper." Lucille felt as if her brain wasn't working right. Had she left something out?

"Is Chief Ferguson considering withdrawing from the race?" It was Chang, from the *Record*.

"Of course not. This certainly isn't his fault!" She heard the snappishness of her tone but couldn't restrain it. "My husband would have done anything to prevent this murder. There was no reason to anticipate the events of this week; at the time, I'm sure he discussed Councilman Tracy's suggestion with his department heads and found it to be impractical." She remembered something Mack had said at the time. "What about the junior high school, and the elementary schools? Why protect one school and not the others?"

Finally the reporters drifted off, leaving her alone. Across the council chambers, Lucille caught Hank Tracy's eye. His shoulders slumped. In the gray light left behind after the cameras were gone, he seemed to have aged ten years.

She'd known him and Lena for a long time, at the yacht club. They'd been surprised when she married Mack Ferguson. People never expected a woman of fifty-one to have secret hungers; it never occurred to them she might have married for sex.

Had she?

Lucille walked out, her mind full of Sunday's dinner. They couldn't afford to cancel it. Assemblyman Gorwins was scheduled to speak, and given his prominence, that was a rare coup. Besides, the guests had already paid. The press coverage was arranged. To cancel it now would be tantamount to dropping out of the race, and then where would they be?

If he could just solve this thing, Mack could still come out a hero. Lucille forced herself to stop frowning. She had a Republican Women's luncheon at the club today. She wanted to be smiling when she walked in.

46

Artie Ballard's answering service said he was out of town and would be back in his Newport office on Thursday. Would Diane care to leave a message? After a split second's indecision, she decided she would not.

No use alerting the guy to what she was up to. She'd have to go by there in person, the way she'd done with Bruce Jorgas. A reporter could get a lot done over the telephone, but there were limits.

Sorting through yesterday's letters on her desk, she slipped off her left shoe and flexed the pinched toes. This weekend she would definitely have to buy a new pair of pumps.

Diane looked up at Barry. He was just getting off deadline, standing up from his seat beside Rand Franklin. He caught her gaze and came over, surveying the area quickly to make sure they wouldn't be overheard.

"Seems to me we have some unfinished business from last night." The lines in his face relaxed a little, his coming-off-deadline look. "How about dinner at my house this time?"

She nodded. "Why not?" Unfinished business. She could already feel the heat of his nearness and taste his mouth.

"Still scared?"

"Witless."

His hand covered hers. "We'll take it slow. No pressure."

She tilted her head at him skeptically.

159

"Your buttons are safe with me. I promise."

"We'll see." The lump in her throat surprised her. Damn it, she wanted Barry, needed him. Also liked him and trusted him. What the hell was wrong with her?

"How's the investigation into our resident psychic going?" He'd apparently decided to change the subject. Relieved, Diane told him about the interview with Bruce Jorgas.

"It's odd how everyone seems to think he's such a great guy." Barry tapped his fingers against the desk top. "He didn't make much of an impression on me last night, one way or the other, but maybe that's because I was worried about Lara—and you."

"I'm all right," Diane said.

Ardrey Glenn's secretary came by to tell Barry the publisher was ready for their lunch date, and he had to excuse himself. "Tell me more later," he called as he left.

Diane fetched a grilled cheese sandwich and strange-smelling French fries from the newspaper cafeteria. She'd forgotten that they changed the deep-fat only once a week and it was already three days old.

Someone had dropped off today's mail on her desk. There was an envelope with the return address of South Coast Repertory, and Diane opened it, pleased to find the information she'd requested about the summer theater workshop.

In spite of Lara's protestations, Diane wasn't entirely convinced she might not decide to run away again. It was a good thing they'd arranged to get together after school today. Diane had a lot of things she wanted to talk about, and maybe the theater information would help.

One of her dreams came back from last night. Oddly, she remembered more of it now than she had on waking up this morning. Lara was floating in the ocean, far out, and Diane saw a shark coming toward her. She screamed and began swimming as hard as she could, trying to reach Lara, but the water lapped into her face and the girl kept getting farther and farther away, until Diane couldn't see her. She knew the shark must be getting closer . . .

"Romantic daydreams, or was the cheeseburger drugged?"

160

Jimmy plopped onto the chair beside her desk.

"Oh! Just—nothing." Diane shook her head to clear the dream away. "Listen, I don't know how to thank you for last night. You don't know how relieved I was, seeing you drive up with Lara."

"My pleasure." He grinned. "Hey, I like being in the middle of things for a change, instead of always in back of a camera. How's Lara doing? Thoroughly reformed, I hope."

"I haven't had a chance to talk to her yet." Diane waved the press release. "I'm picking her up after school to discuss acting lessons. Maybe that'll help tide her over the next few months, anyway."

"Well, if there's anything I can do, you let me know." Jimmy sprang up. He never seemed to stay in one place for long.

Finishing her lunch, Diane decided she'd put off the tedious task of digging through the files long enough.

The *Record*'s library, like the rest of the newspaper, had grown more or less unplanned, spilling from one back room to another. Shelves lined the walls, crammed with *Who's Who* and *What's What* and *Current Biography*. Filing cabinets created a maze in the center of the room.

With help from one of the librarians, Diane found that the Dana Point case would be listed under "Murders," followed by the name of the victim, which she didn't know, so she had to dig through all the murder files. It was shocking how many of them there were, dozens of victims, each one somebody's child . . .

Finally Diane reached the name Cassandra Starling. Inside, she found a blurry high school photograph of a young girl with pixie bangs and an impatient smile. A glance at the headlines confirmed that this was the right story.

Diane checked the envelope out of the library and took it back to her desk, clearing a space in which to lay out the clippings.

They were organized in reverse chronology, so she began at the back.

DANA POINT—The sheriff's department is asking the public's help in finding Cassandra Starling, 16, a junior at Dana Hills High School, who was last seen Tuesday hitchhiking on Street of the Golden Lantern.

Diane skipped the rest, flipped past a story about the offer of a reward, and came to the headline "'Psychic' Joins Search for Missing Girl."

DANA POINT—Real estate developer Eduardo Ranier of Citrus Beach, claiming he has received psychic impressions about a teen-age girl missing for more than a week, has volunteered to join the search for her.

Sheriff's deputies expressed skepticism but said they would welcome any additional help in locating Cassandra Starling, 16.

"Believe me, I'm aware that I may be exposed to ridicule for claiming to be a psychic," said Ranier, 31. "At first, I considered staying out of the whole thing, but my conscience wouldn't let me."

You hypocrite!

Ranier and his partner, Artie Ballard of Santa Ana, were the developers of Casa Bellita, a Capistrano Beach condominium complex that filed for bankruptcy earlier this year.

Asked if his participation in the search is related in any way to his real estate dealings, Ranier said, "Absolutely not."

He declined to give any details of his "visions" involving Starling, saying he did not want to distress her family by discussing the case publicly.

Diane slapped the article down in the stack. The sheer gall of that man! He knew all the right things to say, didn't he? He'd been smooth last night, too. It was easier to be objective reading about him in a musty stack of clippings than facing him in person.

The next few stories reflected the reporter's frustration at being unable to pry out any more details of Eduardo's "psychic" search, but the writing was filled with skeptical innuendos.

There was a sidebar, an interview with a psychic who'd worked with police in Los Angeles County. She walked a fine line, saying—of course—that clairvoyance really did exist and that she had used it successfully in several cases, but that such insights were unreliable, particularly to anyone who wasn't trained in interpreting them.

Diane turned to the next clip and read the headline. Even here in the newsroom, with the drone of voices and keyboards providing a reassuring background, she felt cold.

Body of Missing Girl Found in Field

DANA POINT—Following a tip from a self-proclaimed psychic, sheriff's deputies today found the body of a missing 16-year-old girl in a field near Dana Hills High School.

Cassandra Starling was last seen two weeks ago, hitchhiking home from school on Street of the Golden Lantern.

"The information that led to the discovery was provided by Eduardo Ranier," said sheriff's spokesman Lt. Daryl Foxworth. "We are talking with Mr. Ranier to learn how he developed this information."

Coroner's officials said the girl apparently died of strangulation at about the time of her disappearance.

The family had no comment on the participation of a psychic in finding the body of their daughter.

Diane read quickly through the next few articles. Deputies interviewed Ranier extensively, but could find no evidence to link him with the girl. No suspects were identified, and the case remained unsolved.

Further clippings detailed Ranier's rise to a measure of prominence, his appearance on television shows, his announcement that he would be writing a book about his experience.

Then came Chief Ferguson's outspoken criticism. "For all we know, this man may have had some other means of finding the body, some connection with the crime itself," he said in a speech to the Citrus Beach Rotary Club.

The clippings stopped there. Shuffling the strips of paper into their original order, Diane took the envelope back to the library and found another much thinner one labeled with Ranier's name.

It contained only a paltry assortment of speaking announcements and an article about the start of his radio program. Nothing more about the girl. No more bodies located in fields; no more brilliant flashes.

The only item of interest was his predictions for the previous year worldwide. Reading them, Diane noted that several had come true, but they were couched in such general terms—a monsoon in Southeast Asia, the overthrow of a South or Central American regime—that she could have dreamed them up herself with equal success.

The obvious conclusion was that Eduardo Ranier was a fraud.

But was he a murderer?

47

I t wasn't easy avoiding Kris at lunchtime, but Lara managed to dodge away while he was talking to one of the teachers about plans for the concert.

Her heart thumping, she dashed across the park strip to the pay phones by the library.

The business card, dented from lying on the bottom of her purse, even smelled a little like Eduardo, musky and exotic. Lara inhaled it for a moment, remembering his eyes fixed on hers last night. If only he'd been the one to find her! They could have talked . . . but at least he'd had a chance to slip her his card.

She'd had to make sure this morning that she got change, after losing all her money yesterday. Her father had been ridiculously understanding; it almost embarrassed her. Sammy had fixed breakfast, Dave washed the dishes, and Gerry got himself ready for school, his small round face shining as he cast himself in front of her for approval.

Damn it, she loved those creeps. Lara sniffed, glad no one was around to notice.

She dropped the coins into the phone and dialed. Oh, please don't let me get an answering machine, she prayed silently. Please let him be home.

Miraculously, he was.

She would have known that voice anywhere. It had a

165

warmth to it that was lacking on the radio; it seemed more, well, vulnerable somehow.

"I've been hoping you'd call." He sounded like he meant it! "Lara, you know what I said last night—that I'd seen danger around you?"

"Yes?"

"It's still there. I want you to be careful."

Was that the only reason he'd asked her to call? "Sure. Okay. I won't run away again." She wondered if he could hear the disappointment in her voice.

"As a matter of fact, there was something else I wanted to tal to you about." He hesitated a moment—oddly, it reminded her of Kris, the first time he'd asked her for a date. "I wondered if you were free this afternoon. I thought you might want to come watch me tape my radio show."

"Hey! That sounds terrific!" She did some quick mental calculations. Would her dad object? But she'd be safe and accounted for, after all, and it would be an educational experience. Only, what would he think of her running around with an older man? Maybe she should say she was going out with Kris.

"I usually tape about five o'clock. That gives me time to make corrections before we go on the air. If you like, I could pick you up straight from school, if you don't mind riding around with me while I run a few errands."

"Oh." Lara bit her lip. "I, uh, I'd arranged to meet my friend Diane, you know, the lady who was at my house yesterday. But you could come too, if you like. We won't be long. She's just got some information for me about an acting class. We'll probably go have fries at McDonald's, that's all."

She remembered what Diane had said on Monday, that she wanted to be present if Lara got together with Eduardo. Well, see what a good girl I'm turning into? she told herself wryly.

"I wouldn't want to get in the middle of anything. I have the feeling Diane might not be too impressed with me." He gave a rueful chuckle. Just like a kid! Lara thought, and realized she felt comfortable with him, the way she'd imagined she would. "Maybe I'll come by a little later, after I finish a few odds and ends. Do you mind waiting?"

"No—I'll be in front of the high school," she promised.

"I don't want you to do anything you feel is wrong, but it might be better if you don't tell your friend about coming to the radio station with me. People put the narrowest interpretation on things."

"Yeah, I know." She didn't, exactly, but she sensed he was right. Besides, she didn't want anything to interfere with tonight. "No, I won't say anything. I'll call home and tell them I'll be out with Kris—this guy I know—so they won't worry."

"Good girl," he said. "Now remember what I said, about being careful."

"Oh, I will." She hung up the phone and gave an excited hop, and wondered if this was how it felt to fall in love.

48

"The problem with our killer is that he isn't very original. Not in the way he kills, anyway."

Mack poured himself another cup of coffee and offered one to the mayor, but she declined. It was the first time he could ever remember seeing Patricia Reilly in his office. Usually she summoned him to hers.

"I do watch police shows, Mack. I know murderers usually have a trademark of some kind. Are you telling me this one doesn't?" The mayor was a stocky woman, but not homely, he reflected. If you squinted, maybe she even looked a little like Sharon Gless. He wished he had a glass of bourbon instead of this damn coffee.

"It's hard to tell from one body. You know, some aberration could be accidental, or it could be on purpose." He knew he wasn't coming off like much of an expert. Somehow in front of Patricia Reilly he felt the way he had when he'd first begun dating Lucille, as if he came from the wrong side of the tracks. "Of course, sending a photograph and a threatening letter to a newspaper is definitely out of the ordinary."

"I suppose it's too much to ask for fingerprints," she said, and he nodded.

A silence fell between them. Why had she come? If she wanted information, she could have telephoned for it. Mack wished Lucille were here, invisible, sitting behind his shoulder to give him advice.

"You know, I've had reservations about the way you run this department for a long time." Shit, here it came. "Don't you think it's time you promoted Mario De Anda?"

He tried to think of a reasonable explanation. "Actually, I was planning to move one of the other captains into detectives. Pyne, for example."

"Your good buddy Pyne is barely competent and you know it, and I'm well aware that he's the reason for all this game-playing." Patricia Reilly was a self-made real estate broker who ran an office of nearly forty agents, and Mack felt as if she were about to foreclose on him. "As for stationing an officer in front of the high school back when Hank first asked for it, I won't fight with you in hindsight. But find this guy, Mack. Find him real fast. Or I'll have your ass."

As she strode out of his office, Mack wondered why he'd ever thought a woman would be too soft for the job of mayor. This one probably ate nails with her Wheaties.

He went down to De Anda's office.

"The mayor's after my ass," he said. De Anda looked unsympathetic but diplomatically refrained from rubbing it in. Under the circumstances, he was entitled, Mack reflected. "I'm making you captain."

De Anda blinked. "Now? Thanks. Who's my new lieutenant?"

Mack ran his fingers through his thinning hair. "Who's on top of the list?" For promotions below the rank of captain, officers were tested and ranked by an independent assessment center.

"Shit." De Anda shook his head. "Terry Hewett. He's tops, but he's in court all week. Well, it's nice to have the title, anyway." And the raise, of course, but De Anda was too smooth to mention it.

They went over the evidence again and the computer printouts. There were dozens of unsolved more-or-less-similar murders around the state, going back for decades. A cluster in

Berkeley a few years back had never been solved, but there hadn't been any threatening notes to the newspapers. Besides, the victims were street people—a couple of prostitutes, a runaway, an old woman.

The Tracy girl's body had yielded little evidence, and the reported sighting of a van wasn't much to go on. The note and the photograph were a bit more helpful.

"He's somebody ordinary-enough looking to walk into the *Record* office without attracting attention." You had to hand it to De Anda; he wasn't rubbing Mack's nose in the promotion. It was business as usual. "You have to assume he printed the picture himself, and it's not a snapshot either, so he knows something about cameras."

"We could try to trace where it was printed."

De Anda frowned. "If it were some weird kind of paper, maybe, but it's good old Kodak. Could have been done anywhere, say, at someone's home. I used to develop pictures myself; anybody could do it."

"Maybe the patrolman's noticed something going on at the high school, nothing obvious, but a hint of something, if he thought about it hard."

"Not so far. I talked to him today myself." De Anda leaned forward, his elbows resting on a stack of reports. "I have a feeling about this, Chief. I think this guy is somebody who lives around here, who people see a lot. Somebody they wouldn't notice because he's part of the scene. Could be a teacher, a janitor—hell, even a newspaper reporter, if you're going to consider all the possibilities."

"Well, whoever he is, we've got to stop the bastard before he kills two more women like he says he will!" It irritated Mack, to have De Anda crossing him at every suggestion. The guy's job was to get the crime solved, not put up stumbling blocks.

"What if he's somebody they know and trust?" De Anda looked up and their eyes met. "Right now, every woman in Citrus Beach is in danger. Your wife. My wife. That dumb girl who ran away from home last night."

170

Mack stood up. "Let me know if anything new comes in."

"There's one thing I can say. If there *is* another victim, it'll help us develop a pattern."

"That's real nice." Mack didn't bother to keep the sarcasm out of his voice. "That'll be a big comfort to her family."

"Just thought I'd cheer you up," De Anda said.

49

Was Eduardo Ranier a murderer?

Diane sat motionless over the small stack of clippings, staring across the newsroom without seeing anything.

A sixteen-year-old girl had disappeared after school and been found dead in Dana Point two years ago. The same thing had happened to a seventeen-year-old girl in Citrus Beach this week.

Eduardo Ranier had found the body of the first girl. He'd been on the high school campus on Monday. He'd talked to Jeanette, maybe fixed those eerie light-blue eyes of his on her. The way he'd done with Lara. Diane hadn't missed the look that had passed between the two of them last night, after Jimmy brought Lara back. The girl was intrigued, probably flattered by his attention—maybe a little mesmerized. Diane shuddered.

Should she go to the police?

Immediately, with her reporter's objectivity, she examined her arguments from their viewpoint. The man might, for all she knew, have a perfectly good alibi for where he was at four o'clock Monday afternoon. Even if he didn't, could he have walked into the *Record* office Tuesday morning and dropped off that photograph without attracting some attention? He was kind of a celebrity, and an unusual-looking man as well.

172

Of course, he might have an accomplice, but she had the sense that Eduardo was strictly a loner.

And what about the photograph? She had no idea whether Eduardo Ranier knew anything about photography.

Then she remembered. His uncle owned a camera store.

She didn't seem to be able to breathe properly. This wasn't what the district attorney would consider an open-and-shut murder case, she reminded herself; it was just a handful of suspicions. But God, she hadn't connected the camera store until now.

Last night at Lara's house, she'd sat only a few inches from Ranier, talking with him. It was hard to imagine an ordinary man doing a thing like that to Jeanette Tracy. But then, he wasn't exactly an ordinary man, was he?

She couldn't go to the police with a few coincidences. At best, they'd add Ranier to what was undoubtedly a long list of people whose friends and neighbors suspected them.

Diane's hands felt dry and puffy, as if the skin might crack. She wanted to do something, to shake some sense into Lara, to keep Eduardo away from her. Why wasn't instinct enough? In a reasonable world, it ought to be. But this was a rational world, not a reasonable one, and it needed facts.

Could she dig something up through her own investigation? Lara was in no immediate danger. After last night's escapade, she'd seemed thoroughly subdued.

But I'll mention it to her this afternoon, Diane decided. I'll warn her. She won't believe me, but maybe she'll have a few doubts. At least she'll avoid being alone with him.

And after all, Diane reminded herself, maybe it wasn't him. Maybe she was letting her anxiety cloud her judgment. Maybe she simply didn't like the idea that a man of his age was showing so much interest in Lara.

The reporters and photographers were drifting back from late lunches. She noticed an air of restlessness about Chang as he came in and paused in the doorway, staring at the bulletin board without appearing to focus on its assortment of announcements and humorous clippings. Diane always made a

173

point of maintaining a pleasant distance from the police reporter, who tended to take everything too personally. Barry had pointed out once that Chang must have had a difficult childhood, the product of a marriage between people from different cultures. And it couldn't have been easy, coming to Southern California from Hong Kong as a child. He was an outsider, like Eduardo Ranier. How much did the two of them have in common?

She watched Chang wander over to the desks in front of the photo lab and say something she couldn't hear to Meyer Krantz.

"No, he's still in the darkroom." The photo chief wiped sandwich crumbs from his mouth, smudging ink on his cheek in the process. "Why, where did you think he was?"

"That's what I wanted to know." Chang leaned against a desk and swung one leg back and forth. "I saw him talking to Hank Tracy for a minute after the press conference. If he was asking questions, I want to know what was said. I'm the reporter on the story, you know."

Meyer didn't try to hide his exasperation. "He was asking Tracy whether he wanted his first name listed as Hank or Henry. That okay with you, Chang?"

The reporter ignored the question. "I'd like to see the photograph of the girl, the one the killer sent. Maybe there's something in the background. It doesn't seem to me we've made enough of it."

Diane dropped all pretense of not listening. Was Chang onto something? Anything he came up with, combined with her own suspicions, might be enough to take to the police.

"There's nothing but part of a couch." Meyer reached into a drawer and pulled out a clear plastic envelope containing the velox. "See? The damn thing doesn't even have flowers on it, just your average plain sofa."

Chang held the picture up to catch the light. "You notice the white spots on this picture? A couple of flecks here in the corner, and some more down there. Was that from our dust or his?"

"Who knows—maybe it's part of the dot pattern when

they screened it." It was Jimmy, who'd come out of the darkroom drying his hands on a paper towel. "The cops have the original. But that wouldn't do us any good without another photograph printed on the same equipment, would it?"

Chang dropped the envelope on the desk. "You guys are the experts. Right?" He went back to his seat. Jimmy made a face behind his back, and Diane smiled wryly, trying to disguise her disappointment.

She caught sight of the wall clock. After two-thirty. She'd better get a move on if she was going to be at the high school by three.

The telephone rang and she answered it reluctantly. A commanding female voice erupted into her ear. "Oh, my dear, I'm so glad I caught you in. The most terrible thing has happened to me and you're the only person who can help me."

"Can I call you back tomorrow, Mrs. Belster? I'm—"

"Diane, this is urgent!" The tone was reproving. "I just bought a package of luncheon meats and when I opened it, there was this yellow gunk all over . . ."

Jimmy strolled by, shaking his head sympathetically, and went out of the newsroom. Diane sighed, and settled in to listen to Mrs. Bluster's latest complaint.

50

You'd think, after how hard Kris had worked looking for her last night, that Lara would show a little gratitude, but she'd been ignoring him all day. He hadn't been able to find her for the first half of lunch period, and then he'd discovered her sitting outside on a bench staring into space, wearing a glassy half-smile.

Now, as the bell rang dismissing them for the day, Kris had to grab his books and practically chase her out of the chorus room.

"Wait a minute!" He scooted alongside, catching a whiff of her perfume. It was something kind of floral and sophisticated, not the Intimate he'd given her for Christmas. "What's going on with you?"

"Oh, nothing." She was smiling, but not directly at him.

"You act like you just won some kind of prize." He stared at her suspiciously. "They didn't decide to do *West Side Story* after all and you're keeping it a secret?"

She shook her head. "You're really batting a thousand today, aren't you?" They reached her locker, and she swung it open, flinging her books inside.

"No homework tonight?" He didn't know why he was pushing her. She was likely to fly off the handle, but damn it, he'd had a rough time yesterday, starting with finding Jeanette's body and ending with not being able to sleep half the night, still keyed up after the search for Lara. The least he expected was a little sympathy. "I mean, maybe I could help with your algebra."

"I think I'll skip it." She slammed the locker shut, twirled the dial on the combination and strode ahead of him out the front doors.

"Let's go get something to eat." Damn it, they needed to talk. Or maybe he just needed her to be there. Sometimes he wondered if she liked him anymore.

"I can't. Diane's picking me up." Lara inhaled deeply and faced him. "Look, Kris, I appreciate what you did last night, I really do, and maybe tomorrow we can do something to celebrate."

"Oh?" His breath caught for a moment. They'd come close to making it a couple of times, but Lara had always pulled back. She was afraid of getting pregnant, she said. But they both knew there were things you could do to prevent that.

"Yeah. Like we could go ice skating at the mall. My treat." She gazed at him expectantly.

"Oh, terrific."

"Or bowling, whatever you want."

"You know what I want."

He could see immediately from the hard set of her jaw that he'd said the wrong thing. "There are plenty of girls around who'll do that. If you want one of them, that's fine with me." She turned sharply away.

"Oh, come on, Lara—" He started to follow and then halted. "Well, have it your way. Maybe I will, you know that? Maybe I just will!"

He stalked around the building toward the football field. Who did she think she was, the only girl in the world? Okay, maybe she *was* kind of special, but that didn't mean he had to act like a lap dog.

Some of the girls jogged in the afternoon and he liked to watch them, their round breasts bobbing up and down sort of off-rhythm with their stride. There was this one girl named Felice who put out for practically everybody. Maybe she'd like to have a Coke. Somebody would probably see them together and tell Lara. That ought to make her think twice.

Mr. Gfeller had gone out to the parking lot without his briefcase, and Mrs. Arbor trotted after him, barely catching him as the Oldsmobile started to pull out of its reserved slot.

"Sorry about that." The window rolled down and he took the soft leather case from her hands. "Thanks, Greta."

"My pleasure." She stepped back and waited as he backed out. He'd hardly glanced at her, but then, he was a busy man. How frustrating it would have been if he'd gotten to the district headquarters without his notes! And it was an important meeting, too, about tightening security at the schools.

Mrs. Arbor took her time walking back, soaking up the sunshine. There were so many young people outside today, laughing with their friends, poking each other, the boys watching the girls and the girls eyeing the boys while pretending to ignore them. She'd seen a whole generation of youngsters come through this school. They hardly ever recognized her afterward, but she enjoyed watching them in the grocery store with their toddlers. It saddened her sometimes when she'd see them a few years later, their faces strained, the rings gone from their fingers, the children older and impatient.

Now there was that pretty Lara Ryan, standing near the curb as if she were waiting for somebody. Mrs. Arbor wondered if Eduardo Ranier had ever gotten hold of her yesterday. She thought about asking Lara, but just then the girl looked over at one of the cars. There was a real crush today— all the parents were picking up their kids, since that terrible thing happened to Jeanette Tracy.

Lara walked over, bending and talking to someone through the window. Mrs. Arbor had the impression it was a man. Maybe it was Lara's father. Or it might even be Mr. Ranier himself. He seemed like such a nice person on the radio, and she'd like to ask him about her husband, whether it would help if they went to UCLA for the arthritis instead of UCI, but she didn't want to go over there now and butt in. It might look as if she were nosing into Lara's business. If he was going to help with Lara's career, well, the school would hear about it soon enough. Lara would never know she'd had a secret helper in the office.

The secretary swung smartly about and went up the steps. If there was one thing nobody could accuse Greta Arbor of, it was snooping.

51

D iane stood uncertainly in front of the high school, Kris
at her side. "Honest, it was maybe fifteen minutes ago,
I left her right here," he said. "She told me she was going to
wait for you."

He didn't seem to mind that she'd dragged him away from
a conversation with a well-endowed young woman by the
athletic field. In fact, Kris looked as worried as Diane felt.

*I've been through this before. Monday. And it turned out all
right. I was only a few minutes late. Please, God.* "Let's ask the
kids," Diane said. "Somebody must have seen her."

With Kris's help, she quickly covered the dozen or so students still clumped about, waiting for rides or trying to figure
out what to do with the afternoon. Nobody had noticed when
Lara had left or who she was with.

"Where's the patrolman?" Diane shaded her eyes to look
around. "Isn't he supposed to be in front of the school?"

Kris pointed. A man in a blue uniform was standing to one
side by the bicycle rack. They walked over and told him the
situation.

The policeman gazed around while they spoke, as if expecting Lara to materialize. He was in his twenties, not much out
of high school himself. "I didn't see anything funny going on.
Nobody who didn't look like they belonged here."

Diane decided to take a chance. "You didn't happen to see

180

a man in his early thirties, tall, with light blond hair, did you?"

He reflected for a moment. "Nobody like that. Mostly mothers picking up their kids. Would you like me to call in a report?"

Diane hesitated. "Let me telephone her house first."

"I'll do it." Kris headed across the park strip toward the phones by the library.

"Boy, I sure hope nothing's happened to her." The young cop ran a nervous finger over the smooth butt of his holstered revolver. "Everything was so normal. I've really been keeping an eye out."

"No one's blaming you." Diane felt faintly sick. This couldn't be happening, not after last night. The crisis was over. Lara had been so happy to be home.

A dark shadow fell over the water. The shark was coming up on Lara, getting bigger and bigger until it blotted out the sky and she was a tiny speck, screaming for help. But the tide was against Diane, the waves tumbled her over and over, and she heard the sickening crunch of tires . . .

Kris came back shaking his head. "I'll go check out McDonald's." He took off running.

"Did you ask around?" the policeman said.

"Yes." Diane glanced up at the head of the steps. "You don't suppose she could have gone back inside? Maybe she left something in her locker." Without waiting for an answer, she hurried up. The double doors stood ajar, and, inside, the arch-ceilinged front hall was empty except for the echoes.

After glancing down the hallway and seeing no one, Diane went into the office. There was a gray-haired, slightly plump woman behind the counter. "Do you know Lara Ryan? Have you seen her this afternoon?"

"Well, as a matter of fact, yes, about ten minutes ago." The secretary wore an eager expression, as if she'd been waiting all day for someone to ask her for information. "She was talking with a man in a car. Actually, I'm not absolutely certain it was a man, but I had that impression."

"Did you see her get in?"

"No, no, I didn't."

"What kind of car?"

"I really didn't notice, I'm afraid. I don't like to pry, you know."

Diane didn't want to ask the next question, but she had to. "It wasn't a van, was it?"

"Oh, no." The woman sounded very definite. "No, I would have noticed that. It was a sporty kind of car. I don't know what color."

"Thank you."

Diane went out. Kris had come back from McDonald's, breathless, to say she wasn't there. Diane explained what she'd learned.

"I think I'd better report in." The policeman walked over to his black-and-white and reached in the window for the radio mike.

The blood seemed to have drained out of Kris's face. "It must have been somebody she knew. What you asked—do you really think it was that Ranier guy?"

"I don't know, Kris." Diane clutched the strap of her purse, as if that too might disappear. "Oh, God, I don't know."

52

"Wasn't she the girl who ran away last night?" Chief Ferguson angled his rear end with obvious discomfort into the narrow wooden chair in De Anda's office. "Sounds like she's done it again."

"I don't think so." De Anda refrained from saying what he sensed, that Ferguson was grabbing at straws. "Apparently the school secretary saw her talking to a man in a car. Unfortunately, she didn't get a description, except that it's a sports car, not a van."

The chief's florid face took on a gray undertone. "We'll have to treat this as a kidnapping, then. There's nothing to indicate it's the same man—but the circumstances are too much alike. Damn it!"

As he put out the APB, De Anda felt an unaccustomed uneasiness. Jesus, this was a weird case. Was the girl just running away again? And what about Kris Lender? He'd been one of the last people to see both girls. If it weren't for the school secretary, that kid would be hauled in here right now.

He realized his hands were cold. If it had been Kris . . . If he, De Anda, had let the killer go . . .

No. No way it was that kid. He couldn't have kidnapped the girl in a car and been hanging around the school at the same time, unless he had a twin brother nobody knew about.

183

De Anda realized he was praying silently. Not another one. That stupid kid. If she's playing games with us . . .

His instincts told him this was the real thing. He'd never believed much in instincts before, but these were screaming at him.

Lara Ryan. Somebody had told him she was in danger, or had he imagined it? When she ran away yesterday, the name had sounded vaguely familiar. Of course, she'd been a witness in the Tracy case.

He couldn't even feel excited about being promoted to captain. For one thing, he was still doing the same work he'd done all along, at least for the rest of the week. Besides, he didn't like starting his new position with a psychopathic killer hanging over his head.

Sgt. Terry Hewett—make that Lt. Terry Hewett—ambled in wearing a stiff polyester leisure suit and a wrinkled tie, looking like a mongrel dressed up for a kids' dog show. "Judge had a doctor's appointment so he let us out early," he explained.

De Anda filled him in. "Well, Lieutenant? Any brilliant ideas?"

"Seems like I ought to have some, doesn't it? Thanks for calling me at lunch about the promotion. Made my day." Hewett tilted back the wooden chair and put his feet up on the desk. He looked a lot more comfortable sitting there than the chief had.

Two detectives had already been dispatched to the high school to begin interviewing witnesses. Now De Anda and Terry went over the sketchy information, looking for angles. Maybe someone else had noticed the car. Maybe the man had been seen by some of the parents at the curb.

"What bothers me," De Anda said, "is that we had our own patrolman right there and she disappeared under our noses."

"Unless of course she really did just run away again." Hewett lit a cigarette, unfiltered. "But let's assume the killer's got her."

"Then we're probably already too late." Amazing how

calmly he could say things like that. De Anda tore his thoughts away from the memory of the Tracy girl's waterlogged body, the limp golden hair sticking to her.

"Yeah. Hard to figure this one." Hewett was staring at the ceiling, his eyes narrowed against the acrid smoke. He was one of the sharpest guys in the department, in spite of his generally rumpled appearance, and De Anda was glad to have his input. "This guy walked into a newspaper office and nobody noticed. He pulled up to a high school where everybody's paranoid as hell, and nobody noticed."

"Maybe we've got Casper the Friendly Ghost here."

Hewett flicked his ashes on the floor. "Who knows?" He gave De Anda a lopsided smile that was almost a grimace. "I'll tell you one thing. I have a feeling when we catch this guy, there's going to be a bunch of shocked people around this town."

It was about an hour later that the phone rang. It was Emma. "There's a man for you on three-three-oh. Says he knows something about the Ryan girl."

De Anda grabbed the phone.

He recognized Eduardo Ranier's voice immediately. "I just heard on the radio . . . Lieutenant . . ."

"It's captain now."

"I beg your pardon?"

"I got promoted."

"Oh." The man sounded slightly dazed. "You know I sensed danger around her . . . It was very strong . . ."

"Look, Mr. Ranier—"

"No, wait, please. I just—I got a flash from her—very strong, just a few minutes ago." Maybe the guy was on drugs. He sounded like he was having a hard time breathing. "She's still alive. She's terrified. This man—he's tied her up. She's in a small room, very small, maybe a closet."

"Where is she, Mr. Ranier?"

"If I knew, don't you think I'd tell you?" There was a thread of something like hysteria there—or maybe the guy was just one hell of a good actor. "I wanted to tell you that

185

she's still alive, and I thought, from her being tied up, that maybe he isn't going to kill her right away. I was afraid that— I drove by the high school a half hour ago, just, just by chance, and I saw the cops and—I was afraid you'd think she'd run away again and you wouldn't take it seriously."

The guy was definitely a basket case. He'd said nothing provable. They didn't have grounds for an arrest, but he had to be questioned. "Mr. Ranier. I'd like to discuss this with you further. Are you at home?"

"No." Calmer now. "I'm at the radio station. I'm about to start taping my show for tonight."

"I'd like to come by and talk to you."

"I don't know anything else." The man sounded faintly irritated, a complete switch of tone. "If I did, for God's sake, you wouldn't have to pry it out of me."

"All the same—"

"Look, Lieutenant—Captain—I'll call you if I pick up anything else."

"Mr. Ranier." De Anda spoke quickly, afraid the man was about to hang up. "I'd like to come by your house tonight and talk to you."

A brief pause. "I have a consultation tonight. It could run fairly late. Make it tomorrow morning. About ten will be fine."

De Anda took down the address. "All right. Tomorrow at ten."

He didn't have enough for a search warrant, he knew, standing up and shaking a kink out of one leg. But he could take a drive by Ranier's house now and talk to the neighbors.

If Lara Ryan was there, someone might have seen her go in.

53

Dinner at Barry's house was a largely silent affair, interrupted by the occasional squawk of the police radio. There was no word on Lara.

"You know, it's possible that she really did run away." Barry cleaned up the last of the homemade lasagna on his plate. It had been delicious, Diane was sure, but she'd hardly tasted it.

She'd been over this ground a hundred times in her mind. "No. She was out there waiting for me, Barry. I don't understand why she would leave. What could be so important?"

"Maybe she got tired of waiting."

She wanted to snap at him, but she reminded herself that he was trying to help. This situation certainly wasn't his fault. He wasn't Sol. And Lara wasn't Mark. She was old enough and smart enough to look out for herself. But wasn't that what they'd said about Jeanette?

"If I sit here much longer I'm going to explode." She jumped up and carried her dishes into the kitchen. "Barry, thanks for everything, but I'm not in much of a romantic mood tonight. I'm not even in the mood to be passably civil. Isn't there anything we can do? I'd go through this town one house at a time if I thought it would help."

He brought in the rest of the dishes and arranged them

187

neatly inside the dishwasher. "Let's assume she's run away. Where would she go?"

They ruled out the possibility of a friend—Diane knew them all, and had already called them—and after last night, Newport probably offered no allure. "Hollywood, I guess," Diane said.

"Fine. Let's go cruising." When she hesitated, he added, "It's better than sitting here, don't you think?"

She agreed it was.

During the hour's drive, she sat stiffly, willing them to move faster. *Let this be over soon. Let her be there, where we can find her. Please let her be safe.* Then something occurred to her. "What if we do see her and she's with someone? You know, a pimp, somebody really tough. Barry, he could hurt her, or us. By the time we got help . . ."

"Calm down." He took one hand from the steering wheel and cupped it over hers. "Do you remember a couple of years ago, the series we ran on Western Food and Amusements?"

"I think that was about the time I came." She had a vague image of an editorial but couldn't remember what it said. Why was he bringing it up now?

"They moved out from Vegas, trying to take over management of the yacht club and expand it. We did some digging and found out they had mob connections. There was even a suggestion that a few of the planning commissioners were getting their palms greased."

The traffic on the San Diego Freeway slowed near the intersection with the Santa Monica Freeway. Diane wanted to scream at a truck that pulled in front of them, going forty-five.

"I got some anonymous phone calls, not-too-veiled threats." Barry shifted them over a lane and sped past the truck. "I started taking precautions—Silly Putty under my hood so I could see if it had been opened, that kind of thing—and I talked the sheriff out of a gun permit."

Diane glanced at the glove compartment. "Is it loaded?"

"The first cylinder's empty. You want to see it?"

"No." The thought of a loaded gun gave her the shivers. But she was glad it was there.

They took the Sunset Boulevard off ramp and wound through the green hills of Beverly, past the UCLA campus. Gradually the road straightened and widened, and the billboards loomed overhead. Barry turned north on a cross street.

It was after nine o'clock and Hollywood Boulevard was just getting into full swing, she saw when they reached it. Neon signs jagged back and forth overhead, music blared from the doors of record shops, and movie marquees proclaimed the latest in porno.

But Diane wasn't looking at them. She was studying the people.

Bodies packed the sidewalk. Young bodies, most of them, scantily or gaudily dressed—black bodies, brown bodies, white ones, so ripe you could almost smell them through the thick layer of exhaust. The faces were unlined, heavily made up, and hard, except for here and there a couple of obvious tourists, or a young girl, wandering, eyes wide. The crowd seemed to engulf the solitary ones—another girl, a guy, a couple would start a conversation. Diane didn't need to hear the words. "You need a place to stay? You hungry? Hey, I know somebody . . ."

The older people looked not so much aged as worn out, their skin sagging and yellowish, their eyes puffy. They shuffled and leaned, not going anywhere.

A tall figure swaggered along, a man dressed in a flashy suit and a snappy hat, his cuffs glittering. He walked by a blonde girl who looked about fourteen and swatted her on the rump, not affectionately, but in something like a warning.

Diane swallowed and kept looking. They stopped at a light, and a crush of people sauntered across in front of them. No use asking if anyone had seen Lara; they wouldn't notice one more runaway, and if they did, they'd never tell. *They'd think I'm her mother. Oh, Lara.*

Cops had parked their units in the center turn lanes and were waving the traffic on, trying to keep it moving. Vehicles full of kids ignored them, youngsters leaning out to call to their friends. Sometimes at a stop light a kid would jump out of one car and run to another.

Diane strained her eyes searching for Lara's dark hair and bright face. Even this Goya-esque pit was better than being caught by . . . that man.

Once Diane thought she saw Lara. She called out and started to open her door as Barry pulled quickly to the curb, and then the girl turned and Diane saw that she was Hispanic.

"I'm sorry." Barry headed for the freeway after a fruitless hour of cruising. "I thought she might be here."

"At least we did something." Diane closed her eyes, feeling the sting of the salt. "We tried."

"Home?"

"Yes, fine. Maybe the police have heard something."

As soon as they came within listening distance, they tuned the radio to KCIT. The after-school rock shows had given way to easy listening, and Diane let a Linda Ronstadt song float around her.

The information from South Coast Rep was still sitting on the seat of her car . . . Lara had such a beautiful voice, throaty and true, only a little rough around the edges . . . She was going to be all right, she had to be. Jimmy would come driving up with her in the car . . . What was Diane going to do with that damn material from the theater? . . . Mark had died less than a month before Christmas. She'd already wrapped the presents. Afterwards, she just stuffed them into a closet. Months later, near the end of the divorce, she'd opened the closet and a package fell out, the paper ripping to reveal a teddy bear, and she'd started to cry . . .

On the radio, someone finished shouting about a once-a-year sale at a sporting-goods store, and then the deejay said, "For the next fifteen minutes, one of the most popular programs on radio, *Ranier Reflects,* with our own resident psychic, Eduardo Ranier!"

Diane sat up sharply. She reached out to switch the channel and then stopped. Barry glanced at her briefly but said nothing, concentrating on the cars edging in from the Long Beach Freeway.

"Hello, friends." Diane tried to picture the man from last

night, but he eluded her. "I'm sure you've all heard about the disappearance of a second Citrus Beach teenager . . ."

He went on to talk about how he'd met Lara at the high school Monday and helped search for her Tuesday night. "I want to tell her loved ones that she's in great danger, but she's still alive."

"Damn you!" Diane slapped the dashboard. "Oh, damn you!"

Eduardo's oily voice went on, oblivious. "She's contacted me twice this afternoon, since her kidnapping. I saw her very clearly. I'd rather not disclose too many details here, but I have been in touch with the police."

"You son of a bitch!"

"So I want to say this to the killer: let her go. You're going to be caught if you keep her or if you harm her. Just let her go and leave this town. That's the only way you'll escape me."

Barry leaned over and turned off the radio. "That's enough of that shit. Diane?"

"I'm all right." She felt as if she might rocket straight up through the roof of the car. Right at this moment, she hated Eduardo Ranier even more than the killer. Unless he *was* the killer. "How can anybody be so cruel? He's just exploiting this whole thing. 'In touch with the police.' I'll bet! Can you imagine? Chief Ferguson would boot his rear end all the way to Santa Ana!"

Barry was staring fixedly at the road ahead of them. "I can't help wondering, too . . . Diane, you don't think. . . ?"

The question hung in the air between them for almost a mile of freeway. They were isolated on a ribbon of artificial light in the midst of darkness.

"I'm going to try . . ." She shuddered. "Barry, I'm going to talk to his former real estate partner tomorrow. There won't be time to track down his mother in San Diego, but maybe I can find his uncle. I'll write the story tomorrow and show him up for the phony exploitive bastard he is. That son of a bitch!"

She was still fuming when they reached her apartment, and

she was glad when Barry offered to come inside. The visit to Hollywood, the sight of so much youth decaying in front of them, had left Diane shaken. Then there was Eduardo's brazen cruelty, his pronouncements taking on the semblance of authority by the endorsement of radio—had the world lost all reason?

What if some drunk ran into Barry going home? What if she never saw him again? It could happen. There was no safety, anywhere.

They had a glass of sherry, sitting in the living room. "Don't go home tonight," Diane said.

They moved closer together and she relaxed a little, feeling the human warmth of him. She tried to memorize everything about Barry, the faint scent of after-shave lotion, the calluses on his ink-stained fingers, the tenderness in his face when he looked at her.

Afterwards, lying together in a tangle on the pulled-out sleeper, she clung to him, feeling as if she stood blind on the last safe pinnacle on earth.

54

He gave the girl a drink of water in the little room off the garage, holding the knife next to her throat in case she tried to scream. She asked him again about the insulin and he told her to shut up. It was making him nervous, keeping her alive this way, but he had to do the videotaping in daylight.

If she'd just been a good sport about riding up to the Heights with him, he wouldn't have this problem. But no, she'd gotten suspicious and tried to jump out of the car. He'd had to hit her really hard and get her back here fast. It was a good thing that snoopy Rita Beth hadn't been hanging around.

Lara finished the glass of water and started to say something. He shoved the rag into her mouth, pulling it so tight she whimpered. He let her use the dirty john while he watched, and then tied her up, pulling the cord hard against the white skin of her wrists. She smelled good, more natural than the other girl. Jerking on the cord and seeing her flinch got him hard.

His mother was in the bathtub, the water oily with some kind of perfume rolling in droplets down her breasts. She'd left the door half-open on purpose, and she giggled when he came in.

They played a game where he caught her hair in one hand and pulled her head back to the water, almost but not quite under-

193

neath, so her breasts jutted up. With his other hand, he squeezed at them and she would gasp and moan and beg him to stop, and then laugh.

They were having such a good time he didn't hear the front door open and didn't know the man had come in until someone gripped him, jerked him up, and slammed him against the tile wall, and the man cursed at him with breath that stank of alcohol.

His mother began crying incoherently. He wasn't sure whether the man knew what had been going on, and it didn't matter. He was only twelve and the man seemed to be twice as big as he was. He still remembered the helpless rage as a fist slammed into his cheek. Then he tried to squirm past but the man caught him and threw him onto the bed and shook him really hard, so his teeth chopped together and his muscles felt like they would never function again.

For a minute, he thought the man was going to kill him, and then suddenly the man got up and let him go.

When he thought about it afterwards, he knew the man must have wanted to beat him up really bad. Maybe the man was some kind of pervert like they warned you about at school, who enjoyed hurting young boys.

The girl watched him. He could see her mind working. She would be fun, lots of fun. They were going to do this one slowly, up at his house in the hills where he wouldn't have to be so worried if she let out a yelp. She'd try to outsmart him all the way. It would make winning that much more exciting.

He turned out the light, locked the door and walked back to the house.

Time was getting short. He wouldn't be able to get away until tomorrow afternoon, and then he still had to catch another one and kill her too by Saturday. It would have been a lot easier if he could have caught two of them at once.

The thought stopped him.

His heart beating faster, he went in through the kitchen door. Of course! He'd catch another one tomorrow and take them both up to the Heights together. A double murder—yes—he'd need daylight, time to position the camera—but that would simplify things a lot, and he could torture them both together, and let them watch each other. Oh, God, it was terrific!

The problem was, the high school was out of bounds. Too risky after today. That cop standing by the bicycle rack hadn't noticed him, he was sure of it, but the guy would be more alert tomorrow.

He might be able to pick up a hitchhiker. But suppose someone noticed and wrote down his license number? Besides, he didn't want some little nobody. Jeanette Tracy had been a coup. Lara Ryan wasn't so special, but there were enough people who cared about her to make a fuss. The next one had to be even better . . .

They'd be expecting him to go for another girl. But he wouldn't. He'd surprise them. It would be a woman, someone who mattered, but also who could be easily persuaded to get in his car. Maybe he'd say he knew where the girl was . . . or he might not even need to mention that. He'd play it by ear. He was good at improvising.

He rolled the rubber band off the afternoon paper and sat down at the kitchen table. Flipping through the second section, he came to the consumer column with its flattering line drawing of Diane Hanson.

Yes, she was going to be perfect.

THURSDAY

55

As she stepped off the elevator, Diane paused in the lobby of the Newport Center bank building, blinking against the strange ochre light glaring in from outside. The sky had been a funny color all morning, what people in the Midwest called cyclone weather; or maybe her eyes were just sore from a mixture of tears and sleeplessness.

Her hair had picked up the reek of cigarettes from Artie Ballard's office. Damn pompous asshole anyway. He'd had a slick explanation for everything. He and Ranier had been the victims of soaring interest rates. They hadn't meant for their investors to lose everything. It had looked like a sure thing, a terrific condo development, best architects, etc., etc., and then belly up, well, these things happen. As for Eduardo, they were just business associates, didn't mix socially, far as he knew Ted was a hell of a nice guy.

She'd half-expected Artie to offer her a bottle of snake oil on the way out.

Diane moved closer to the carpeted wall to let a couple of businessmen by. She wasn't ready to go back to the paper and write her story. There was still too much missing.

It was hard to think straight. All night Diane had wavered between images of Lara in torment and waves of hope that the girl really had just run away again. This morning, Barry had fixed breakfast. Just having him close comforted her, and then her thoughts would go back to Lara, and to Eduardo. And Jeanette.

Eduardo's phone number and address were unlisted. Besides, surely he wouldn't be stupid enough to keep the girl in his house where anyone might come across her.

Or maybe, Diane admitted, she was on the wrong track entirely. Maybe he was exactly what he seemed, a semifraud operating just this side of the law, but otherwise harmless. She wished she could believe that.

Diane walked over to the bank of pay phones and dropped a quarter in. Meyer Krantz answered, and gave her Jimmy.

"I need to find Eduardo's uncle," she said. "Does he still have that camera store?"

"No, I heard he sold it a while back." In the background, the newsroom hummed and chattered. "But maybe the new owner could tell you. Citrus Beach Camera, on Lemon Street."

Diane fumbled through the vinyl-covered phone book and made another call. Yes, the new owner remembered Jeb Raines. Just a minute, here was the phone number, but he didn't have the address.

She called, got an answering machine and hung up. The phone book listed the same number for Jeb Raines, but no address.

Panic edged up her throat. She couldn't reach him; he might be out of town, or just not answering the phone, and she didn't have his address. Diane wasn't hot enough on Eduardo's trail, and Lara might die because of it. Like Mark. Those nightmares had persisted for months, the horrible feeling of helplessness, of not being able to move fast enough, the desperate need to have come home just five minutes sooner, one minute, thirty seconds.

This isn't doing Lara any good.

Diane flipped through her purse address book and called the public relations officer at the phone company. He greeted her like an old friend; Diane checked with him frequently on complaints and questions from readers. It only took him a minute to check his crisscross and give her the address.

200

She recognized it as an apartment complex on Las Flores in Citrus Beach, not more than a mile from where she lived. She thanked the man and thrust her way out through the heavy glass doors into the eerie filtered light.

The announcer on the radio was predicting a heavy storm by tomorrow. It suited her mood perfectly. Last night with Barry—had it been a mistake? It didn't feel like a mistake. And yet she knew he wanted more than she could give him. Oh, God, she was going to let him down, wasn't she? The way she'd let down everyone in her life who ever mattered.

The drive from Newport back to Citrus Beach took twenty minutes. The complex turned out to be a maze of lettered buildings, and it took Diane another ten minutes to find B-11.

She could hear the squawk of a television set as she knocked. Had Eduardo's uncle fallen asleep? Or had he gone out and left the TV on? For one irrational moment, she wondered if he was dead. Then footsteps creaked across the floor and the door opened.

The man who stood there was in his late sixties, light-complected like Eduardo but with sunken cheeks and a jaundiced cast to his skin.

"Mr. Raines?" Diane tried to sound pleasant and normal as she introduced herself and explained that she was writing an article about Eduardo for the newspaper.

"Oh, come in." His courtesy gave her a momentary twinge of guilt. He obviously thought she was a friend.

The furnishings of the apartment were sparse and mismatched, like something a recent fire victim might have amassed from Thrift shops. The only exceptions were the photographs on the wall: splendid full-color posters encased in clear acrylics. There were four different versions of a girl standing in a meadow, each shot with a different colored filter, and Diane realized the pictures must be handouts from a camera company.

She accepted a seat on a lumpy chair, declined a cup of coffee, and pulled out her notebook as her host turned down the TV. It was tuned to an old movie. Beyond it, she noticed the telephone sitting on its answering machine with a red light glowing, indicating messages.

"Mr. Raines, I understand your nephew got in a few scrapes when he was younger. Anything serious?" Maybe that was starting out too boldly, but she had no patience left.

A slow shake of the head. "I wouldn't say so. Ted was always a strange boy, kept his own company. My sister wasn't much of a mother to him, I'm afraid. Mostly he got into high jinks, trying to prove he was somebody special. Can't really blame him. I never understood much about kids, even though he lived with me for a while. I'm a bachelor myself, you see."

Diane scribbled down a few notes, just to look busy. She didn't want to hammer this point so hard she offended Jeb Raines, but she knew there must be something he wasn't telling her. "Did he ever tell fortunes, predict the future, anything like that?"

"Couple of times he warned me not to do things," the old man said. "I didn't do 'em, so I can't rightly tell you whether he was right or not, can I?"

"After he found that girl in Dana Point, there were some questions raised." She studied his reaction, but he was nodding placidly. "About how he came to find her. You never had any suspicions that there was anything wrong, did you?"

"Well, now." Thin fingers tapped on the arm of Jeb's chair. Blue veins puffed up from the back of his hand. "Not exactly, no."

"But?"

"Well." He cleared his throat. "Mind you, I like the boy. He's a good nephew. Comes to visit me every couple of weeks, always brings a gift, and I know things ain't so easy for him in the money department, in spite of the way he dresses and that car he drives."

Diane leaned forward, trying to speed him up.

"Uh, anyway . . ." Jeb Raines looked slightly embarrassed. "He did, uh, always like young girls. Not real young; I'm not saying he's some child molester, it's just he doesn't feel real comfortable with women his own age, I guess."

"Can you give me an example?" She was taking his words

down as fast as she could write, using her own shorthand to get it exactly.

"About eight years ago, it must have been—seven or eight—well, he was twenty-five, I guess—there was a spot of trouble over some sixteen-year-old girl. I guess he was taking her out, turning her head, and her parents threatened to call the police unless he stopped seeing her. So he did." There was a slight quiver in the hands folded in the old man's lap. "Now this was all with her consent, mind you. Ted never hurt anybody, not that I know of."

"I'm glad to hear that." But she wasn't glad at all. Lara at fifteen was exactly the kind of nymphet Eduardo Ranier liked. Diane shuddered, and hoped Jeb didn't notice.

A few minutes later, walking back to her car, she wondered what Eduardo would do when he found out the kind of questions she'd been asking.

56

I t was nine-thirty and Capt. Mario de Anda was getting ready to go out when Emma buzzed in to say Eduardo Ranier was waiting to see him.

"Here?" He cursed silently. "We had a ten o'clock—all right, send him in."

Now he had no way of getting inside the guy's house. De Anda rubbed his eyes, which felt dry and flaky. He'd spent about an hour in Ranier's neighborhood last night, questioning neighbors, trying not to imply Ranier was a suspect. Nobody reported seeing anything suspicious.

He noted the approaching footsteps. The man didn't sneak around in rubber soles, at least. In fact, the shoes that appeared in the doorway were expensive leather, maybe Italian. De Anda took in the wool suit and tailored shirt, all the way up to layered ash-blond hair. A twenty-dollar haircut, at least.

"Thanks for coming by." He stood up and they shook hands. The man's grip was firm.

"I want to help, Captain."

The thing about Eduardo Ranier that bothered De Anda was the way the man looked unwaveringly at him. Usually people glanced around the room, or lowered their eyes, or fidgeted. Ranier just stood there, probing at him with those pale eyes. Damn spooky son of a bitch.

They both sat down. "Do you know where Lara Ryan is?"

"She's in Citrus Beach." The tone was matter-of-fact. "I heard from her again this morning. Excuse me, Captain, you understand that I didn't literally hear from her over the telephone. But I've never seen anyone more clearly. She's weaker than she was yesterday. Does she have some kind of illness?"

"She's diabetic." Shit, what if the chief walked in here and found him treating this crap seriously? "Listen, Mr. Ranier, pardon my skepticism, but you seem to take an extraordinary interest in a girl you hardly know."

A faint pink flushed across the high, almost Mongolian cheekbones. "Frankly, she seems to have chosen *me*. I find these—communications—very disturbing. It's frustrating to me, too, Captain, to know she's out there and needs help, and not to be able to find her."

"Where were you about three-thirty yesterday afternoon?"

"Running errands. Dry cleaning, shoe repair, that kind of thing. I'm sure some of the clerks could identify me." The guy was a cool customer, you had to hand it to him. Nothing but that one brief blush revealed any emotion.

"Why did you go to the Ryans' house Tuesday night?"

"As I said before, I felt danger around her. Captain, there's more. This man isn't finished yet."

De Anda felt as if something cold and slimy had just crawled up his arm. Was it possible the killer was sitting right in front of him, coolly revealing his plans, and reveling in the fact that the police couldn't do a damn thing about it? "So he said in his note."

"I felt something else this morning. The killer is going to act again, very soon, maybe while Lara's still alive. His target is someone close to her. I get a hint and then—I can't quite put it together. I feel like I should know who it is." Ranier shook his head in frustration.

Jesus, the guy really seemed to believe all this garbage. "She doesn't have a sister, Mr. Ranier."

"I know." The eyes looked straight at him again, and De Anda thought he glimpsed anguish in them. Or was it laugh-

205

ter? "But it's a girl close to her. Captain, I hope you plan to put a guard on her friends."

"We'll look into it." And he would, too. "Mr. Ranier, would you mind if we searched your house?"

He wished he could have filmed the half-dozen emotions that flashed across the blond man's face in the next few seconds, because it was impossible to identify all of them so quickly. Disbelief, anger, frustration, contempt. "You really think I kidnapped her?"

"It's a possibility." De Anda stayed alert, watching for any sudden movements. "You have to admit, your behavior raises certain questions."

Ranier spread his hands. "I suppose that's true. Captain, I wouldn't mind but I'm not going to be home until this evening, and I don't want people pawing through my place when I'm not there. Frankly, I came in early because I'm on my way to Los Angeles for a television interview, and then I've got some consultations lined up. Give me a call about, say, ten o'clock tonight, and if I'm home, you're welcome to come by."

De Anda nodded. He'd put a stake-out on the house, and if anything turned up, they'd go for a search warrant. And he suspected Ranier knew that.

The fact that the man didn't seem nervous wasn't an encouraging sign.

De Anda was beginning to think this was their man. And he was beginning to wonder if they were going to be able to nail him.

57

Someone was in the yard.

    Lara woke up to the sound of a twig cracking. Or maybe she hadn't been asleep, but in a kind of smoky daze. Her head hurt and her stomach felt as if it were turning over and over, churning away at its own emptiness. Her hands and feet had gone numb and her mouth felt like the Mohave Desert. She could have drunk the entire Colorado River.

He'd left the house; she'd heard his car. How long ago? Minutes, maybe hours?

Another twig cracked, and she heard a low hum, an unidentifiable human voice. Maybe the meter reader was walking through the back yard. If she could make enough noise . . .

She tried to work the gag free with her tongue, but he'd tied it so tight it cut into the corners of her mouth. When she shouted, all that came out was a faint moan, and the strain made her abdomen hurt.

Even with her eyes adjusted to the dim light, Lara couldn't see much. He'd stuffed her into a tiny room off the garage that smelled of dust and old chemicals and piss, because there was a toilet at one end of it. It made her want to throw up.

She was wedged underneath some shelves stacked with oil cans and rusty gardening tools. If she could knock one down . . .

Shifting her weight onto her back, Lara jammed upward with her tied feet. Her shoes scuffed at the bottom of a shelf. With a grunt, she tried to thrust harder but succeeded in making only a faint shuffling noise.

It was hard to hear over the gasping of her own lungs. Her ears strained, but there was no reaction from outside. Had the meter man left? Had she just imagined she heard somebody?

A tear slid down her cheek. She felt stupid and angry at herself. *Why did I ever believe him? Why didn't I figure it out before it was too late? Please, please get me out of here.* God, she was so thirsty. And hungry. But mostly, she needed insulin.

A puppy yipped in the yard. Oh, shit! It was just a damn dog!

Lara sagged against the wall. He was going to kill her; she could see it in his eyes whenever he looked at her. And he wouldn't just strangle her the way he'd done with Jeanette. He was going to take her somewhere in that van, and God knows . . . She couldn't even think about it. She hated him so much that she felt as if her hatred could find him like those heat-seeking missiles on the news and blast him to hell where he belonged.

Even Tuesday when she'd been thinking about Jeanette, the reality of death hadn't hit her. Now, lying here, she could see the old Lara like someone in a TV movie, a smartass teenager who snipped at Kris and hauled little Gerry around and ran off into the night all full of herself, making her dad and Diane worry. She still couldn't believe she was really here. She couldn't imagine what the pain was going to feel like.

The humming started again in the yard. That wasn't any dog. That was a girl. Now she was talking in a high singsongy voice to the dog. "Hey, little guy, you want to come to school with me today? Huh?"

Adrenaline jolting through her, Lara flung herself against the wall, humped her body up and down to make as much noise as possible, and growled as hard as she could.

Out in the yard, the puppy barked again.

Harder! Faster! Lara thrashed against the wall and groaned, until her throat felt raw and her shoulder throbbed. Her head was swimming. She'd become separated from her body. The pain didn't matter. Kick! If she could knock the shelf down . . .

"Oh, quit barking!" The voice sounded cross. "You think you're a match for that old possum, huh? Dumb dog." There was another high-pitched bark and then footsteps slapped away, away, away.

Lara lay still, her mind clouded, all the strength drained from her muscles, her chest heaving to draw in enough air. Other people had died like this. She'd read stories in the newspaper—and then there were the history books. There'd been a picture in a book at Diane's house of a Nazi concentration camp when the Allies got there, the piles of skeleton-thin bodies that had once been people. Only they hadn't been real people, not to her, not until now.

She closed her eyes and imagined a naked woman who had been a famous dancer, who was mentioned in Diane's book. The victims felt dehumanized and ashamed because they were naked, that's what the book had said. The woman was being marched into the gas chamber when one of the guards recognized her and ordered her to dance, and as she danced she began to feel human again, and the other people did too, and they attacked the guards and killed some of them.

Lara lay with her eyes shut, imagining the woman dancing, seeing the light come back to her face.

She knew she wasn't very strong or experienced, either. But if she could, if he gave her the least little opening, she was going to kill him before he could kill her.

58

B arry had found excuses to walk out to the lobby of the *Record* twice that morning. Each time, he glanced around to see if there were any strange men. Each time, he checked under the scattered newspapers on the front counter to see if another envelope had turned up.

So far, nothing.

It was after eleven, and he couldn't leave his desk any more, not until the last page dummy had been sent to the backshop. Why did he have the feeling the killer knew that?

This is paranoia, he told himself.

And then there was Diane's empty desk. She'd reminded him this morning what she was up to, as they unscrambled their clothes and shoes in her living room and he demonstrated his talent at burning the toast and eggs. There wasn't much harm that could come to her, driving down to Newport to talk to Ranier's former partner, was there?

Still, she'd been gone longer than he expected. She should be wandering in any minute now. Last night she'd been so beautiful, sweet and fiery in his arms. He'd better not think about that now.

A few desks over, Meyer Krantz was tapping a pencil on his desk in a loud rat-a-tat pattern. Halfway across the newsroom, one of the reporters burrowed through old papers trying to find something, turning the pages with a windy rustling that went straight to the roots of Barry's teeth.

The whole newsroom was on edge about this last disappearance. The killer had been here sometime Tuesday morning; he'd left a note threatening to strike again; and now it had come to pass.

The reporters weren't even telling their usual bad-taste jokes, the kind that sprouted up about everything from AIDS to Mideast hijackings. Give them another twenty-four hours and they'd be at it.

Damn. He'd been staring at the same headline for five minutes and he still hadn't figured out how to fix it. Too passive. Right. Use an active verb. Not "Tax Hike Approved" but "Tax Hike Squeaks By . . ."

Why hadn't Diane come back by now? Where was she?

Chang wandered up, peering over Barry's shoulder at the A1 dummy to see how his story had been played. It went right across the top, under a banner. Guy ought to be pleased.

The reporter cleared his throat. "Oh, by the way, they've called a press conference for two o'clock."

"What about?" Barry swung around, irritated. Everybody at city hall knew that would be too late for the *Record*'s deadline. Couldn't they show a little consideration for the hometown paper?

"De Anda says they're not sure, but the TV stations want something to show at six o'clock, so he's going to stand up there and update everybody. Nothing we don't already have, unless something breaks in the next three hours."

An instinct told them both to turn at that moment and look at the doorway. Maybe it was because everybody else in the newsroom was turning.

Jimmy stood there, his face white, holding up a manila envelope.

"Looks like something just broke," Chang said.

59

Mack had already gone down to the press conference when Assemblyman Gorwins called his office. Michele put the call through to Lucille.

"Well, hi, Greg." She projected as much trusting enthusiasm as she could. As if this were just a friendly social call.

"What the hell is going on down there?" She could picture him—a big man, like Mack, slicker and more sophisticated but with the same roughness at heart. Before she married Mack, Greg had made a pass at her once and she'd considered taking him up on it, but then his wife came into the room, and that was the end of that.

"You mean the, uh, murder case?" She tried to inject just the right note of casualness.

"Look, I've got my anticrime bill coming up for a key vote in committee next week. How's it going to look when I stand up there Sunday and throw my weight behind a guy who can't even keep order in his own town?"

You had to say one thing for Greg Gorwins—he didn't beat around the bush.

"This could happen to anybody, Greg." She felt as if she'd been repeating that line nonstop all week. "It's just rotten timing. We've got one girl dead and one kidnapped, but she's still alive."

"How do you know that?"

"There was a note that came this morning. As a matter of fact, I was just on my way to the press conference."

"What does it say?"

He was going to find out on tonight's news anyway. "He's threatening to kill the girl and catch another one tonight. It, uh, it's kind of a challenge to Mack. Like the killer's daring the police chief to catch him. It almost looks like a setup, like . . ." She stopped herself just in time. Greg would think she'd gone loony. Nobody went around murdering people just to embarrass the police. "Well, he's obviously a psycho."

"Any leads?" There was another voice in the background and his tone took on a hurry-up edge.

"Yes, I think so. As a matter of fact, Mack does have a suspect in mind, but it's not something they can release yet." There, that would make Greg feel better. He liked being in the know.

"If they get this thing wrapped up by Sunday, he could wind up looking like a hero. But I'll tell you this, Lucille, if he falls on his ass, I'm not going down with him. I like you, lady, and I've got nothing against your husband, but politics is politics."

"I understand, Greg."

By the time she got to the press conference, most of the seats in the council chambers were taken. Lucille recognized quite a few people in addition to the press—city workers and some of Mack's political supporters. In one corner Hank Tracy sat surrounded by friends, including Mayor Reilly.

Mack stepped up to the lectern. Behind him, Lucille saw Captain De Anda take a seat as bright lights flooded the platform. She was glad Mack had let her put a little powder on his face; even so, he was clearly sweating. He looked smaller than usual, from where she sat at the back of the room, but there was a confidence about him that strengthened her.

"As some of you know, another note was received from the killer this morning." Mack had picked up the impersonal inflection of a TV announcer. Polish, that's what he was getting, just as Lucille had hoped. "I can't show it to you—it's an

213

important part of our investigation—but I can read you its contents."

Chairs creaked as reporters bent forward, ready to write.

"'I have Lara Ryan. She is alive but not for long. Tonight I will take another one. Your town has a—'" his voice caught for a fraction of a second—"'"pervert for a police chief and he can't catch me.'"

Questions flew at him. Fingerprints? None. How had the killer managed to drop off the envelope twice without being seen? No one knew. Did they have a suspect? There was no one in custody.

A woman from KCIT asked why Mack thought the killer had singled him out in the note. "We think this man has a hatred of authority figures." Lucille smiled; she'd come up with that line herself. "But we're checking into anyone who may have reason to hate me. I've sent a lot of people to jail over the past fourteen years."

Good, that was a nice plug. Lucille hoped some of the stations would use it.

There was more after that, about what precautions were being taken and how Lara's photograph was being distributed around town, but Lucille didn't pay much attention until the Oriental reporter from the *Record* stood up.

"Yesterday I called your attention to an escaped rapist named Colin Bregman who used to hang around the high school. Is he a suspect?"

Mack signaled to De Anda, who came over to the bank of microphones. "I'm glad you asked that, Guy. Just a few minutes ago, I got a teletype saying Bregman's been picked up in Colorado. That doesn't mean he couldn't have been in town Monday or Tuesday, but we're going on the assumption that the killer dropped off the note at your paper this morning."

As the questions died down, Lucille glanced nervously at Hank Tracy. Was he going to say anything? No, he was talking quietly with Lester Logan from the chamber.

As she walked across the parking lot, she thought about what she'd overheard this morning.

They did have a suspect, someone named Ranier. They

214

were watching his house. But they didn't know if that was where he was hiding the girl. In fact, they still weren't absolutely sure it was him.

He must have another house somewhere, a place he thinks is secret. Surely they can track it down. She stopped short of her car and turned back to the police station to tell Mack.

60

"Yes, Captain De Anda is in now."

Thank God. Diane rested the telephone against her shoulder, trying to ignore the stack of mail she'd opened without being able to focus on it.

Ranier always liked young girls. "Captain? This is Diane Hanson over at the *Record.* Remember me?" *She could still hear Jeb Raines saying, "Ted never hurt anybody, not that I know of."*

"Yes, Ms. Hanson?"

"Captain, I've been doing some digging for an article I'm writing about a man named Eduardo Ranier. I've come across a few things I think you should know." She spilled it out— the slain girl in Dana Point, the real estate misdealings, his uncle's story about the teenager. She blurted it in a breathless rush, afraid that he'd stop her, afraid he'd blow away all her carefully gathered information like a house of cards.

When she was done, he said, "Ms. Hanson, can I tell you something in complete confidentiality?"

"Absolutely."

"We have Mr. Ranier's house under surveillance now. We don't have any hard evidence yet, but there's enough reason to keep an eye on him."

"You haven't been inside?"

"Without a search warrant, you realize we can't do anything, and we haven't got enough hard evidence to get one.

216

But I talked with the neighbors and, between you and me, took a look through the windows, and there didn't seem to be anything amiss. We're looking into the possibility that he may have another house somewhere."

Diane's hand began to shake and she forced herself to steady it. "Do you really think he's the one? Is Lara all right?"

"The answer to both questions is, we don't know." She remembered De Anda's face from when he'd interviewed her Tuesday, a dark-haired, well-groomed man with compassionate brown eyes. She felt safer knowing he was on Eduardo's trail.

"Captain, would it hurt anything if I went ahead with this story? Maybe somebody reading it will remember something that could help us. I suppose it's a long shot . . ."

"As long as you don't mention that he's considered a suspect. I think he's got some idea what we're up to, but I'd rather not confirm it. Besides, we could be wrong. We don't want to try a man in the newspapers."

After she hung up, Diane sat for a moment staring into space.

I know she's still alive. If she were dead, I'd feel it. Wouldn't I? But she hadn't known Mark was in danger, not until she saw him running into the street. Why hadn't she sensed it sooner? Wasn't a mother supposed to have those instincts?

"You okay?" Jimmy leaned across her desk. "You look pale, kid."

"It's Lara." She swallowed, remembering that she wasn't to tell anyone about the police. But she could discuss her own suspicions, couldn't she? "I can't help thinking—you know I've been looking into Eduardo Ranier. I just have this feeling . . ."

Jimmy's eyes narrowed thoughtfully. "I wouldn't have figured it, myself; I mean, I remember him as kind of odd, but not dangerous. I guess you can never tell."

"I'm going to write my article tonight. I've got to get it done. Jimmy, somebody out there may have seen him with Lara and doesn't realize what it means."

He seemed to be thinking something over. "I could find out where Ted lives. Maybe you should confront him with what you've got, Diane. If we go together, we'll be all right."

And the police will be watching. "Do you think he'd let us inside?" she asked. "Suppose he's got Lara tied up somewhere?"

"You might notice something—some detail that anybody else would miss. It's worth a try, don't you think?"

Diane nodded slowly. She'd better not tell Barry. He'd have a fit. "Okay. I should be home about eight. You remember how to get there?"

"Sure." Jimmy grinned. "Don't worry. We'll find that kid."

Watching him walk away, Diane realized for the first time how tired she was. God, it was only five o'clock. She felt as if she'd been running all day, spinning her wheels. *The pen is mightier than the sword.* Bullshit. One damn story in tomorrow afternoon's newspaper wasn't going to stop Eduardo Ranier. But what else could she do?

Just as she noticed the "MSG PENDING" light blinking on her computer, Ginny Hertz walked by. "Hey, you got a call while you were on the phone. Did you get my message?"

Diane hit the keys and the note appeared on her screen. It said, "Eduardo Ranier. Will call back." The hope that Jimmy had inspired flickered like a candle flame in a chill wind; they'd obviously lost the element of surprise. "Did he say anything else?"

"He wasn't at a number where he could be reached." Ginny stuck her pen through her hair, a tangled orange pile that next week might be pink or purple. "He said something about an article you were writing on him, that he wanted to talk to you."

He was probably furious. On the other hand, Eduardo certainly had a right to tell his side of the story. Diane supposed Barry would have pointed that out tomorrow morning if she'd written the article without it. "Okay. Did he say when he'd call back?"

"He said he'd try again in an hour or so and if he didn't

reach you, he'd call in the morning. Oh, there's my phone!''
Ginny dashed off.

Diane felt strange, now that her investigation had come out
in the open. Who'd told Eduardo? His uncle? Cissy Greenspon? Most likely Bruce Jorgas last night when Eduardo went
in to make his radio broadcast, she thought.

*On the other hand, this gives me a perfect excuse for dropping in
on him tonight. If he doesn't reach me first. And if he does, I'll say
I wasn't satisfied to write the story without seeing him face to face.
Oh, God, what if Lara's there? What if I can't find her? What if he
pulls a gun? But Jimmy will be there, and the police are right
outside.*

Barry hadn't missed any of the comings and goings around
Diane's desk. She was up to something, and he was willing to
bet it had to do with her investigation of that damned psychic.

Why was she so certain the man was involved with Lara?
Maybe there was something to it, but she hadn't been objective about this from the start. He should never have approved
the story.

After Ginny retreated, Barry made his way to Diane's desk,
trying to act casual. ''How about dinner, gorgeous?''

She blinked up at him as if awakening from a reverie. ''Oh,
hi. Gee, Barry, I'm just going to catch a snack from the machines. I want to get my story done tonight, on Eduardo.
You'll run it tomorrow, won't you?''

''That depends on what you write.'' He lowered himself
into a chair. ''Diane, have you talked to this man himself?''

''I'm going to, tonight. He called and he's supposed to call
back.'' She was flustered, trying to reassure him—as if he
were her enemy, or at least an obstacle.

''Diane, if he really is the killer, this man is very, very dangerous.'' Barry had to restrain the impulse to reach for her
hand. Half the newsroom was probably watching them.
''Maybe you ought to knock off the story for now. You're
anything but objective.''

An opaque expression came over her eyes and she shook

her head tightly. "No way, Barry. I'll write it. If it's a piece of shit, you don't have to run it. But it won't be. Somebody out there must know something. Maybe tomorrow afternoon will be too late, but maybe it won't."

"You're not going to meet this man somewhere? You're not going to be alone with him?"

"I'm not a fool!" She caught herself. "I'm sorry. No, Barry, I promise I won't do anything stupid."

"Maybe you should tell the police what you've found."

"I already have." She shrugged. "Who knows what good it'll do?"

He glanced at his office, which he'd already locked up for the night. He supposed he could find some excuse to hang around and be sure she was all right.

She'd resent it. And of course there was a guard on duty at night, patrolling the paper, although he was an old guy and liked to linger over his coffee. Barry scratched behind his ear. Besides, Saturday was Elizabeth's birthday. She'd asked for a red-white-and-blue silk scarf and he'd promised it. He'd meant to buy it tonight and express mail it up to Stanford tomorrow. Otherwise it wouldn't get there till Monday . . .

"I'll be fine, Barry." Diane was studying him with a new-found tenderness. "Believe me, I won't try to deal with this man myself."

She was a grown woman. If he tried to hold her too tightly, he might lose her. Damn. Every instinct cried out for him to protect her, to keep her safe, but you couldn't do that, not with a woman like Diane.

"I'll be home," he said. "Call me if you need anything."

She said she would.

61

The sheriff's department was cooperating fully with information from the two-year-old Dana Point slaying, but the fact that the girl had been dead two weeks when they found her meant there hadn't been much to go on.

"Listen," the sheriff's homicide detective told De Anda over the phone, "The guy didn't have to be psychic; all he really needed was a good sense of smell."

Graveyard humor didn't sit well with De Anda just now, but he thanked the guy for the information and hung up.

Chief Ferguson wandered in after dinner. He looked like hell, gray and haggard. De Anda wondered if the chief had heart problems.

He sank heavily into the wooden chair. "What's new?"

"Not much." De Anda told him what he'd learned about Ranier and Dana Point. "As for anybody else, there's a couple of guys who might have it in for you. Remember that dope bust last summer, the guy got off on a plea bargain? He made some threats to his cell mate about how he was going to stick it to you."

Ferguson waved his hand. "The guy was a cream puff. Who else?"

There was a suspected child molester who'd gotten routed to the wrong wing of prison and ended up having his private parts reshaped with a dull knife. He'd gotten an early release, and he'd been suing everybody from the state Department of Corrections on down.

"Naw. He wouldn't kill anybody; he'd have his lawyer do it."

As he went on through his notes, De Anda wondered about the chief. Sure, the election was at stake; that much was obvious. But what else? He'd always wondered why a classy dame like Lucille would marry a redneck like Ferguson. It wouldn't surprise anybody if she dumped him after this.

In spite of himself, De Anda felt a twinge of sympathy. The chief might be a jerk, but he didn't deserve to have his entire life fall down around his ears.

He reached the last name on his list. Last but not least, as Lester Logan would say in one of his long-winded speeches at civic events. "And then there's Ranier. You did a little tap dance on his career, as I recall."

"Career, hell." Ferguson exhaled heavily. "Con game is more like it. What do we have on him?"

"Just some suspicions, circumstantial stuff. We can't afford to put everyone on him, because if we're wrong . . ." De Anda didn't need to finish the sentence.

"You found that second house, the one Lucille thinks he has?"

"We're checking on it. But it could be in another county. If he has one at all." Orange County was wedged between Los Angeles, Riverside, and San Diego counties. Any one of them could be reached in less than forty-five minutes.

They sat and stared at each other across the desk. The killer had threatened to kidnap another woman tonight. They'd beefed up patrols, canceled vacations, authorized overtime. And they both knew it wasn't likely to do any good.

The phone rang. De Anda started, and then he picked it up.

"Huntington Beach just called." It was the watch commander. "They've got two guys they think did the minimart murder."

"I'll send somebody right over." De Anda hung up and told the chief.

"One down," he said.

222

62

On his way back from the press conference in Huntington Beach, Chang found himself planning how he was going to write it up—two weasely kids caught trying to hold up another store, a pair of obvious losers. How could anybody be stupid enough to keep a murder weapon around and use it in another robbery? The guys had practically signed their own death warrants.

Yeah, he'd have to get that revolver into the lead. Of course, the ballistic test results weren't available yet, but the cops were pretty sure it was the same gun. Some kind of off-model street weapon. Probably stolen. And they'd used what looked like the same car. Real dumb guys. Dumb. Dumb.

Not like the Citrus Beach killer. Chang swung his car off the freeway onto Citrus Avenue. This guy was tough. He was actually daring the whole city to catch him, almost as if he didn't care if they did. What was the guy up to, anyway?

Chang never got involved in his cases, but this one had him on edge, and he wasn't sure why. Maybe it was because the killer had actually come to the newspaper, twice, or because Chang had seen the Ryan girl with Diane a couple of times, so she was more than just a blurry face in a photograph.

Or maybe it was the weather. He glanced up at the dark-on-dark clouds against the night sky. The air crackled with the heavy threat of a storm.

He couldn't get it out of his mind that there was some vital clue they'd overlooked.

There had to be something about the note and the photograph. He knew the cops had tested both of them in every way known to man. There were no fingerprints.

Meyer and Jimmy both swore there was nothing to be done about the specks on the print. But they always dismissed anything Chang said.

Impulsively, he made a right on Lemon Street and halted in front of the Citrus Beach Camera Shop. The store was brightly lit, high-tech glossy and touched with sharp colors. Even the half-dozen people inspecting camera equipment had a finished sheen to them.

The manager, who looked younger than the clerk who fetched him, gave his name as Tom Grace. "What can I do for you?"

Chang identified himself. "I had a few technical questions about the photograph the killer left with us, just of a general nature." He waited for Grace to suggest he talk to the paper's own photographers, but the man apparently didn't think of it.

"I'd be glad to help out any way I can." Grace led the way back to a small but surprisingly tidy office, with a fake oak desk and stuffed chairs.

Grace told Chang more than he wanted to know about high-contrast papers like Agfa, which didn't help much, since he already knew the killer had used Kodak.

"That's pretty common," Grace agreed. "You guys probably use it yourselves. Comes in individual sheets or in rolls, for a commercial printer."

"Could you tell anything by looking at a print?"

"Depends. Let me show you something." Grace jumped up and led the way back into the store. They passed a black-haired girl who was sorting and filing little packets of photographs in a drawer, humming tunelessly to herself. She glanced up at Chang and smiled, but he ignored her.

"See, here's a commercial printer." Grace pointed to a black-and-silver piece of equipment about the size and shape of a Xerox machine. "The paper moves along those tracks there. If you let the chemicals get low, you might see a faint indication of those little teeth that keep it on the track. Of course, that wouldn't tell you which commercial printer the thing was made on, just that it wasn't printed in trays in somebody's garage."

The task was beginning to seem impossible, but as long as he'd come this far, Chang pressed on. "What about specks on the print?"

"From dust?" Grace considered. "You'd have to have something to compare it to. Another picture printed at the same time on the same machine."

"What about the enlarger? Couldn't that leave dust specks too?"

"Yeah. It could." The manager shrugged. "Any kind of glass will collect dust, on the enlarger or the printer."

"How often do photographers clean those things?"

"Depends." Grace spread his hands. "If you want really high-quality prints, every day. Most people probably do it every few days, once a week."

Chang was out of questions. "Thanks."

"Don't know how much help I've been." Grace walked him to the front of the store. "Say, did that other reporter from your paper find Jeb Raines all right?"

Chang asked what other reporter and who Jeb Raines was, and Grace told him.

Why would Diane be looking for the former owner of the store? Why would she need to talk to him for a consumer story?

Chang decided to find out first thing in the morning.

63

By the clock on the newsroom wall, it was almost nine-fifteen. Diane paused and glanced around. Despite the bright fluorescent lights, the emptiness of the large room gave her an eerie sense of displacement.

Where had the time gone? It seemed like only five minutes ago that she'd called Jimmy, saying she'd have to postpone their confrontation with Eduardo until later. Yet she knew she'd made that phone call two hours ago.

One elongated story below, the pressmen must be churning out advance sections of the paper, but they might as well have been on another planet for all the noise that penetrated here. Even the circulation department would be closed by now, no longer taking calls from angry subscribers whose papers hadn't arrived.

Besides, the way the Record building had grown, with one addition slapped onto another, the newspaper had become a kind of labyrinth. From where she sat, Diane couldn't hear anyone moving. Not even a telephone was ringing. The piles of papers, books, files, and note pads on the desks around her gave the place an abandoned air, like a city after a neutron-bomb blast.

She glanced down at her screen. After almost four hours of steady work, she had the story organized and largely written.

Now if only Eduardo would call in, she could get this thing done.

A blinking light caught Diane's eye. Across the top of her screen flashed: "MSG PENDING."

The oddness didn't strike her for a moment, and then she realized that there wasn't supposed to be anyone at the paper right now to send her a message.

Her throat tightened, and then she scolded herself for being ridiculous. Maybe Barry had come back to check on her and was being cute. Smiling, she pressed Control and Msg.

The cryptic sentence said: "Three strikes your out Ms. Hanson."

Diane stared at it. What the hell?

At the bottom was the log-on: Rodrig. Who was Rodrig?

It took her a moment to remember that Rodrig meant Celia Rodriguez in Lifestyles. Their log-ons were limited to six letters.

Swallowing hard, Diane stood up and walked between rows of desks, her footsteps sounding abnormally loud in the silence. She passed the bulletin board, turned down a corridor, and hurried as she neared the Lifestyles room.

The department was slightly smaller than the newsroom. Filing cabinets clustered against the walls, and about two dozen desks sprawled across the center, covered with the usual litter of photographs, entertainment releases, and newspaper sections.

"Celia?" Diane didn't see anyone.

She walked between the desks, glancing at the screens, until she came to one that was in the operating mode. The log-on read: Rodrig.

From the neat stacks of files on the desk, it was obvious that Celia had gone home for the day. Gone home and forgotten to log off. Anyone could have sent that message from this terminal. But what did it mean? "Three strikes your out Ms. Hanson."

This afternoon's edition had been tossed onto a corner of

the desk. The bold black headline read: "Killer Vows To Strike a Third Time Tonight." Someone had circled it in red.

Diane picked up the phone and dialed the number for security. It rang ten times without an answer. The guard must be on patrol.

This was ridiculous. How could someone attack her here at the newspaper? The killer didn't operate that way. He lured young girls into his car at the high school. Everybody knew that. She picked up the phone again to call Barry.

From down the hall came the sound of heavy footsteps, slow but certain. He must have known she'd come here, to Celia's desk in this trap of a room.

Diane's fingers hesitated on the buttons and lost their place. The number . . . What was Barry's number? Jesus, the killer couldn't be in the newspaper, could he? The man was coming this way, coming closer. She dropped the phone and ran.

She made it out the door. There was no one in sight, but the way the corridor twisted, she couldn't see more than twenty feet in either direction.

The footsteps had come from the area of the newsroom. She ran the other way, trying to keep her low heels from tapping too audibly, trying not to let panic squeeze the breath out of her.

Deep in the heart of the building, the printing presses were rumbling. If she could just reach the men down there, she'd be safe.

The corridor jagged past the art department, its easels standing empty. Diane nearly tripped on a pile of newspapers someone had left sitting in the hall.

Maybe it's nothing. Somebody might be playing a joke. But it didn't feel like a joke.

Still, she slowed a little, trying to stay in control. No one around. God, it was quiet here. She padded through the worn backshop area where the lineoleum floor covering was bared to its slate-gray backing. On her right, the paste-up room with its long, slanted tables stood empty.

Diane's lungs ached. Behind her, she couldn't hear any

sounds of pursuit. But how could she, over the noise she was making herself?

Past the backshop, she reached the mailroom, a cavernous dragon's den with half a dozen rooms jutting off it, piled with new and old sections and inserts. A great assembly line snaked like a roller-coaster track through the middle.

"Ms. Hanson?"

At the masculine voice, Diane's mouth flew open but she found she couldn't scream. Jesus, this was like a bad dream, standing here paralyzed, watching the lean, well-dressed figure of Eduardo Ranier step from behind one of the machines.

"I'm sorry if I startled you." He flashed her a smile that might have been engaging under other circumstances. "I told the guard we had an interview lined up, which was more or less true, but then I got lost. This place is really a maze, isn't it?"

The light blue eyes studied her intently. Yet his words sounded so normal that Diane found herself able to speak again. "Yes—yes, it is."

"I understand you've been questioning some of my friends, Ms. Hanson." He hadn't moved, and yet he seemed to have come closer. Where was he hiding Lara? In a secret house? A hotel room? How crazy was he? Could she talk him out of it?

"I, uh, received an inquiry about you—for my consumer column—and so, well, I've been wanting to talk to you." Diane backed up a step. They were in the most isolated part of the newspaper. There wasn't even a telephone around. *Dial 8 to get out and then 911. That was all it would take.* "Maybe we should go back to my desk and I could ask you a few questions."

His eyes took on a luminous quality, like a cat's in the night. "Ms. Hanson, I feel a very strong aura of danger. I don't think you should go back to your desk. I think you should come with me."

Oh, God. If she screamed, would anyone hear her? Where the hell was the security guard?

He was still staring at her, and beyond her, as if seeing

229

something she couldn't. "Ms. Hanson, I knew the third one would be somebody very close to Lara, but I didn't realize until now it was you."

Was that how he lured Lara, warning that she was in danger and offering a ride? Play along with him, Diane. Play along. "Why don't we call the police? There are phones back in the newsroom. You could wait with me till they get here."

He didn't move, and Diane realized he was standing between her and the corridor. "That won't help. This threat, it comes from very close to you. It might be a neighbor, someone like that. The police would escort you home and leave, and there you'd be . . ."

"I'll take my chances, Mr. Ranier." Diane tried to brush past him. "Let's just go back to the newsroom, shall we?" *Oh, God, just let me get out of here. Please let someone come.*

With a shock, she felt Eduardo catch her elbow and force her to face him. He was much taller than she was, even taller than Barry. "Wait a minute. I know the police suspect me. Maybe you're planning to call them to come get me. Is that the idea?"

"Mr. Ranier . . ."

A set of footsteps approached down the hall. Diane's knees felt as if they might give way any minute. She thought she would die of relief when a familiar voice said, "Hey, what's going on here?" and she saw Jimmy hurrying toward them.

Eduardo released her arm. "Look . . ."

"No, you look, Mr. Ranier." Diane glared at him. "You had no business coming here and threatening me."

"I wasn't . . ."

Jimmy reached them. "Is anything wrong?"

She caught his arm for support. "Let's just get my purse. I—I can finish the story in the morning." They left Eduardo standing there, staring after them.

"What was that all about?" Jimmy asked as Diane logged off her terminal and picked up her purse.

"He—he tried to get me to go with him." Now that the danger was past, she was trembling all over. "Jimmy, I think I

230

should go to the police. That man—he was stalking me. He said I was going to be the third victim."

"Jesus. Why don't you drive over there now?" He walked beside her to the parking lot exit, his easy normality restoring a little of her shaken confidence. "It's a good thing I decided to stop by and make sure everything was all right. I'd expected to hear from you again before now."

"Oh, God, what about Lara?" Diane stumbled on a step and Jimmy steadied her. "He's got her somewhere and now he's going to kill her!"

"You probably shouldn't think about it. It's just making you more upset." They reached her Volvo, its green color looking faintly gray in the wan light. "I'll hang around till you get this thing started."

"Thanks." Diane clung to him for a moment before she got in the car and inserted the key.

Nothing. Not even a click. "Oh, shit," she said.

"Try again."

She turned the key. Dead silence. "Damn it!" Diane smacked the dashboard furiously. "Why me? Why now?" To her fury, she started to cry.

"Hey, it's no big deal." Jimmy leaned down to speak through the open window. "I'll figure out what's wrong tomorrow. Come on. I'll give you a ride."

Diane leaned her head back for a moment. She felt so helpless, so frustrated, just like . . . No, she wasn't going to think about Mark now. Or even Lara. She was going to go to the police station and tell them about Eduardo Ranier. "Thanks, Jimmy." She grabbed her purse. "Let's go."

64

He'd never made such a mess of anything in his life. Except maybe for that damn condo deal, and that hadn't really been his fault.

Ted Raines shoved the door open wearily and flicked on the light. He dropped his mail on a glass table and closed the door behind him. No need to open the envelopes; he knew they were bills.

The police were watching his house. Did they think he was too stupid to notice the van stationed across the street? Well, they'd get bored with it, sooner or later.

Why had he gotten mixed up with this business in the first place? What he needed to do was make some money, not get himself arrested.

He walked over to the black lacquer bar and poured himself a Dewar's, straight. For once, the elegance of the setting provided no relief. The stark white carpet and walls, the Chinese red couch and the black accents were beginning to give him a headache. Maybe the fact that he was two months behind on his payments had something to do with it.

He emptied the glass.

Ted poured himself another Scotch and sank down onto the sofa, kicking his Italian leather shoes under the coffee table. How had he managed to turn the evening into such a catastrophe?

He should have just called that Hanson woman. But hell, she was doing a hatchet job on him with that article; he could tell from what Bruce and Uncle Jeb had said. And then he'd gotten lost in the newspaper building. It was embarrassing; when you were psychic, people expected you to be Houdini into the bargain. Well, he wasn't.

When he realized he'd startled her, he'd meant to smooth it over. Instead, he'd seen the black cloud settling around her and realized she was in danger. Only Christ, she hadn't believed him. And he hadn't seen clearly enough to know exactly where the danger lay.

What if she went to the police? What if she called them tonight and said he'd threatened her? They might be coming for him any minute. Well, there wasn't a damn thing he could do about that, was there?

Ted rested his head against the arm of the sofa and thought about Lara. Lord, she was pretty. So pretty, and so young. He knew he could get into trouble, messing with her, but sometimes he couldn't help himself. And she'd been willing; he'd felt her vibrating toward him over the phone lines. When he'd driven by the school yesterday and she wasn't there, the disappointment had cut through him like a blast of cold air.

Why did the goddamn killer have to get his hands on Lara?

Until this week, Ted hadn't had very many psychic episodes in his life—mostly about people he was close to, except for those unexpected glimpses of that girl's murder down in Dana Point. He'd done his best to capitalize on it. For two years he'd been half-faking it, milking the few insights he did get, and nobody'd noticed. God, people were gullible. "Ranier Predicts the Events of the Coming Year." Who couldn't, given a modest amount of intelligence and a little research?

He'd never expected it to work against him. Cops, newspaper reporters, they all figured him for a fake. Which hadn't mattered, until this week. Until the flashes became real again, and no one would listen.

Ted twisted, trying to get comfortable. His head throbbed. What he needed were a couple of Tylenols. What if the police got here and hauled him off to jail before he had time to take anything? It felt as though the top of his head were coming off.

And then he saw her, so clearly she could have been sitting across the room. Limp brown hair fell across her face, and the room was dark, dark, lit only by a fragment of moonlight coming through the boarded-up window. Her thoughts were more jumbled than they'd been earlier, as if she were ill. Diabetes, the detective had said. She was pleading for help. The intensity of her despair swept over him as if it were his own.

Ted tried to send to her, pressing his forefingers tight against his throbbing temples. *Where are you? Lara, where are you?*

She didn't seem to hear. She was thinking about something—a van; that's right, the newspaper had said the killer had a van. He was going to take her somewhere in it. He was going to kill her somewhere else. But where? Why?

And then she was gone. Had the killer come back? Had she fainted? Was she going into some kind of coma?

Ted slipped off the sofa onto the carpet. He lay there, dazed, without the energy to get up.

In the distance, a siren wailed through the streets of Citrus Beach. He listened, expecting it to come closer, but it faded into silence.

Somehow his hand found the glass on the coffee table, closed around it, and brought the Scotch to his lips. A sip steadied him, and he sat up, very slowly.

She hadn't believed him tonight, that Hanson woman. Had the killer caught her already? He massaged the back of his neck with one hand. What good was being psychic if you couldn't get there in time to help?

Ted closed his eyes. Maybe he would just sleep here on the floor.

It didn't seem as if the police were coming. Apparently Diane Hanson hadn't called them after all.

65

"**T**he police station is the other direction."

"I know." Jimmy grinned at her. "I thought you might want to calm down first. Diane, if you walk in there now, you're going to get hysterical."

She could feel that he was right, and yet the urgency to help Lara pressed on her. Still, the police were watching Eduardo's house; they already suspected him; what more could she add? "I suppose a cup of coffee wouldn't hurt."

She hadn't driven through Old Town in a while. During the day, it had always struck her as charmingly raffish, but at night there was a seedy quality to it that she hadn't noticed before. It was funny, but in the ten months since Jimmy joined the *Record*, she'd never seen his house before, although he'd visited her apartment several times.

Finally the car stopped. Jimmy got out and held her door open.

"Boy, you're certainly being a gentleman tonight." She sighed, relieved to have someone else take charge. The encounter with Eduardo had left her shaky. "Jimmy, you don't know how much I appreciate this. If you hadn't come along . . ."

"But I did, didn't I?"

The trees in the yard were overgrown, Diane noticed, but what else could you expect from a bachelor? Then he swung open the door and she took in the shabby sofa, the flowered carpet, and the scratched coffee table. In the glare of an unprotected overhead bulb, she could see a thin layer of dust on the TV set.

"Pardon the mess." Jimmy waved at a couple of boxes stacked in one corner. "I just invested in some video equipment. Haven't had time to put it away yet."

He went into the kitchen, and Diane could hear him running water into a pot. "Gee, I wouldn't want to say anything about your housekeeping, but since you've been so nice, I might pay you back by coming over this weekend and tidying up a little."

"Hey, would you?" He was clattering around in the cupboards, searching for cups. Diane smiled to herself. She'd forgotten what it was like to be very young, nearly broke, and just winging it through life. She would have been willing to bet that the mugs wouldn't match—and sure enough, when he brought them out, they didn't.

The coffee tasted halfway decent. "At least you don't boil yours in a frying pan." She'd told him earlier about Cissy Greenspon, and Jimmy laughed appreciatively.

"My mother did teach me a few things."

"I'm sorry I never knew her." The coffee wasn't doing anything for the fog in Diane's brain. "She died about a year ago, didn't she?"

He nodded. "Left me a nice insurance policy and a run-down house in La Habra Heights. Unfortunately, it's too far to commute."

Oddly enough, instead of perking up from the coffee, Diane found herself getting sleepier. "Boy, I don't know what's wrong with me." She forced herself to stand up. "I think I'd better get some fresh air."

"Let me show you the back yard." He jumped to his feet. "Maybe you can make suggestions about what I should do with the landscaping, if you can call it that. Right through here."

As she navigated the narrow kitchen, Diane caught a whiff of Ivory soap. It smelled just like Lara. Instantly, she visu-

236

alized Lara as she'd looked when she got home Tuesday night, climbing out of Jimmy's car and glancing apologetically at her father and Diane.

Oh, God, I'm just torturing myself. Diane opened the side door.

There's somebody here.

Ted awoke with that thought in his head, and he wasn't sure if it was his or someone else's. He was lying on the carpet, propped against the couch, and his back hurt.

He glanced at his watch. He'd only been asleep about five minutes.

It was Lara. The impression was more fleeting, less vivid this time. He listened. Voices. Someone was there with the killer. Lara was trying to reach whoever it was, to warn them, but the gag was wedged tightly in place.

"Where are you, dammit?" He didn't realize he'd spoken aloud until he heard the frustration in his own voice. "Lara?" But there was nothing more, only the buzz of silence.

Sinking back onto the sofa, he cursed what Cissy Greenspon called his "gift."

As soon as she opened the door, Diane knew that had been a mistake. She was too dizzy to step out in the open without any support.

"Jimmy?" she murmured. "I don't feel well."

She started to turn back. There was a sudden movement behind her. She caught a glimpse of Jimmy's face, with a strange light in his eyes, and then something heavy crashed against the side of her head and she blacked out.

FRIDAY

66

It was seven-thirty on Friday morning when Ted slipped out the back door of his house, leaving it unlocked. He never carried keys or a wallet when he went for his morning walk, just a small transistor radio in his upper left shirt pocket, a few bucks in case he got hungry, and a business card so they'd know who he was if a truck hit him.

The morning was dark and dense beneath sullen clouds. He'd seen through the bathroom window that the police were still camped out across from the house, but they wouldn't notice him slipping out this way, down the alley that led past his neighbor's purple-and-green patch of winter vegetables. It felt good not to be watched.

He hadn't heard from Lara all night.

Ted tuned the radio to KCIT, which was still playing its overnight quota of bland pop music. It helped quiet the noise in his mind.

He didn't want to hear from Lara again, dammit. He didn't want to have to watch her die.

Over a clutch of short, fat palm trees, he noticed the giant cow begin its morning rotation on top of the drive-in dairy. The air smelled like rain. From the other side of the alley came the shrill of raised voices and the clatter of breakfast dishes. Ted quickened his stride to get that blood coursing and those lungs working the way the doctors said you should.

He'd tried jogging back when it was a big fad, but it hurt his knees. He'd never been particularly athletic, even though Uncle Jeb used to say he was tall enough to play basketball.

On the radio, Karen Carpenter was singing "We've Only Just Begun." Syrup of ipecac, that's what he'd heard really killed her. Using it to make herself throw up, and it had weakened her heart.

He should have been smarter on Monday. The minute he felt the darkness hovering near Jeanette and Lara, he should have hustled his ass out of town for the duration. He didn't need to have his mind torn in half, didn't need the anguish of a dying teenager radiating through his nervous system. But goddammit she was pretty, and she would have felt good in his arms, and now she'd worked her way into his head somehow.

Ted reached Las Flores and turned left toward the harbor, wondering if he'd have time to make his usual circuit before the rain hit.

The first thing Barry saw when he pulled into the parking lot was Diane's car. The first thing he thought was that she'd worked all night.

Then he remembered that she'd been having problems with the damn thing.

Disturbed, Barry went inside. The circulation department was still largely empty as he passed it on the way to his office. There was no one in editorial at all. He walked back to the art department, found an illustrator, and had her check the ladies' lounge, but it was empty.

Diane must have taken a taxi home. Why hadn't she called him? Maybe it had been late. But she must have known he wouldn't have minded.

He phoned her apartment, but there was no answer.

Barry walked over to Diane's desk, looking for a printout of her story on Eduardo, but he didn't see one. Uneasily, he sat down, logged on, and checked her queue. There it was.

He opened the story and scanned it. There were no quotes from Eduardo himself, which meant Diane had left without finishing. Maybe she couldn't reach him until too late, he told himself. That meant she'd probably be in early this morning to wrap up the story. Any minute now.

The phone was ringing over in photo. Meyer Krantz emerged from the darkroom and answered it. Barry heard him say, "Yeah, it's been going around. My wife's been sick with it all week," and then, "Take care of yourself, Jimmy."

Why hadn't he followed his instincts and come back to the paper last night? Barry closed the file and logged off. Damn it, he'd been so reluctant to push Diane for fear of driving her away that he'd failed to protect her.

Or maybe he was blowing this whole thing out of proportion. She'd probably be here any minute.

There was nothing floating by the old pier this morning, no hair spread like seaweed on the water, no glimpse of sodden material.

Kris Lender stared out to sea for a moment, unmoving. He'd come here yesterday and again today. He kept seeing the pier the way it had looked Tuesday morning when he'd found Jeanette.

Out to the curve of the horizon, the world was dying in the jaundiced light, Catalina Island forming a great black hulk that loomed from the flatness of the gray ocean. At breakfast, Arnie had offered to bet that the coming storm would wipe out the rest of the old pier. Kris sure as hell hoped so.

He walked back and caught the bus on Citrus Avenue, feeling as if he were riding to prison. Jesus, he couldn't bear it, another day of sitting in class, not listening, wondering what the newscasters were saying, whether Lara's body had been found. He didn't want to hear about it third-hand, with half the school knowing before he did.

There was no point in going to school anyway. He hadn't learned a thing yesterday and he wouldn't again today.

Kris got off at Calle Cortez and turned right to walk the long blocks to the *Daily Record*. Diane would understand. She'd let him hang around the paper. Maybe it was the sense of a storm coming, but he had the feeling that whatever was going to happen would happen today.

Captain De Anda had just settled down with a cup of coffee and a stack of reports when the call came from Barry Wheatley over at the newspaper.

One of his reporters, Diane Hanson, was missing. The same Diane Hanson who'd been at the high school when Jeanette Tracy disappeared. The same Diane Hanson who'd called yesterday with her suspicions about Eduardo Ranier.

"I finally went out and checked her car and it was tampered with," the editor said. "Somebody removed the distributor cap. I called her landlord and he said there was no sign she ever came home last night; her kitten acted like it was starving."

De Anda glanced out at the other detectives. Jane Amboise was freed up since the minimart arrests. "We'll be right over," he said. "Was there a guard on last night?" Yes; the man didn't have a telephone, but someone had been sent to fetch him, the editor said. "Fine. Round up anyone else who might have been working late. It'll save time when we get there."

De Anda put in a call to Chief Ferguson and explained why he and Amboise wouldn't be at briefing that morning.

"Shit." De Anda would have been willing to bet season's tickets to the Rams that Mack was more worried about his damn fund-raising dinner Sunday night than about Diane Hanson. "Well, there's always people coming and going around that paper. Somebody must have seen the killer, if it was him. You should get a lead on him pretty fast."

"Right." Now the son of a bitch has two of them, De Anda thought. Just like he said he would.

"Call me as soon as you know anything," Ferguson said.

"Will do."

Ted stopped by the Rainbow Cafe for a cup of coffee and a doughnut. The waitress said, "Looks like rain, huh?" and he nodded.

244

He was wondering why he hadn't heard from Lara. If she were dead, he'd know it. Damn, he'd almost forgotten what it had been like with that Dana Point girl. The horror, the disbelief, the agony of reliving her death. He'd wanted to run away from it, just as he wanted to run away from this.

Two years ago, he'd been flat broke, and he'd been willing to risk the ridicule for the chance to make a few bucks. And he'd have made a lot more than that, if it weren't for the damn police chief—oh, hell, you couldn't blame the guy. Anybody'd have thought the same thing in his place. Diane Hanson sure as hell did.

Ted gave the waitress a faint smile as his coffee arrived. He took a bite out of the chocolate doughnut and drank the thin black brew.

If he didn't think it would look too suspicious, he'd take a long vacation, starting now.

By the time he arrived at the paper from his rounds of the police station, Guy Chang already knew about Diane Hanson's disappearance.

What he hadn't known was that Jimmy Owens had called in sick. He didn't believe it for one minute. The SOB had looked healthy as a horse yesterday.

Chang created a new file in the computer and then sat there tapping absent-mindedly at the keys, watching Captain De Anda and Detective Amboise take one employee after another into Barry's office. The men were strangers to him—printing press operators, truck drivers, people like that.

It didn't take a genius to figure out what Jimmy was up to. Ever since he'd arrived at this paper ten months ago, he'd been trying to prove he was not only a good photographer but a good reporter. Right this minute, Jimmy was probably sniffing down some clue about Diane, something only a close friend like him would know.

Chang's stomach tightened. He didn't like the way this was shaping up. First Diane had been conducting her own investigation. He'd heard enough to know she suspected that so-called psychic, Eduardo Ranier. Everybody else knew that, too.

There must be some other clue, somewhere. Something he could find before Jimmy did. Something he'd already been thinking about . . .

He looked up as the door to Barry's office opened and the detectives came out. Barry joined them and they walked away toward the cafeteria. Probably getting a cup of coffee before the night watchman arrived, the key witness.

Dangling his steno notebook, Chang wandered over past the copy desk. No one gave him more than a casual glance. The mood in the office today was subdued, everyone turning inward to face his own unease that the killer had come here twice with his envelopes and now he had reached right into this building and claimed his third victim.

Through the glass, he could see Captain De Anda's briefcase sitting open on Barry's desk.

Chang strolled inside and sat down, flipping open his notebook as if awaiting their return. After all, he *was* the reporter on the case.

No one was paying any attention.

Chang leaned over and peered into the briefcase. He wasn't interested in the stack of reports. He found what he wanted near the bottom: a plastic envelope holding the photograph of Jeanette Tracy's body. The one the killer had printed.

He tucked it under his arm and slipped out of the office. There was no sign of the detectives yet. One of the copy deskers gave Chang a puzzled look but he ignored her.

At his desk, hidden by a mound of books and papers, he examined the photograph. There was nothing identifying in the background, that was for sure, but the scattering of white dust specks was much clearer than on the velox.

And running down the sides were the faint track marks of a commercial printer.

The woman at the front desk insisted that Diane Hanson wasn't in.

"Well, can I wait for her?" Kris wondered why the woman was looking at him so strangely.

"Do you have an appointment?"

"No. I'm—sort of a friend."

She told him to sit down, and made a phone call. A few minutes later, a young woman came and led Kris through a maze of corridors. He'd only been inside the newspaper once before, on a tour with one of his classes, and he'd forgotten how confusing it was, with desks stuck everywhere, stacks of papers on every empty chair, and people walking around shouting at each other. Yet they all seemed to know what they were doing.

Waiting in an office were Captain De Anda and a hard-faced woman who had to be a cop too.

"What's going on?" Kris felt as if he'd walked into another dimension. Why were the detectives here when they should be out looking for Lara?

"Suppose you tell us what you know about Diane Hanson's whereabouts," the captain said.

Kris stared at him blankly and then he realized what the man meant. "She's missing?"

"When was the last time you saw her?"

"Wednesday afternoon, at the high school. When Lara disappeared." He sank down into a wooden chair. "What's happened?"

The detective said Diane had vanished sometime last night from the paper.

"She—at the school, she asked the cop, I mean the policeman, if he'd seen a tall pale man—she meant Eduardo Ranier." Kris shivered, remembering that Ranier had been among the searchers Tuesday night. "She suspected him."

"We know. What are you doing here?"

"I hate sitting around that damn high school. Diane's the closest person to Lara other than me and her family. I thought she wouldn't mind if I hung around, and if anything happened, I'd find out about it right away, here at the newspaper."

He was relieved to see the captain's grim expression ease a little. "All right. If you remember anything else, let us know. You'll be around here?"

"I sure will." Kris walked out, feeling lightheaded, as if

he'd smoked too much grass. Barry Wheatley looked up from his desk and waved him over to a seat. Without words, the man seemed to understand how Kris felt. From the strained set of his eyes and the harsh lines around his mouth, he looked as if he felt the same way.

There was a flurry of movement at the door to the newsroom. Someone was bringing in an old man, maybe in his sixties, with baggy, worried eyes.

"Thank God." Barry stood up and called over to the detectives. "The guard's here."

Celia Rodriguez was late getting to work because her little boy had spit up on himself and had to be changed, and then the lady at the day-care center wanted to talk to her about how Davie had been throwing his food around and screaming at the other children.

A tight band was pressing around Celia's skull by the time she reached her desk, and she was afraid maybe one of her migraines was coming on. She took three Tylenols and hoped for the best.

It didn't make her feel any better to see that she'd forgotten to log off last night. And there was a marked-up paper sitting on her desk, as if someone had been working here after she left.

Apprehensively, she checked her queue. Access to her stories was limited to a few editors and to herself, but of course anyone could have gotten into it from this terminal last night.

Nothing appeared to have been disturbed.

With a sigh of relief, Celia pulled out the notes of the interview she'd done yesterday and began to work.

"A tall, kinda spooky-looking man, yep, that sounds like him." The night watchman nodded earnestly under the intent gazes of the two detectives. "Said he had to talk to her about some article she was writing and that she was 'specting him. He was dressed real nice, not like some of the creeps who come wandering by here at night. I didn't think there'd be anything wrong with lettin' him in."

248

The man paused. De Anda got the impression he was seeking reassurance. Well, that was the guy's own problem.

"Did anyone else come in?"

"No. It was time for my rounds. I left the side door closed—it sticks, kinda, and strangers think it's locked, but the people who work here, they know to just give it a shove. I weren't gone long, just stopped for a cup of coffee from the machines in the lunchroom."

"Hear or see anything on your rounds?"

The man scratched the side of his nose. "Not as I can recall. A real quiet night. I was wondering why I didn't see either of them come out, but then I leave at twelve, and these reporters, sometimes when they're on something really hot . . ." He left the sentence unfinished.

De Anda found a newspaper clipping in his briefcase and held it up. "This look like the man you saw?"

"Yep. That's him." The watchman squinted at the name. "Eduardo Ranier. Ain't he some kind of psychic?"

"So he says."

There was always the possibility, not to be overlooked, that the night watchman himself might be the killer, but after some further questioning, De Anda very much doubted it. For one thing, the early-morning watchman had seen this man at his post at midnight; for another, there was nothing to link him to either Jeanette Tracy or Lara Ryan.

Finally he let the man go and put in a call to Ferguson.

"Jesus." There was a note of excitement in the chief's voice. "This is what we need. Let's pick up Ranier."

"You want to get a search warrant first?"

"Oh, hell," Ferguson growled. "We got to go in the house to get him, right? We'll just make sure we think we see something suspicious, and then we won't need any goddamn warrant."

"I'll meet you there," De Anda said.

Ted had stayed at the coffee shop longer than he meant to, staring out at the harbor. He had no appointments this morning, and no great desire to return to the house where he felt watched at every move.

He'd had two refills of coffee, and the last time, the waitress had slopped some of it onto the table and mopped it up carelessly, a sign of impatience.

He considered walking on up to see Uncle Jeb. The man had held him together sometimes, over the years. Ted had been a mass of exposed nerve endings, or at least that was the way it seemed, looking back. Never fitting in anywhere, not really sure he wanted to, not really sure what he *did* want, only knowing that he ached with longing sometimes for things he couldn't quite grasp. The sight of a red umbrella opening in the rain could bring it on, or the scent of old-fashioned perfume, or an Edith Piaf song. Uncle Jeb always eased him back to earth.

No, he didn't like to go see Uncle Jeb without some kind of gift. The old man was on a tight budget. Sure, Ted was mortgaged up to his ears, but that was different. He was still young. One of these days, he'd make some big money. He'd buy Uncle Jeb his own condo. For himself . . . well, there'd be fast cars, and expensive hotels in exclusive resorts, and lots of girls, young ones with shiny lips and wide eyes.

Drawing himself reluctantly back to the present, Ted paid his bill and left the Rainbow. He took his time walking along the bayside shops, peering idly in the windows. He flicked his radio back on.

They were playing a commercial for a department store, and then the announcer said, "We've just received word from Citrus Beach police that a reporter at the *Daily Record*, Diane Hanson, disappeared last night. Police had no comment on whether Hanson is believed to be a victim of the Citrus Beach strangler."

Ted's breath came shallow. Last night. She'd disappeared last night. Had she had a flat tire on the way home? Had it been a neighbor, as he'd suggested? Even a boyfriend?

Why the hell couldn't he see the things he wanted to see?

He'd lost his taste for lingering near the harbor. Besides, it was starting to drizzle. At a near-trot, Ted moved back up Las

Flores, over Grosvenor, and onto Orange Avenue, coming home from the opposite direction. The Lemon Tree complex was set down in a kind of hollow, and as he approached he checked to see if the police were still waiting in front of his house.

He stopped dead.

There were three cars in addition to the van. You didn't have to be psychic to know they belonged to cops too, even though they weren't marked.

They hadn't come to talk to him; they'd come to arrest him.

The night watchman. He let me in. Didn't he see Jimmy? Didn't he see them go out together? Just my rotten luck. Ted stepped back, behind the shelter of an overgrown camellia bush.

Without warning, pain twisted through his head, so hard he nearly doubled over. The neatly marked lawns and curving streets of Lemon Tree vanished and he was staring at a shaggy hill dim with rain, half-dead roses tangling up to the roof of a ramshackle house. He could almost smell the decay rising from a fallen tree that had barely missed the edge of the house.

They're there. Both of them. And the killer. Where the hell is that place?

It wasn't around here, that much was for sure.

The pain receded, leaving him weak. Ted wanted nothing more than to stagger home and sink down on the sofa with a glass of Dewar's.

The police were waiting for him.

With a low groan, he turned and struggled back up the street to the bus stop on Orange Avenue.

67

The rain grew steadily heavier as the van rolled along the freeway. Despite the throbbing in her head and the rawness where the rope cut into her wrists and ankles, Diane tried to focus on where they were going.

Beside her, turned on one side in the fetal position, lay Lara, her skin flushed, her breath coming in shallow gasps. Her eyes fluttered opening now and then, looking into Diane's with a depth of sorrow that indicated she knew what was happening, in spite of hovering near a diabetic coma.

Oh, damn. Damn it damn it damn it. How could I have been so stupid?

She knew they'd gotten on the 405 Freeway; they'd turned right, which meant they were going south, and then curved up to the left, which would put them on the Costa Mesa Freeway, unless she'd lost track somehow. And then they'd gone west, but that could have been on any one of three freeways, and by the time they changed again, Diane was completely lost.

Do they know I'm missing yet? She had a feeling Jimmy would have made up some clever excuse. What about her car? Had he gone back and moved it, or was that taking too much of a chance?

What bothered her most was that she'd failed Lara. She'd been so damn wrapped up in her suspicions about Eduardo that she'd never seriously considered he might be telling the truth.

He knew I was in danger. He can't be in league with Jimmy; at least, I don't think so. That means he really is psychic. Oh, sweet Jesus, please let him figure out where we are, because nobody else will.

She herself had helped put the police on the wrong track. She'd pointed long and hard at Eduardo. *Even if he knows where we are, will they believe him?*

She wished there were some way to reach out and comfort Lara. Yet maybe that wasn't necessary. Diane had always felt an undercurrent of strength in Lara and now, looking into the girl's half-open eyes, she sensed that it had intensified. Or was that an illusion born of desperation? Even as Diane watched, the girl's body jerked convulsively as she retched. It was a good thing they hadn't eaten this morning; with the gag on, Lara might have choked if she'd brought anything up.

The van slowed and came to a stop, then turned left. They were off the freeway. *But where?*

The nausea had passed for the moment. Lara wished her head would clear up. She'd felt this way once when Kris's parents had been gone and they'd smoked pot in his room and had some wine. After a while, she couldn't even hold her head up. It had occurred to her then, blearily, that if he were a real jerk he could have had sex with her and she couldn't stop him; but he hadn't done it.

God, she missed him. Why had she been so cranky with him Wednesday? He was her friend, somebody who stuck by her, like Diane. Diane who was lying here in the same damn painful position, trussed up, her blonde hair all rumpled and the makeup smeared under her eyes.

I probably don't look any better. Lara tried not to think about the twists of pain in her abdomen, or the acres of water she wanted to drink, or the way she didn't seem to be able to take in enough air.

She still couldn't believe she'd been so stupid on Wednesday, when Jimmy came by and told her Diane had asked him to pick her up. She hadn't even questioned it. But why should she? He hadn't done anything Tuesday night . . . but then, there had been that patrolman, the one who'd stopped them in the car. Jimmy must have planned to kidnap her then, before the cop loused him up. Well, she'd sure given him a second chance, hadn't she?

That rain was really coming down. It sounded almost like hail, clattering on the metal roof of the van. All that water and nothing to drink. Maybe they'd skid and have an accident. Maybe the highway patrol would come along.

Yeah, and maybe Superman would fly down from Metropolis and rescue them.

Lara knew Diane wanted to comfort her, but that was ridiculous. She wasn't a child; she knew what was coming. And it wasn't some guy with a big S on his chest.

Diane's purse was lying a foot away, half open, the way Jimmy had tossed it in. Maybe the switchblade was still there, down at the bottom. But with both of them tied up this way, it might as well be on the moon.

Her eyelids wouldn't stay open. She let them sink shut.

When Jimmy slid open the side panel, Diane stared beyond him. It was hard to see much in the rain, but obviously they were out in a hilly area, overgrown and unkempt. It didn't look like any place she'd ever been before.

He slung her roughly over his shoulder. Diane's head pounded mercilessly from the blow it had taken last night, and her hip ached where his shoulder dug into it. The downpour made her clothes stick to her body, and water ran down her face, blinding her. The ground was soft beneath his feet; he lurched once and nearly dropped her. She couldn't see any more; the blood was rushing to her head, and she felt as if her nose would burst.

The air pulsed with lightning, followed within seconds by the deep snarl of thunder.

His shoes scraped up some steps, and she realized they were at a house. The clink of keys—a door creaking open—

and then he dumped her onto a dusty sprung sofa and went out again.

A minute later, he was back with Lara, plopping her into a chair.

"Like it?" Jimmy grinned at them. "Nice place, huh? My mom left it to me."

He looked and sounded so much like his old self that Diane felt momentarily reassured. Then, as he went out again, relief turned into fear. He had to be insane. He'd been keeping up this pretense for the entire ten months since he'd arrived at the paper, and all the while he must have been planning this. It had the feel of something intended, something with a purpose—*but what?*

When he slogged back in, not bothering to wipe his muddy feet, Jimmy was carrying a box from the van. She hadn't paid much attention when he'd loaded it in there last night, but now she saw it was his new video equipment.

He'd taken a photograph of Jeanette.

Oh, dear God. It couldn't be what she thought.

Another trip, another box. Lighting equipment, she saw from the drawing on the side of the box.

Except for the few pieces of furniture in the living room, the house had a sparse, unoccupied feel to it. Probably no telephone.

As if she had any way to free herself and get to it, even if there were.

Lara stirred sluggishly. She seemed to be nodding at their purses, which Jimmy had dumped in the corner. *He doesn't want to leave any evidence lying around anywhere. Or maybe he wants our ID, as proof. Why is she looking at me that way?*

"You might be wondering—" Jimmy pried open one of the boxes—"what I intend to do. Of course, you're the hotshot reporter, Diane. Maybe you've already figured it out."

And I thought he was my friend. Oh, my God. She'd had only seconds to realize Mark was in danger, not long enough, not fucking long enough. With Jimmy, she'd had ten months.

With Lara, maybe three days to figure out the danger. She'd failed. Oh, Jesus, there wasn't even a Sol to blame this time.

"In case you're trying to figure out how to escape, don't bother. There's no one around for quite a ways, and I'm in a lot better shape than you are." He set the camera up on a tripod and then stared at the plug. "Oh, shit. I forgot to get a battery . . . well, never mind. We won't need it." He plugged the cord into an outlet and set up the lights. "Nice, huh? My own little studio. Never make it in Hollywood, but what the hell?"

This is all a game to him.

Jimmy went back out to the van. He returned with a tape and slid it into the camera. "It picks up narration, too," he said conversationally.

He walked around the room squinting, then adjusted the lights. As nonchalantly as if he were staging a class photo, he aimed the video camera at the floor just in front of Diane. "Not a very snazzy background, but then, these fat cat Republicans need to see how people really live, don't you think?"

Diane watched him steadily. Behind her back, she tried to work her fingers loose, but the blood had gone out of them.

Jimmy walked over to Lara and stood in front of her, legs apart. "Not much of a live wire, huh?" He reached down and squeezed her breast. Diane winced, then pulled furiously at the ropes until her wrists burned. Lara's head came up and she glared at Jimmy. "That's better."

He walked away, leaning against the wall as he drew a pouch from his shirt pocket and rolled himself a joint. The sweetish smoke revolted Diane. "You're going to enjoy starring in my own private snuff film. It's really something of a work of art. Lara wanted to be an actress, didn't you, kid? Well, here's your big chance."

Where is Barry right now? Is he worried yet? This is going to be such hell for him. And Lara's father. And that poor little Gerry.

"I hope you're not modest." He smiled at them slyly, his eyes narrowed against the smoke. "About having people see you naked, I mean. And sex. Republicans need to see that. Not that they don't already know. My stepfather knows all

256

about sex. He used to get real hard for my mother. And me, too. You didn't know that, did you? Maybe he'll get it up watching the tape.''

Mack Ferguson's fund-raising dinner was day after tomorrow. It was beginning to make a bizarre kind of sense.

Jimmy, watching her, nodded approvingly. "Oh, yes. You've figured it out, haven't you? Smart girl, Diane. Mack Ferguson killed my mom. Oh, not so anyone would be able to pin it on him. He turned her into an alcoholic. He used to do weird sex things with her—that was what drove her crazy. The one she really wanted was me. So did he.'' The bantering tone warped into a whine. "Right before I went away to college, he saw me coming out of the shower naked, and he started hitting me. Like, for no reason, just grabbed me and punched me out and knocked me around until he got his rocks off, you know? The fucker killed my mother. After the funeral I got somebody I knew at the fire department to show me the pictures of the car after she smashed it up, and she was lying there with her legs spread wide open, you know, like she was waiting for him. So I came back. I came back to get him.''

Instinctively, Diane wanted to try to talk him out of it, to point out that killing innocent people to ruin Mack's career was insane—but of course, that's exactly what it was, and talking wouldn't do a damn bit of good, even if she didn't have this gag digging into her mouth.

"Just so you know, I'm going to do Lara first. Because you'll be more fun; you'll fight more.'' A strange light seemed to glow in back of his eyes. "I'm already hard, Diane. Want to see?'' To her disgust, he began unzipping his pants. "I'll bet Barry isn't that big, is he?'' She tried not to look at his penis. There was something so juvenile and pathetic about him, and yet he was going to kill them.

Unless she could think of something . . .

The way she lay there looking up at him reminded him of his mother. Rubbing himself, he thought about that day after

257

graduation when he'd come home from the beach and found his mother on the couch reading.

He'd gone over and touched her the way he liked to, but she'd acted strange, pulling away, and then she'd ordered him to leave the house, told him he wasn't welcome to live there anymore.

You goddamn bitch! Who do you think you are, playing Miss Holiness with me?

He grabbed her wrists, and saw the fear in her eyes, and felt her struggle like a moth he'd caught once and held in the cage of his hands, how wildly it had fluttered until he crushed it. But she didn't scream.

In the bedroom, he found some heavy packing tape in Mack's desk, the kind with threads running through it that you couldn't break. His mother was scratching at him, trying to wrench away, but it was easy to lash her to the bed frame. Once she'd been so much bigger than him. Once he'd come out of that place between her legs, the place he was going back to.

At some point she started to sob, and he liked her tears, rubbed his whole body over her face to wet it, and then he did what he'd always wanted to do, what she'd always wanted him to do, what she let Mack do. He could hear her whimpering, whispering "Oh, dear God," as if anyone were listening. His cock got so big it filled up the whole world, and heaven rioted through him, and she lay there like a used-up old bag when he was through, and he didn't even bother to untie her when he went in to clean up.

Jimmy didn't hear anything until he stepped out of the shower, still wet, and Mack was standing there, his big beefy face contorted with fury. The man grabbed him and started throwing him around the bathroom, and Jimmy couldn't get a grip on anything. The towel bar smashed into his ribs and his breath wouldn't come and then Mack jerked him into the bedroom and started pounding him, one blow coming so fast after another that Jimmy couldn't see anything but a big blur.

He could hear his mother crying, still crying, damn her, and Mack was saying, "You bastard mother-fucker," and smashing him, and Jimmy could feel blood spurting out of his nose, and he tried to pull himself up but Mack was holding him down and the

258

pain jolted through him, and the anger, and he wanted to kill Mack, kill him right then. And afterwards there was blood on the bed, and a shocked look on Mack's face, and his mother was still lying there, not making any more noise, still spread-eagled and tied, waiting for anybody who wanted her.

His legs shook on the way to his room, and somehow he shoved things every-which-way into his suitcase, and cleaned himself up, and got out to his car.

He had the university send them the tuition bills. Mack always paid them. They'd never spoken again, not even at the funeral. But Jimmy hadn't forgotten. And he was going to make sure Mack never forgot, either.

Staring down at himself, Jimmy realized he'd almost come and then pulled back just at the brink. Perfect. He wanted to save it for these two bitches.

The rain was slamming into the side of the cabin really hard. He hoped it wouldn't mess up the sound on the tape.

Putting his cock back into his pants, he switched on the floodlights. The women blinked. "Hurt your eyes?" He walked over to Lara and untied her. She shifted listlessly. "Come on!" He jerked her onto the dirty braided rug in the middle of the floor, where he'd focused the camera, then went to check the viewfinder to be sure he had the angle right.

Diane was moving around; he could see her trying to get loose. "Don't worry," he said. "There'll be plenty left for you."

Lara didn't struggle much as he stripped off her blouse and jeans. She was wearing a pink lacy bra and panties, and the bright light picked up the green in her eyes. A real pretty one. The Republicans ought to enjoy watching this.

"Don't." Her voice came out a whisper when he pulled off the gag. Jimmy went over and switched on the camera. "You'll have to speak up, Lara. Oh, come on, plead for them. Mack Ferguson likes to hear people plead. It gives him a hard-on."

He stepped into camera range himself. "Beating up kids is what Mack Ferguson really likes. Assemblyman Gorwins, be sure to ask him about that."

It was different than when he'd imagined it. In his fantasies, the camera had taken care of itself, but now he saw he'd have to be careful to keep them both in the right place, and not block the lens at critical moments. Like now, as he reached for Lara Ryan's bra. Those Republicans were going to drool in their salad, looking at her breasts.

White light flared through the room without warning, and thunder boomed right overhead, and then the one thing happened that he hadn't counted on.

The lights went out.

68

De Anda led two men to the front door while Terry Hewett went around the back with another couple of officers. De Anda stood well back as he pounded on the door, ready for a gunshot to come flying through.

He heard nothing inside—no footsteps, no chair scraping, nothing.

The lights were still on in the kitchen and bedroom, and the car was parked in the driveway. That didn't mean Ranier hadn't gone out on foot. Or that he wasn't lying in wait for them inside. Or that they wouldn't enter and find a house full of bodies.

He pounded again, and then withdrew, telling Hewett on the walkie-talkie to keep watch in back.

"Playing possum?" Chief Ferguson was waiting by the squad car, holding a shotgun, his thinning hair slicked down by the drizzle. "Looks like we'll have to use tear gas on the son of a bitch."

De Anda didn't bother to hide the disgust in his voice. "Yeah, well, before we go grandstanding, Chief, maybe I could try using the neighbor's telephone."

Reluctantly, Ferguson nodded.

Dammit, why did the chief have to be so hung up on making himself look like a hero? Sure, De Anda thought as he headed for the house across the street, it was understandable, with the sheriff's campaign, but it wasn't good law enforcement.

Besides, there was something about this whole situation that bothered him.

The killer was a sly one. Too damn sly to walk right into the newspaper with the night watchman as a witness.

On the other hand, he'd obviously had some sick reason for vowing to kill three women in one week. Maybe once he'd accomplished his goal, he didn't care if they knew who he was.

That was one thing about being a cop. You could get inside the head of a dope dealer, or a robber, or a burglar. But a cold-blooded murderer, that was something else again.

A fiftyish woman in a print bathrobe, who'd obviously been watching out her window, quickly let him in and pointed the way to the phone. De Anda dialed Ranier's number and let it ring ten times. Then he dialed it again, and waited.

He had a feeling the guy had given them the slip. One way or another.

Mack fingered the trigger on the shotgun as he watched the house from the shelter of the car seat. The rain was really starting to pour down now.

Part of him wanted to shoot the guy when he finally came out, but it wouldn't look good. Yeah, he knew a bleeding-heart judge would probably let the guy off because some juror was clicking her knitting needles during key testimony or some damn thing like that, but hell, the press didn't like it when you went around blowing people away.

Well, he could keep a lid on it. Just as long as they caught the guy. Just as long as they had the son of a bitch in jail by Sunday.

A Mustang drove slowly by along the street. Mack's head jerked up. Dammit, he'd told the dispatcher to keep off the open channels. He didn't want any asshole press coming in here and turning this thing into a circus.

262

The car passed them and pulled into a driveway. It was white, not silver.

Mack exhaled slowly.

After seven years, it shouldn't bother him so much every time he saw Jimmy, but it did. God, the kid was such a bastard—he'd had to teach him a lesson, but he hadn't meant to lose control; he could have killed the boy. That unrestrained violence was a dark legacy from his own father, and he hated it in himself. Mary's way of forgetting that day had been drinking. Mack's had been working eighteen hours a day. It had turned out to be a deadly combination for Mary.

He wished Jimmy hadn't moved back to town after she died. The damn kid was like some kind of a ghost, a living reminder of the shadowed side of himself that Mack had sworn off long ago.

If the creep ever decided to go public, he could really make it look bad. Child abuse was a big issue these days. And Mack would never tell anyone what Jimmy had done to deserve it; it would be too degrading to Mary's memory.

The walkie-talkie crackled. It was Hewett. "Chief, I tried the back door and it's open. You want we should go in?"

"Wait till De Anda gets back."

Ferguson made some noises about leading the men, but De Anda pointed out—with as much tact as possible—that the chief's instincts might not be quite as sharp as they'd once been, and he might endanger them all.

"Besides, we need you to cover the front," De Anda said.

He circled around through a neighbor's yard. They'd evacuated the people on both sides in case any shooting started, and a paramedic unit was on its way to stand by, but he didn't really believe anybody was still in that house.

Not anybody alive.

69

B arry didn't even try to get any work done; he would let Rand Franklin take care of the newspaper today. Instead, he sat at the desk next to Rand's, staring over the newsroom, thinking about Diane.

The detectives had rushed out of here as if they were on their way to a fire. He'd questioned the guard himself afterwards, learned that it was Eduardo Ranier they'd gone to get, and then told the man not to discuss the matter with anyone else.

The cops obviously didn't want a bunch of reporters following them over to Ranier's house. And dammit, neither did Barry, not if there was even the slightest chance it would interfere with getting Diane back safely.

Oh, God, why hadn't he come by here last night to check on her?

At the desk beside him, Kris ruffled distractedly through yesterday's paper. He was a handsome youngster, kind of cocky the way he moved, and it would be easy to lump him as a typical smartass teenager, but after seeing the way he'd searched for Lara Tuesday night, Barry knew better. And Kris had found Jeanette's body. It was more than a kid his age ought to go through. Hell, it was more than a guy Barry's age ought to go through, for that matter.

Instinctively, he reached in his pocket for a cigarette. Oh, shit. He turned to Rand, and then remembered that Rand didn't smoke.

Maybe he ought to drive over to—where the hell did Ranier live, anyway? Just to find out what was going on. Maybe the women were there . . .

Barry glanced at Chang's desk. Now, that was funny. Chang was gone, but his screen had some squiggles on it, which meant he hadn't logged off.

Of course, it would be just like the reporter to chase after the detectives. But Barry hadn't seen him around when they'd gone tearing out of here.

Chang was probably just visiting the men's room, he told himself, and then he froze.

Eduardo Ranier was standing in the doorway to the newsroom.

Oh, sweet Jesus. There was no sign of the police anywhere around.

The first thought that went through Barry's mind was that Ranier had a gun, that he was planning to go out in a blaze of bloodshed. The son of a bitch must have charmed his way past the receptionist. Oh, God in heaven . . .

But Ranier wasn't holding anything as far as Barry could tell. He looked wet and uncertain, as if he were seeking someone and wasn't sure of his reception.

Chang came out of the darkroom and did a double take. Barry stood up, peripherally aware of Kris dropping the paper and standing, too. "Should I call the police?" the boy asked softly.

Ranier's eyes met Barry's and the pale man actually looked relieved as he started across the newsroom, Chang trailing after him holding a photograph. "Not yet. I want to find out what the hell this is all about."

Ranier reached the desk and Barry saw that his fists were clenched, not with anger but tension. "The police are at my house," he said. "I came here because I didn't know where else to go. I'm the wrong man. And if they waste any more time, it's going to be too late."

The entire newsroom was staring at them. Barry could feel

the intensity of Ranier's gaze. The only thing he could think was, *As long as he's here, he isn't doing anything to hurt Diane and Lara. Unless he's already killed them.*

It wasn't until after he'd gotten off the bus, walked several blocks in the rain, and persuaded the receptionist that he had urgent business with Barry Wheatley that it occurred to Ted that he hadn't the foggiest idea of what he was going to say. He didn't know who the killer was or even where the women were, except that it was a rundown house and it wasn't near here.

The inside of the building looked a lot different in daytime, full of people and the clack of computer keys and the ringing of phones. He felt out of control here, surrounded. For a minute, he wanted to run. Goddamn, why was he messing in something that was none of his business?

Only it was his business. The police had made sure of that.

He could see the suspicion in Barry's eyes even as they shook hands. Instinctively, Ted knew his radio persona with its slick paternalism would get him nowhere, would make him even more suspect.

"Your uncle used to own a camera store, right?" It was the slim Oriental man who'd followed him across the newsroom.

"Yes." *Why are you asking me about camera stores at a time like this?*

"You must have a lot of equipment—professional stuff."

"Chang," Barry said warningly, but the younger man ignored him.

"Ever see this before?" He handed Ted a black-and-white photograph.

It was the girl Jeanette, obviously after she'd been killed. "No." He handed it back impatiently. "Wheatley, I admit I was here last night, but I didn't leave with Diane."

"Do you own a commercial printer, you know, the kind that runs the paper through on a track?"

"Chang, what's all this about?" Barry looked as annoyed as Ted felt.

266

"Well, the killer took this picture, and it was printed on a commercial printer . . ."

"I don't own one and I've never used one and frankly, the only camera I know how to use is an Instamatic." Ted turned to Barry. "She left with Jimmy Owens. I'm surprised he hasn't already told you that."

"He's out sick today." Barry was already punching commands into his computer and reaching for the telephone as the number came up.

"He probably doesn't even know she's missing yet." Ted felt some of the tension seep out of him. "He'll tell you. And the police. He ought to know where she went from here." And then he realized that Barry was just standing there, listening to the phone ring, and nobody was answering it.

"That's funny." Barry hung up. "If he's home sick, he ought to be answering the phone."

"Home sick my ass," said Chang. "He's out trying to chase this story down on his own."

"Isn't there some way you can reach him?" Ted was beginning to feel like a man in a nightmare, trapped no matter which way he turned. Where the hell was that kid, anyway? He was Ted's only alibi. Christ, he had to turn up.

Chang waited restlessly while Barry dialed the number again without reaching anyone, and finally the editor took notice of him. "Where'd you get the photo, anyway?"

"I swiped it from De Anda's briefcase." Chang didn't see any point in playing coy. "I think it might be some kind of clue. How many people have access to a commercial printer—and could walk into this newspaper twice and leave envelopes without being noticed—and could lure three women to go with them, even in the middle of all the paranoia? It's got to be a short list."

He could see a faint tinge of red creeping up Ranier's neck. The guy had managed to talk his way in here last night and again today, all right. But why would he have come here now, if he was the killer? No, whoever had done it, Jimmy

Owens was hot on his trail, and if there was a way to beat him, Chang sure as hell intended to find it.

Meyer Krantz wandered over. For that matter, half the newsroom was drifting by, trying to listen in.

"Is that what you were doing in the darkroom?" Meyer took the photo from Chang and examined it.

"Yeah, I thought I'd start by seeing what our photographs look like when they come off the printer, but they don't have those track marks."

"That's because we refilled the chemicals Tuesday." Meyer held the photo up to catch the light better. "We were getting crap like this on Monday."

"How many people have access to your darkroom?" Ranier asked.

"Just our own photographers—unless of course somebody managed to sneak in here late Monday night. Like you, for instance." Meyer started off with the photo.

"Hey—" Chang grabbed for it and missed.

"Touchy, touchy. Just thought we ought to dig up a few photographs that were printed that night. We could see if the track marks were the same. And the dot pattern, for that matter."

There were about a dozen pictures in Tuesday's paper that had been printed in the lab on Monday. Some of them were filed in the library, where they belonged; others had been lost or discarded. Only seven could be found.

Three of them matched, dust spot for dust spot, track mark for track mark.

"Holy mother of God," Meyer said.

Barry kept staring at one—the picture of a smiling Jeanette Tracy that had been taken at the high school that same afternoon.

Taken by Jimmy Owens. Printed by Jimmy Owens. Jimmy who could easily have planted the killer's envelopes at the front desk—hell, he'd "found" the second one. Barry could still see him standing at the entrance to the newsroom, holding it.

Jimmy who had been the last one to see Diane last night. Jimmy who wasn't home this morning.

"I don't believe this." Chang kept gazing at the two pictures of Jeanette. Before and after. "I was sitting at my desk while he printed this. I remember he took a long time about it. He said something about sending a picture to AP . . ."

"Do you think they're at his house?" Meyer asked.

"No. They're at—sort of a cabin." In his shock, Barry had almost forgotten Ranier was there. "It's not around here. It's kind of run down, in a hilly, overgrown area."

"Climbing roses?" Meyer said.

Ranier nodded quickly. "You know where it is?"

"Up in La Habra Heights. Jimmy inherited it from his mother; he had a beer blast there right after he joined the staff." Meyer pulled out a map book and flipped it open. "Little winding street off East Road. Orange Hill, I think it's called. Here. There's only four houses on the whole street and it's way down at the end."

Barry picked up the phone and called the police.

The dispatcher turned him over to the watch commander, who said the chief and Captain De Anda couldn't be reached. He promised to relay the message as soon as he got hold of them.

"Whose jurisdiction is La Habra Heights?" Barry asked the dispatcher.

"LA county sheriff. That should be the City of Industry substation."

"Thanks."

He called the sheriff's department. The dispatcher sounded suspicious of his story, and part of Barry couldn't blame her even though most of him wanted to shake her violently.

"I'll have somebody swing by," she said finally, "but it may take a while. The power's out up there, it's pouring like crazy, and we've got some hills starting to slide."

"Two lives depend on this. Would you send a car out there right now?" Barry had to force himself not to swear, knowing he'd only antagonize the woman. "And paramedics, please. The girl has diabetes."

"I'll see what I can do."

He hung up and started for the door. "Goddamn bureaucrats. I'm going out there."

Ranier, Kris, and Chang came with him.

70

I n the faint light that seeped through the windows, Diane watched in mingled relief and fear as Jimmy let go of Lara and stepped back, cursing.

He walked across the room and pulled aside the tattered curtains. The room brightened only slightly.

"Fuck." He went back to Lara and knelt, beginning to tie her up again. "I'll have to run into La Habra for batteries. Don't worry; it won't take long."

Diane glanced at the now-dark floodlights. Jimmy cursed again. "Oh, yeah. Well, I'll get some hurricane lamps; snuff films are supposed to be grainy anyway, aren't they? Thanks, Diane. I might not have remembered. You saved me a trip." Flashing her a grin, he made a dash for the truck. The door slammed shut behind him.

How long would it take? He'd mentioned La Habra, so they must be up in the Heights. Couldn't be more than ten or fifteen minutes each way, although in the rain, things might be slowed down. And then he'd have to find a place that carried the right kind of batteries . . .

"He forgot to gag me." Lara's voice was soft in the semi-darkness. "I tried to . . . to tense myself up, like I read Houdini used to do, to make the ropes loose . . ." The words trailed off as she bent over, retching again. *Oh, please let her be all right!*

Lara straightened, breathing hard, and then there was a rustling movement as she began trying to wiggle free. Jimmy hadn't spent much time tying her, Diane remembered. A healthy person ought to be able to get out of those ropes fairly easily. But Lara wasn't healthy.

"My whole body hurts and I'm so thirsty." Lara was breathing hard. "I wish you could talk to me."

So do I.

"I know!" Lara edged closer. "Turn your head. Maybe I can pick the knot loose with my teeth."

Diane obeyed. She wanted to tell Lara to work on the ropes, not the gag, but she couldn't.

The girl's breath came hot on her cheek. Diane could feel Lara struggling, feel the blood surging through the girl. Oh, God, they were both still alive, there was still a chance for them.

Now, in slow motion, she had the precious seconds back, the seconds she'd needed to save Mark. Time took on a thickness it had never had before. Diane could feel the hands of an unseen clock vibrating slowly in the room, ticking forward notch by notch as Lara fought with the gag. The moisture from her mouth turned alternately hot and cold on Diane's face.

By now, Jimmy must have reached a store. Maybe they'd be out of batteries, or wouldn't carry the right kind, or didn't stock the lamps. Would he pay in cash? By credit card? They'd have a record that way. But of course he didn't care. Jimmy was putting himself in the tape. He wanted the world to know what he was doing.

Lara paused for a moment, panting. Even if they got help, would it be too late for her? How long did it take to die from diabetes? It wasn't like insulin shock, Diane knew that much; Lara had carefully instructed her long ago in the urgency of providing instant glucose. But they'd never talked about diabetic coma. There'd never been any reason to.

This was an ugly room, an ugly place to die. With her head tilted this way, Diane could see a spider web at the corner of the ceiling with several indefinable blobs in it, probably flies.

Oh, God, Jimmy must have made his purchases by now. Unless there'd been an accident on the road and traffic was blocked. But it was the middle of a weekday. How much traffic could there be, even in the rain? They were going to die here, she and Lara, their bodies violated, their dignity stripped away, naked in front of a camera, while Jimmy spouted his madness out loud . . .

The gag came loose.

Diane tried to speak and began to cough. Finally she found her voice, rough and unfamiliar. "Can you get your hands free? Here—turn around—maybe I can get you loose."

Lara obeyed. "Do you still have the knife?" She sounded amazingly calm. Determined, that was the word for it.

"The. . . ?" Diane remembered. "It's in my purse." She bent to work on Lara's bonds. The angle was awkward, and the rope felt stiff and unyielding in her teeth. It was hard sorting out which strand was which, and getting a grip; when she began tugging, she felt as if her teeth would snap off at the roots.

If Jimmy hadn't been in such a hurry and hadn't been so sure of Lara's weakness, it would have been impossible. But gradually Diane felt the rope began to give, and then, miraculously, Lara's hands were free.

The girl turned and began to tug feebly at Diane's bonds. It seemed like hours before the pressure eased and the ropes slid off and the blood prickled into her fingers. Trying to ignore the pain, Diane struggled to remove the ties from her feet, then reached over to help Lara.

How much time had passed? She checked her watch, which said it was 9:48. But she didn't know what time Jimmy had left.

"You'd better go for help." Lara was still on the floor, sagging against the edge of the sofa. "I can't walk, Diane."

"I'll drag you." She caught Lara beneath the arms and strained to lift her, but managed only to shift her awkwardly onto the couch. Diane cursed her own weakness.

Lara pushed her away. "I'm too heavy. He'll catch us both. Please. Hurry."

Diane wavered. Her feet and hands still throbbed agonizingly, her head ached from the blow last night, and all her movements felt forced and leaden. She could barely walk herself, much less drag Lara.

"Here." She found her purse and dug in it for the knife. "Hide it, and then use it if he comes back. Lara—"

"I'll be all right." The girl took the knife. "Just—please—I'm so thirsty . . ."

Diane dashed into the kitchen, filled a cracked plastic glass with water, and brought it to Lara, who swallowed it in a great gulp. Then, after checking around the cabin quickly just in case there was a phone, Diane staggered outside into the rain, which was pouring down with blinding force.

Slogging to the edge of the road, she realized her dilemma. They were at the end of the street. If she walked down it, Jimmy would see her as he came back.

Through the slanting rain and the thick brush, it was impossible to see any other houses. But there must be some. La Habra Heights. It seemed to Diane that she'd read somewhere the lots up here were about an acre. That wasn't so big, was it? She stumbled across the overgrown yard and peered down into a thick stand of cypresses.

She couldn't see any lights. Oh, damn—of course there wouldn't be any, in a blackout.

The hill was steep. It would be easy to slip and break a leg. There might not even be anyone home at the next house, if she managed to reach it.

I've got to go. There isn't any other choice.

And then Diane heard the sound she dreaded. The sound of Jimmy's van churning up the road.

71

R anier's house was empty. It was a classy place, De Anda noted in passing, with its art deco furnishings, everything neat and tidy. No sign of any struggles; no whiff of perfume; nothing at all to indicate the women had ever been here.

Gun drawn, he led the men from room to room, checking inside closets, behind drawers, calling out "Police!" as he went. The funny thing was that, on the dresser in the bedroom, he found Ranier's wallet. His driver's license and fifty-three dollars were inside, along with a scattering of credit cards. Why would the guy leave without his wallet?

He called Ferguson on the walkie-talkie and told him what they'd found.

"Get back out here." The chief sounded angry, frustrated, ready to pound on something.

At the car, as De Anda ducked under an umbrella, Ferguson told him they'd had a call from the watch commander.

"Our friend Eduardo Ranier showed up at the newspaper this morning, insisting that he's innocent and that he wasn't the last one to see Diane Hanson last night."

"Who was?"

There was a strangled pause. "Jimmy Owens."

"You don't think—" De Anda took another look at the

chief's face. It was obvious that was exactly what he did think.

"Apparently the photograph the killer took of the Tracy girl matches dust speck for dust speck with one Jimmy printed Monday night. He was in the right place at the right time to kidnap all three women. And God knows, he had the motive."

Motive? De Anda knew better than to ask what that might be. But Jesus Christ. What kind of reason could a kid have to murder a girl and and maybe two others just to get back at his stepfather?

"We're notifying the LA county sheriff. Jimmy inherited a house in La Habra Heights." Ferguson spoke coldly, almost mechanically. "Let's get the hell up there."

"Right, chief." De Anda slid behind the wheel. "I think I'd better drive."

Ferguson only nodded.

72

I t hadn't taken as long as Jimmy had thought. He'd gone into La Habra by Hacienda Boulevard and within a few minutes he'd found a hardware store that carried everything he wanted.

He cursed at the rain, coming back, finding he had to drive slowly on the winding streets to avoid a skid. His cock got hard every time he thought about Lara lying there, ready for him. He was certainly ready for her.

It was funny to think about what was probably happening back in Citrus Beach right now. He'd managed to get in and out of the paper without the night watchman seeing him; that meant the logical suspect was Ted Raines. Which dovetailed perfectly with everything Diane had been telling people all week.

And then there was that girl in Dana Point. Jimmy smiled to himself. He'd come down on a free-lance assignment to cover the swallows' annual return to Capistrano; nobody around here had even known he was in town. What a kick it had been, reading in the newspaper about how Ted Raines solved the case with his psychic powers. The guy must have stumbled over the body or something and decided to play it for all it was worth. Anybody could see the cops had thought Ted was the killer. Just like this time.

They might even have the poor slob locked up right now.

He could imagine Mack, his fat red face full of self-importance, trying to interrogate the guy.

It was just going to make him look that much worse come Sunday.

Jimmy had to get the tape done by three-thirty today. That would give him plenty of time to get it by five o'clock to the messenger service in Anaheim, which had promised to make a special delivery for him on Sunday. Assemblyman Gorwins would get it as he sat at the head table. He'd open the wrapping paper, puzzled, and then see the card that said, "The inside story of the killer Mack Ferguson created." They always had video equipment at those big hotels; Gorwins wouldn't want to wait to find out what was on the tape . . .

It was too bad Jimmy couldn't be around to see Mack's face.

After he dropped off the tape this afternoon, he'd swing by Citrus Beach, put the wrecking-yard pair of license plates on the van, and take off for South America. The only thing he regretted was that he'd have to leave the Mustang behind. But you had to be practical.

As for that little jerk-off Rita Beth, well, it probably wouldn't work out. She'd be eating dinner about the time he got home, and he didn't want to hang around. Too bad. The bitch deserved to be taught a lesson.

Jimmy pulled into the driveway and drove the van right up onto the muddy lawn, churning across it until the bumper rested against the steps. Then he jumped down and darted up the steps, using his body to shelter his purchases from the rain.

When he first opened the door, he couldn't see anything. It sure as hell was dark in there. Well, he'd fix that.

It took only a minute to set up the first hurricane lamp and get it lit. It cast a rich glow around him. There was one woman lying on the couch. He couldn't see anyone on the floor. Oh, shit.

Jimmy lifted the lamp higher, to see the rest of the room. That was Lara on the sofa; where the hell was Diane?

He stalked through the cabin. Not here. She'd gone for

278

help. Not down the street; he would have seen her. There hadn't been much time. To get the bonds off . . . It was a steep climb down to the next house, too. The place was pretty far away; they hadn't even complained of the noise the night he had his beer blast. For all he knew, it might be vacant.

Or maybe she'd reached a telephone. Maybe she'd alerted the police already. They might be on their way up here. Shit. Maybe he ought to clear out.

No. It wasn't enough to have killed one girl. He needed the videotape, and the narration that went with it, the explanation. A little bit of Mack Ferguson's personal history that the rest of the world had never suspected.

Jimmy walked over to the door and shouted out into the rain, "Diane! I've got her! You going to save yourself and let Lara die?"

Off to his left, he detected a slight movement.

Jimmy smiled to himself. The fox. The fox was laying such a clever trap for the wary rabbit.

Stepping back inside and leaving the door open a crack, he lit the second lamp and positioned the two of them so they lit up the center of the room. Jesus, this wasn't going to photograph well; it was too dim and unsteady, but it was bright enough to show the important parts. Bright enough for Assemblyman Gorwins to tell what was happening.

He'd always had keen hearing; now he picked up a slushing sound near the steps. She was coming.

Hurriedly, he fitted the battery into the video camera and set the tripod further back, so it could take in a larger area.

A faint creak on the steps.

Jimmy turned on the camera. She'd be here any minute. He'd have to kill Diane first, after all; Lara would be an anticlimax, but at least he could take his time with her, give the Republicans something to really look at.

He kept his back three-quarters to the door, so Diane would feel safe. Was it possible she had a weapon? But there was nothing in the cabin. Maybe she'd picked up a stick or a rock. But she wouldn't have figured out anything ingenious. He knew Diane Hanson; hadn't he helped her fix her car more than once? Hadn't she cooked him dinner at her apartment as a thank-you? She was clumsier than average, and not good about mechanical things, even for a woman. But she was smart. He wouldn't underestimate her.

He faced the camera and spoke, letting the built-in microphone pick up his voice. "Sorry for the interruption. We had a little problem with the electricity, as you can see, so we'll just have to make do. But I promise you, what you're about to see is really worth it. Lara Ryan is lying right over here. Want to take bets on whether she's still a virgin?"

The door swung open and he turned to meet Diane even before he'd consciously registered the attack. He'd known before he said it that his crack about Lara would bring her in.

In the shadows, with her hair and clothes plastered against her body, Diane looked like a wild woman. She swung at him with a stick—dammit, she'd torn off a dead rose cane. Christ! The fucking thorns tore streaks in his arm.

They faced each other from only a few feet apart. Jimmy wondered how much of this the video camera was picking up. "You like to play rough? Think you're going to kill me with a rose bush?"

"Why don't you just leave?" Diane was breathing hard already. Nearly winded. "Just leave us alone."

"This is going to make a great movie." He smiled at her. "We've got thirty minutes of tape. Why don't you try to reason with me, Diane? Or beg? That really gets 'em." He knew if he taunted her enough, she'd lunge.

But he didn't want to be stupid, either. Diane might be weaker than he was, but if she got at his eyes with that branch . . .

"I told the neighbors." Her voice was high, near hysteria. "They're calling the police. I came back to protect Lara. So why don't you just get out of here?"

"You don't bluff well." He spread his hands and tilted his head. Winsomely. Cute little Jimmy Owens-Olsen, Superman's red-headed pal. Maybe Diane had the hots for him. He'd always suspected it.

280

Lara stirred, her eyelids fluttering open. "Diane . . . I've got . . ."

Diane lashed at him with the branch. Jimmy grabbed it, trying to ignore the way the thorns punctured his skin. Jesus Fucking Christ. He whipped it away from her and dropped it behind him, jagged pain burning along his arm. "Just you and me, babe."

"Jimmy, for God's sake—"

He walked forward slowly, grinning. She was crumbling. She looked so forlorn, so desperate, with her hair all soaked. He could see the nipples showing through her blouse.

As he reached for her wrists, Diane kicked at him. Trying to get the balls, of course. He twisted his leg around hers easily and tripped her, falling on top of her and pinning her to the floor.

"Good girl," Jimmy said. "Now let's have some fun."

He glanced up. The video camera was pointed right at them.

73

They made the trip from Citrus Beach to La Habra in forty minutes, Barry gripping the wheel and pumping the brakes to keep from skidding when red taillights flashed ahead of him. The windshield wipers fought a losing battle with the rain, forcing him to squint at the black shapes of cars and the green freeway signs until he exited at Lambert Road and the force of the water slackened with his speed.

"Can you see them? Are you picking up anything?" Kris kept asking Ranier from the back seat. "Oh, God, you really knew all this was going to happen, didn't you?"

"More or less." Seated beside Barry, Ranier looked even paler than usual. "I wish this damn rain would let up."

Chang just sat in the back, staring out the window on the left side. Barry could almost feel the intense silent power of his will, pushing them toward their destination. *Before anybody gets killed? Or before the deputies get there and put a lid on things?*

Barry turned onto State College Boulevard, which metamorphosed into La Habra Boulevard. He hated the acrid smell of rain on asphalt, the wetness in the air. Everything seemed to clutch at him, slow him down. Maybe he should have Ranier pull the gun out of the glove compartment so they'd be ready when they got there. No, some cop might see them and get the wrong idea.

"But can't you see what's going on?" Kris leaned forward toward the blond man. "Can't you get one of your flashes?"

"No. They come when they will." Ranier turned on the radio and adjusted the dial, trying to find some news, as Barry reached Harbor Boulevard and followed it until it twisted into the hills.

They came around a bend at forty-five miles per hour and he slammed on the brakes, skewing the car sideways as they halted in a line of humming autos with brake lights glowing in the downpour.

A minute later, Ranier found a traffic report on the radio. The CHP was reporting an overturned pickup truck ahead of them.

"Christ, we'll never get through." Barry glared through the windshield, unable to see past the next bend in the road. "Isn't there another way in?"

"Oh, God, don't tell me we've got to go all the way around on the freeway." Kris was starting to panic. "That could take an hour. How much further is it? We could get out and walk."

"That could take an hour, too." Barry resisted the impulse to press the horn and hold it down.

Ranier was already searching through Barry's map book. The psychic might not be able to pick up what they needed to know, but at least he had a clear head. "A couple of miles east of here, there's another way, Hacienda Boulevard. Can you turn around?"

Cursing under his breath, Barry maneuvered, wishing for the first time that he'd bought one of those subcompact foreign jobs. Irrationally, it occurred to him that he might get a ticket, and he wondered why there was never a goddamn cop around when you needed one.

The explanation for that was simple, he reminded himself. The cops were all up ahead at the accident.

Another car came around the bend toward them, shrieking to a halt and honking madly at Barry's angling. "Go stuff yourself down a hole," Barry muttered, backing one more time and then pulling out.

283

Ranier was slouching in his seat, palm pressed to forehead. Barry shot him a curious glance as they whirred through the puddled water along Whittier Boulevard.

"Well?"

The blond man muttered unintelligibly, then dropped his hand. "She's so damn weak. I think she's got some kind of weapon but she can't use it."

"How much further is it?" Kris jounced edgily on the back seat.

Barry didn't bother to answer.

74

Diane's muscles wouldn't work properly. She wanted to heave Jimmy off her, to claw his eyes out, but she couldn't move. She'd fallen heavily, bruising her head again and hurting her back.

The room had a weird, unearthly quality in the soft wavering light. Above her, she could feel Jimmy moving and knew he was loosening his clothes. Oh, damn him, damn him.

Please let someone come. Even if it was too late for her. Please let them save Lara.

Jimmy was dictating again to his damn camera. "You see, Assemblyman Gorwins, my stepfather has a craving for little boys. Bet you didn't know that, huh? The things he used to do to my mother and me—well, let me tell you . . ."

He was half incoherent, as if making things up as he went along. God, how had he managed to keep up a facade of normality for almost a year?

Diane tried to penetrate the fog in her brain. There had to be something she could do. What had happened to the knife? Had Lara dropped it somewhere on the floor? With her left hand, she fumbled around at the edge of the sofa but came up with only a dust ball, which clung to her fingers for a moment before she managed to shake it loose.

"In case you can't see in this poor light, this female I've got on the floor is Diane Hanson." Jimmy was smiling up at the

285

camera. "Soon to be the late Diane Hanson. Don't you wish this was you instead of me, Mack? Here's my cock. This is for you. Just what you like, remember?"

He lifted his hands from Diane for a moment, and she pushed forward with all her strength, jabbing at his stomach with her thumbs.

"Bitch!" Jimmy slammed her back down against the floor. She thought the back of her head would cave in. But she couldn't quit. Lara was still alive. There was still a chance.

Jimmy was momentarily off balance as he pinned her wrists down, and she writhed, trying to throw him. Just to get him off her. Just to get free for a minute. Maybe she could reach the camera, break the damn thing. Anything to stop him.

She felt him lean away for a second and then he was twisting the coarse fibers of rope around her wrists. Oh, God, he was tying her; she couldn't fight anymore. Her body defied her, limp and useless, as her spirit raged in protest. Diane heard herself scream, a harsh, primitive, hopeless sound that fled her like a banshee, a thing with a life of its own, not a part of her at all.

A spring creaked on the sofa. Someone whispered, "Roll him toward me." Diane wasn't even sure Lara had spoken aloud, but she arched herself with her last remaining strength, so Jimmy swayed toward the couch. Diane caught a glimpse of Lara's face, hideously contorted as if with a superhuman effort, and then she saw that the girl's hand was raised, and the knife was in it.

This was not real. Not this cabin, not these ropes around her wrists, not the pressure of Jimmy's body and his erect penis against her stomach, not the horrible avenging angel that Lara had become, not the downward glide of the knife, not the way Jimmy didn't even notice it, not the way the blade pierced his back, scraped against something, and then went in deeper. This was not the Jimmy Owens who whistled as he came out of the darkroom, the Lara Ryan who half-closed her eyes as she sang along with *West Side Story*. This

286

was not the Diane Hanson who sat at a desk in the newsroom and answered letters about broken toys.

"You can't!" Jimmy half-crouched above her, turning toward Lara, reaching back as if to pull the knife out of himself. "You little slut." The words gurgled in his chest. "Oh, Jesus. I'll get you. I'll squeeze your fucking neck . . ." He choked, quivered, and fell to the floor on his side, body twitching, his penis jerking and spilling something out onto his pants, and then he lay still.

"Lara?" Diane's voice sounded squeaky in the silence, with just the soft hiss of tape noise in the background. "Are you all right?"

There was no answer.

Outside, she heard the chug of a motor halting, the slam of car doors, and Barry's voice calling her name. And there was a siren wailing, no, two of them, slightly off key with each other, and then Diane felt herself slipping into unconsciousness.

75

The story, by-lined Nguyen Chang, in the Friday afternoon *Daily Record* spared no one—not the police who went to arrest the wrong man, not the newspaper that let itself be duped by its own employee, and not Mack Ferguson.

The headline read: "POLICE CHIEF'S STEPSON SLAIN; 2 VICTIMS FREED." Underneath, the subhead said: "*Record* Photographer Is Revealed as Killer of Jeanette Tracy."

There was a sidebar: "Ferguson Withdraws from Sheriff's Race."

The story was picked up by the major wire services and sent nationwide. All three networks used it in their 6:00 P.M. broadcasts.

The anchorwoman was recounting the story with the solemn expression she usually reserved for plane crashes, hurricanes, and acts of terrorism. Lucille paused in the doorway of the den, holding a glass of beaujolais. She could see the edge of Mack's shoulder as he lay on the sofa, staring at the screen.

Damn that smug anchorwoman anyway. You'd think from the way she intoned her words that she'd dug up the story herself. She was an overpaid flunky, an ex-beauty queen who wouldn't know a police report from a hole in her head.

"A videotape left by Owens indicated he planned the murders as some kind of revenge against Chief Ferguson, allegedly for mistreating him as a boy," the woman was saying when Mack pressed the remote control and finally shut her up.

"Would you like something to eat?" Lucille moved forward. From the cans on the coffee table, she could see Mack was on his third Coors.

"Maybe later." He lay there, deflated, as she rounded the corner of the sofa. She didn't like the ruddy tone to his skin, or the heavy lines around his mouth.

"Lupe fixed enchiladas before she left. They're all ready to pop in the oven." Lucille hated enchiladas, but usually Mack loved them. Now he merely lay there as if he hadn't heard.

Damn that Jimmy Owens and his weakling of a mother, the alcoholic who'd dumped a load of guilt on Mack when she wrapped her car around a tree. Hadn't they messed up his life enough?

"We need to talk." His tone was flat.

"Fine. Talk." She sat on the end of the couch by his feet.

"What he said on that tape . . ." Mack took a swig of beer.

"He was pretty incoherent, that's what Captain De Anda told me." Lucille had been grateful this afternoon at the station to find the detective more sympathetic than she'd expected. The man had class, that was for sure. He could have rubbed Mack's nose in this, made a play for the chief's job, but he hadn't. He'd just seemed glad the whole thing was over.

"They probably won't be able to make much out of it." Mack looked momentarily relieved, then his face tensed up again. "But you need to know. I should have told you a long time ago."

He was really quite a man, she thought, taking a sip of her wine. Even in defeat, even after listening to Greg Gorwins sputter this afternoon, even after sitting there at his desk calmly arranging for Sunday's dinner to be called off, there was an aura of power about him that attracted her. Attracted her one hell of a lot.

"What Jimmy was talking about . . ." He swallowed some more Coors, as if it sustained him. "One afternoon I came home early and found that he'd . . . raped his mother." The words came out half-strangled.

"Oh, Jesus." Lucille thought of the skinny red-haired boy with the grin that had never seemed quite genuine to her. "That son of a bitch."

"Well, I—lost my temper." Mack was staring into a point in space somewhere past her left shoulder. "I—I attacked him, Lucille. I—I could have killed him."

"He deserved it." She liked the way her voice sounded, very calm, very assured. She could picture Mack's fists slamming into that nasty kid, paying the boy back for what he'd done to his own mother. The little creep. He'd gotten a taste of his own medicine, that was all. There was nothing wrong with Mack. She knew him too well. She knew there was a fierce masculine undercurrent when they made love, but there was gentleness, too. He should have strangled Jimmy while he was at it; then the Tracy girl would still be alive.

Mack pulled himself up to a sitting position, his legs still draped across the sofa. "Lucille, there isn't going to be any sheriff's race. Not four years from now and not eight years from now. I don't want this brought up over and over again. I'm done with it. I'm not sure I ever wanted the damn job anyway."

He had guts. He wasn't whining away from this, or sniveling after a bunch of goddamn voters, either. He'd thought it out and he wasn't going to waste any tears. They could take their sheriff's job and shove it.

"That's fine with me," she said.

A startled expression crossed his face. "I'm not even sure I can hang onto the chief's job, if Patricia Reilly decides to make a federal case out of it."

"She won't." Lucille set her glass back on the table. "If she mentions one word about that boy's crazy accusations, we'll slap her with a libel suit. You did your job."

"I nearly arrested the wrong man."

"So did Mario De Anda. So would anybody." She stared him down, almost angrily.

290

A faint smile crept across his face. "We should have you on the police force." He set the empty Coors can aside.

"I prefer to do my fighting from the sidelines." She slid along the sofa and felt his strong arms close around her as she stretched against him, her mouth finding his, enjoying the taste of passion mixed with beer.

"Boy, was I scared." Kris pushed his chair back with a scrape, watching the image of Lara being carried out on a stretcher. The hospital TV was positioned high up, and she realized he had to crane his neck to see.

"I don't remember much about it." She rested her head against the piled-up pillows. Boy, talk about lethargic. She was glad there wasn't anyone in the next bed who might have expected her to make conversation. She couldn't even think straight; she kept smelling the spider-webbed darkness of the little room off the garage, tasting the parched desert of diabetic thirst, feeling her teeth tug against Diane's gag.

"Yeah, I thought maybe you were dead. There was blood all over the place." He sounded kind of excited and shook up at the same time. "You know how they say your heart jumps into your mouth? Well, that's how I felt. I kept thinking about how Jeanette looked when I saw her. I couldn't imagine you like that."

"They told me I killed him." Vaguely, she remembered people rushing into the cabin, like something that had happened in a dream. The police hadn't bothered her; she supposed they'd have questions in a day or so, when she was stronger. That was okay. She felt right now as if she were floating, as if she'd smoked grass and nothing really mattered.

"Yeah." His tone was admiring. "I'm sure glad Diane hung onto that knife. Boy, who'd have thought . . ." He stopped as the TV flashed two photos of Jeanette, the one taken at school and the one after she was dead. Both shot by the same photographer. "That creep—so what if he was mad at his old man? Why take it out on you guys?"

Kris's anger felt good to Lara, strong and reassuring. It was pleasant, watching other people have emotions when she'd been washed clean of them. Her eyelids fluttered sleepily. She could still hear the sirens screaming from this afternoon. Vaguely, she remembered the stretcher and the ambulance, and an emergency room, and being transferred down here to Citrus Beach Community, and her father's worried face. And always Kris had been there, in the background. Her friend. He cared about her. Why hadn't she known before how much that meant?

The nurse came in with the dinner tray. "Out," she told Kris.

He stood up reluctantly. "I'll come back tomorrow. It's Saturday. When are you getting out?"

"Don't know." Lara watched the nurse move her water glass out of the way and position the tray on the arm of the rolling table, swinging it into place over the bed. "See you."

"You bet." He backed toward the door, waved, and went out.

"Nice boyfriend." The nurse helped Lara sit up straighter, handed her the needle filled with insulin, and watched sternly as Lara swabbed her thigh and injected herself. "Now, you've got to eat every bit of this, you know. Doctor's orders."

Lara stared down at the food. Weakly, she picked up her fork. The nurse watched her for a minute, then bent over and cut the roast beef into pieces. "Thanks."

"The buzzer's right there by your hand. Let me know if you need anything." The figure in white disappeared out the door.

The TV was showing scenes from a protest march at Los Angeles City Hall. It made Lara's head ache, and she clicked it off.

Halfway through the meal, she heard someone at the door. After a moment, she looked up.

"I can't tell you how good it feels to have my mind to myself again." Eduardo's smile was touched with shyness.

"You could really hear what I was thinking?" Somehow the idea hadn't seemed at all strange when Lara heard about it on TV, about how he'd seen the cabin in a sort of vision. But then, nothing felt real just now.

292

"Yes. It was driving me crazy." He ventured into the room and handed her a card, then sat carefully on the spare bed. "I only picked up bits and pieces—not enough to find you."

She fumbled with the envelope. The card had a picture of a singing mouse on the front and the words, "Good luck on your latest gig." Inside was a picture of the mouse on an operating table, surrounded by rodent surgeons. Underneath was printed, "I hear it's standing room only. Get well soon!"

At the bottom was written, in artful black handwriting that looked almost like calligraphy, "This card is good for ten free singing lessons." There was the name of a studio and a phone number, and then, "Good luck. Ted."

"I called a well-known singing teacher in LA and he referred me to one of his best former students, who has a studio in Newport," Eduardo said. "I already mailed the check, so you'd better take advantage of it."

She nodded weakly. That's right, she was a singer. She'd almost forgotten. These last few days, she'd been somebody else. A woman in a concentration camp. It was over. She'd be going back to school, back to riding on buses and watching gulls circling overhead and being free. Back to being Lara Ryan again.

"You're tired. I suppose I should let you get some rest." He caught his lower lip between his teeth for a minute, like Robert Redford did in the movies.

He was so handsome, with that long lean body and those strange, wonderful eyes. A couple of days ago, she'd thought she might want him for a boyfriend. It was funny how sometimes you had to grow up a little to see how young you really were.

"I'd better leave." He straightened up.

"Will I see you?"

"Around." He gave her the saddest smile she'd ever seen. "Hey, when you're a star, don't forget me."

Outside in the corridor she heard scurrying noises and then her father shepherded Gerry and Dave and Sammy into the room.

"We're illegal. Except for Sammy," Dave said, hanging back. "He's twelve."

"Lara! Lara!" Gerry dashed across the room and up onto the bed, jostling the dinner tray so some milk splashed out and the Jell-o shook. "You're okay, aren't you? You've been gone so long!"

"I'm fine." She gave him a hug and blinked back a couple of big fat tears.

When she looked up again, Eduardo Ranier was gone.

It seemed as if every radio station Ted tried on the way home was blithering about the dramatic demise of the Citrus Beach strangler and the role of a psychic in tracking him down.

Odd, the way it made him uncomfortable. He hadn't felt that way two years ago.

Maybe the difference was that he hadn't had a stake in the outcome then. Or that he hadn't known how inadequate his "powers" were. Sure, they'd helped today, especially the image of the house. But he and Barry, and the sheriff's deputies almost on their heels, hadn't exactly come to the rescue like white knights.

He halted the TransAm in front of his house and leaned against the headrest. Damn, he was tired. Tired of accepting apologies from Chief Ferguson and Captain De Anda and even Diane Hanson as the paramedics carried her out. Tired of acting gracious and noble and forgiving. Hell, he was even tired of hearing his own name on the radio.

A glass of Scotch was beckoning him from inside.

Wearily, Ted climbed out of the car and went up the steps. The cops had dropped him off earlier, apologizing profusely for having invaded his premises; he hadn't noticed anything disturbed when he went in to get his wallet, and now, opening the front door, he was almost glad they'd been there. Hardly anyone ever came here, except the occasional client. Was it possible a house could get hungry for company?

The red answering-machine light was on, but he ignored it as he poured himself a glass of Dewars. The usual bills had come in the mail.

He dropped into a chair, rubbed his aching temples, and wondered what he was going to do next.

The sounds of Lara's voice still reverberated through his head, those agonizing pleas for help. Oh, Christ, why hadn't he been able to help her? When he saw her this morning collapsed in that cabin, sprayed with blood . . . Damn, he was an impotent son of a bitch, wasn't he?

Eduardo Ranier, the great psychic. Why'd he ever come up with a hokey name like that, anyway?

Ted wandered into the kitchen and stuck a frozen dinner in the microwave. He wished he were eighteen again. He wished he could start over.

By the time he finished eating and started on his third Scotch, he was feeling better. Well enough to listen to the phone messages, anyway.

One was from his mother, saying she'd heard the story on TV and hoped he was all right. The rest were from reporters, wanting interviews.

The most interesting message was from *True Inside Story*. They offered fifty thousand dollars for exclusive rights to his life story, to be serialized.

Ted whistled softly.

He thought about Lara, lying there in the hospital bed, her dark hair loose against the pillow. He thought about Jimmy Owens, that freckle-faced kid who used to hang around his uncle's camera store. He thought about being treated with respect by all those police officers, by the newspaper editor.

Strange, but it would feel like a kind of betrayal, selling his story to a scandal sheet. They'd blow it up with screaming headlines and wallow in the gory details.

On the other hand . . .

Ted looked around at the art deco furniture, which was likely to get repossessed if he didn't make his payments soon. So was the car. Hell, so was the house.

Who did he think he was, anyway? The next mayor of Citrus Beach? A ninety-day wonder, that was Eduardo Ranier, and the clock was already ticking his time away.

Ted picked up the phone and dialed the number for *True Inside Story*, collect.

From where he stood in the kitchen fixing chicken curry, Barry could see Diane lying back in his easy chair, reading Guy's story in the newspaper.

It was amazing that she hadn't been more seriously injured. The hospital had released her after treating a few scrapes and bruises and taking a few X rays. Going to be fine, they said. But was she?

For that matter, was he?

He'd never really understood before how she felt at the moment when she saw the truck bearing down on her son, Barry reflected as he cut the raw chicken carefully away from the breastbone. The helplessness, the rage, the sense of a world rocketing out of control.

He'd failed her. If Eduardo hadn't had his visions, if Chang hadn't been suspicious about the photograph, if Meyer hadn't remembered the beer blast up in the Heights; and then they would still have been too late . . .

He washed the chicken fat from his hands and squeezed lemon juice into a measuring cup, then began chopping the apples.

"Whatever you're doing in there, it sounds wonderful," Diane called.

"You're supposed to judge cooking by its smell, not its sound."

"Well, you're not cooking it yet, so I can't smell it, can I?" There was an unexpected note of gaiety in her teasing. The doctor had warned that she might be in emotional shock for a day or two. Maybe this was it.

Barry poured some walnuts into a bowl and carried them out to Diane. "Here's something to nibble on in the meantime."

She set the newspaper aside on the chair's broad arm, the photos of her and Lara folded out of sight. "You're being really nice, taking me to feed the kitten, bringing me back to your house, fixing me dinner."

Setting the bowl on an end table, he sank down onto the sofa. "I feel so useless. Like someone trying to sweep up a volcanic eruption with a broom."

Her gray eyes darkened to a slate color, the way they did when she was worried. "You're taking this harder than I am."

"The doctor said you might be in shock for a while, that what happened might not really sink in."

"It sank in." She gazed at him levelly. "Jimmy's dead. God, for the past ten months, I've been friends with an illusion. I've never known anyone truly mad before. That's what he was, wasn't he?"

Barry nodded. "I don't suppose it's fair to blame Mack Ferguson. Jimmy was probably messed up long before he came along."

Nibbling at one of the nuts, she looked over at a framed photo of his daughter. "You never know how they're going to turn out, do you, or what's going to happen to them? You just have to trust the odds, I guess."

"You're certainly in a philosophical mood."

She turned toward him. "I love you, Barry."

"And I love you. So goddamn much, Diane." His throat felt thick.

A smile softened her face. "I feel as if I've been given a second chance. Isn't that odd? Nothing can ever bring Mark back, but it's almost as if I'd been reborn. I got the chance to help Lara that I never got with my son."

Barry knew what he wanted to say next, and the thought of it frightened him. Automatically, he reached toward his pocket for a cigarette, then drew his hand away.

"That nervous?" she asked gently.

"I want us to get married." The words came out blunter than he'd intended. "We don't have to have children—that's up to you—but . . ."

Her lashes fluttered down, sleepily. "I suppose I'm ready for that. Maybe even for kids. That is, if I don't starve to death first."

Relief flooded through him. "I believe in short engagements. Very short. Like a couple of days." Her only answer

297

was to grope feebly for the nuts again. "Okay, okay, I'll feed you." He started for the kitchen.

"Barry." He turned. "If you really want to smoke, I don't mind. You could run out for some cigarettes."

He didn't even hesitate. "What? And lose my twenty-five bucks in the office pot? I can't afford it. I'm a family man."

"Yes," she said, and smiled.